Bait the Devil

Bait the Devil

A Bounty of Shadows Series

Winter Austin

TULE
PUBLISHING

Dedication

Family. Because it truly is
an important aspect to our lives.

"The line between good and evil ain't always as clear as we'd like it to be."

Pat Garrett

Chapter One

"HE'S COMING OUT the back!"

Dorothy Ybarra bolted toward the rear door from her position next to the dilapidated fence. The hot day stuck to her skin and made her Kevlar vest chafe in all the wrong places. She wasn't going to let it stop her from catching this bastard.

The ancient door flew open, crashed against the side of the run-down home, and swung back in a crazy wobble to smack the three-hundred-plus bail jumper trying to escape. He took a stunned step forward and then toppled down the three steps.

Dot pounced.

"Stay down!" she yelled, grappling for his arms.

With an animalistic roar, he lumbered to his feet.

Off guard, Dot clung to him, managing to wrap her arms around his twenty-inch neck in an effort to keep from sliding off.

"Freddy, you need to sit the fuck down," she yelled in his ear.

Giving another roar, he ran, Dot bouncing against his backside as she hung on. For a man mostly built on cases of soda and boxes of Doritos, he could move. Not wanting to return to jail could be a powerful motivator. He used that weight to his advantage to steamroll the rotted fence, crashing through it and raining shards of wood and boards on them. Still, he lumbered on.

Come hell or high water, Dot would land this bond.

As he barreled through the tangled mess of weeds and shrubs, wheezing with each stride he took in the oppressive heat, Dot managed to get her boots under her and planted them into the creases that were Freddy's hips. Without releasing her hold on his neck, she slowly eased up and back, tightening her arm around his throat.

"Freddy, I'm warning you. Stop now, or I'll put you down."

"Bitch!" Spittle flew into Dot's face.

"That's it!" She yanked back, her crooked elbow clinching down on each side of Freddy's thick neck.

Dot leaned as far back as she could without falling off. Her actions jerked Freddy to a halt. He reached up and clawed at her arm. Dot coiled her hands and locked them together. Freddy wheeled around and whipped about, trying to dislodge Dot. His movements grew sluggish.

"Give up, Freddy."

A garbled response blew from his lips. He dropped to one knee, still grappling to remove Dot's arms out of the sleeper hold. Dot could see his face turning a bright red and deepen to purple. She sensed it when he finally passed out.

She wasn't fast enough to let him out of the sleeper hold and catch him before he toppled forward and landed face-first into the hot earth. Dot scrambled up off him, then checked for a pulse. It was beating away fast and strong.

She stood, bent over, staring down at him and panting. "Damn it, Freddy."

Her partner—huffing and puffing—caught up to them. She peered through her angled elbow. T.J. Roman, drenched in sweat and sounding like a smoker with emphysema, slowed next to her.

"What the fuck," he wheezed.

"Would you cuff this motherfucker before he comes to." Dot backhanded sweat from her forehead.

T.J. dragged out two sets of cuffs and double-cuffed Freddy's hands behind his back, after he turned the man's head to the side so he'd stop breathing dirt.

Dot and then T.J. sank to the ground and sat there waiting for Freddy to wake from his little nap.

Dot twisted around to look in the direction they had come from, cringing at the destruction Freddy had caused in his attempted escape. "Holy shit," she muttered when she noticed how far he'd managed to get with her on his back.

"He's jacked up on coke," T.J. said in passing.

It was the only reason he was able to avoid T.J. and carry Dot this far. She was by no means a small woman either, standing right at six feet and weighing a solid 210 pounds with all her gear on.

She glanced around. There was no good way to get the SUV over here to load up Freddy. They were going to have to walk him back to the house where he'd been squatting to avoid them and the cops for months. God, she hoped the bastard didn't end up having a heart attack on them. If they had to call in an ambulance, they'd lose this bond, and the cops would have custody of Freddy.

"Once he's in county lockup, we're done for the day," T.J. snarled.

"Fine by me," Dot said and flopped back on the dirt. "Don't let him die."

TWO HOURS LATER, they had managed to corral the quickly sobering Freddy into the back of the Suburban, with no more eventful chases, and turn him over to the county jail. Freddy's bail bondsman paid out their fair share of the bond and a huge tip after some hard pressing on T.J.'s part about the circumstances leading up to Freddy's apprehension. Once the check was cashed, a celebratory late lunch at one of the best Basque eateries Dot had found in Boise was the best way to top off a successful day of bounty hunting.

Parked behind the Bar Gernika, she and T.J. sat in the back end of the Chevy Suburban with the hatch up eating chorizo sandwiches with smoked cod croquetas and a bowl of green olives dripping in garlic olive oil. Dot slurped down half of her Coke, then shook the ice in her cup.

T.J. pointed the remains of his smoked beef chorizo at her. "We should register for the SHOT show in Vegas."

"Why?"

"Because we can." T.J. pulled his *duh* face.

Dot rolled her eyes and bit into her sandwich.

"Have you ever been there?" T.J. asked.

She shook her head, wiping smokey chorizo juice from the corner of her mouth.

"The woman raised to be a hunter and a firearms collector has never been to the great SHOT show?" He lowered his reflective sunglasses and eyed her over the top of the rims. "Never?"

"You do realize my family wasn't made of money." Dot popped one of the croquetas into her mouth. "And that's in the dead of winter, when we couldn't just up and run off while we were in the middle of lambing season."

"All the more reason you should go now." T.J. grinned. "A lot of the best bounty hunters meet up there."

Dot scowled at her partner and sometimes bunk buddy. "Lemme guess. You wanna show off your shiny new partner to the boys?"

"Maybe." His grin turned devilish. "Or maybe I wanna see you kick their asses."

Dot wadded up the sandwich wrapper and chucked it at T.J.'s head. "I'm not a toy."

The crumbled ball of waxed paper bounced off his forehead and landed on the Suburban floor between them.

"Really? Then why are you so easy to wind up?"

"You sonofa—" Dot lunged for his throat but was quickly subdued.

Their moment of levity was interrupted by a shrill ring from T.J.'s phone.

"Damn it," he snapped and patted down his body in search for his cell.

Dot found it lying on the makeshift floor behind his hulking frame. She snatched it up and checked the screen. She batted her eyelashes at T.J.

"Don't you dare," he snarled.

She pressed the green icon to answer the call. "Well, hello, cousin dearest."

Lawyer-extraordinaire and covert purveyor of information, Vivian Montgomery was Dot's second cousin. And apparently had earned a spot on T.J.'s contact list under the moniker of Hot Ass Lawyer.

"Dot? When did you start taking business calls?" Vivian asked, her brisk tone underscored by the sound of her heavy breathing.

"What are you doing?" Dot asked. "You sound like you're saving the horse and riding a cowboy."

"Oh, grow up. I'm on a treadmill. Put T.J. on the phone."

"You shouldn't run on those things. They destroy your knees and back," Dot chided.

"When I want health advice from a cigar smoker who jumps from helicopters for fun, I'll call."

"I don't jump from the helo. Unless it's crashing. Even then, that's sketchy shit."

T.J., giving a rumbling growl, jerked the phone from Dot, and pressed it to his ear. "Vivian, what do you need?" He waited a moment, then with another low growl, pulled the phone from his ear and put it on speaker. "You're on speaker."

"I need a huge favor from the two of you."

"When you say huge favor, how huge are we talking?" Dot asked.

"You know, I think I liked you better when you were a brooding, isolated eremite whose main goal in life was equal parts trying to piss off her mother and keep her out of trouble," Vivian shot back.

"Love you too, coz."

"Now shut up and let me finish." The whining sound of the treadmill belt slowing echoed over the phone connection. "I just got a call from one of my colleagues. She had a client fail to appear today."

"Shouldn't the defendant's bail bondsman be calling us?" T.J. asked.

"It's … complicated."

Dot smiled as T.J. groaned.

"Vivian, every time you rope us into one of your firm's problems with their unruly children, we're out money, time, and patience. We're called bounty hunters for a reason. Bounty is in the name."

"Roman, if you keep up the condescending behavior, I'll expose your dirty little secret."

"Dirty secret, huh," Dot piped in. "What's that?"

He thrust a finger at her nose. "None of your business. Vivian, if you so much as breathe out of line, I'll make you regret it."

"Will you do me the favor?"

T.J. stared at Dot, who shrugged as if to say, *Why not?*

"Fine. Mark my words, I'll be cashing in on this huge favor sooner than you think."

"I wouldn't have bothered you with this, expect the guy is a veteran, and you two being veterans yourself, I figured he'd be more likely to work with you than anyone else."

"What's on his file?" Dot asked.

"That's the complicated part. Officially, his file says he was picked up a third time for carrying with the intent to sell. Unofficially, he's … classified."

Dot frowned as she and T.J. locked eyes. As a former army ranger who spent a lot of time flying in and out of forward operating bases in Afghanistan, T.J. knew all about classified situations. Dot, as the main helicopter pilot shuttling him and his team back and forth, though never read in on his actual missions, typically was under strict orders of her own.

"Vivian, I'm not getting fuzzy feelings about this," T.J. said.

"Neither am I. It's why I'm calling the two of you in. The judge wants to issue a bench warrant. My colleague was able to ask for a delay before it's submitted. She was given three hours to present her client or the warrant is released. If you'd rather, you could consider this job PI work instead of fugitive recovery."

The shingle hanging outside their business office did say private investigators. At this point, that title belonged to T.J. and T.J. alone.

"Still not selling me on this," he said. "If there's no bench warrant, there's no cash for catching him."

"Hang on." Vivian spoke to someone, her voice muffled, then she was back. "The firm will pay you a finder's fee."

T.J. continued to stare at Dot. She could sense what he was thinking. He was torn. Take this off-the-cuff job and cash in on the favor department with Vivian to help a fellow veteran? Or say *fuck it* and play hooky for the rest of the day like he'd planned?

Dot didn't really have much of a say in the business dealings of their partnership since she was eight months into the training phase as a fugitive recovery agent and she wasn't a licensed PI. It didn't stop T.J. from pressing her for her opinion, who argued that, because she was about to start taking bounties on her own, she needed to take the reins more often.

"If it helps you make a decision, I've got his last known address and a phone number along with a photo," Vivian said. "This won't be a hard catch."

"Stop saying that. Every time you tell me it's an easy one, it turns into a disaster," T.J. snarled.

"He's right," Dot added.

"Okay, I retract my statement. But, please say yes. Huge favor to me. I'll do anything."

"Anything?"

Dot glared at him.

"Within reason," Vivian shot back.

"We'll do it," Dot said, tired of T.J.'s runaround. "Send us the four-one-one, and we'll go check it out."

T.J. glared at her; his dark eyes flashed a warning. Dot returned his glare with a smug look of her own that dared him to bring it.

"Thank you, coz. Hurry. There's only two hours left before the bench warrant goes out. Then it'll be a free-for-all."

"You couldn't have called us about this an hour ago?" T.J. groused.

"Shut your yap, Roman," Vivian said. "There. Info sent."

His phone dinged.

"His name is Cade Porter. He was a staff sergeant in the Marine Corps." Vivian sucked in a breath. "Oooh."

"Oooh, what?" T.J. insisted.

"If this is right, he was in an artillery unit."

"Oh my God." T.J. groaned.

Dot grinned. Not only did acting on a favor for Vivian chafe T.J. in the chaps, but doing it for a Marine with explosives expertise was going to make that chafe burn. Throughout their long, storied history, there had always been a deep-seated friendly animosity between the army and the Marines. Push came to shove, however, they still had each other's backs.

"If that crayon eater blows us up, I'm going to haunt you," he said.

"I look forward to the visits. Now get going." Vivian ended the call.

T.J. shoved his phone in a side pocket of his cargo pants. "Tell me again why we let Vivian help us out?"

"Because," Dot said as she scooted out of the SUV's backend, "she's good for the money. And I trust her intel more than I would some of your bail bondsmen."

"You say that because you're biased."

"*Nire familia da. Garrantzitsua da.*"

T.J. paused before closing the hatch. "I speak Pashto, Arabic, some Spanish, and Oklahoman. I do not speak Basque."

Dot chuckled. "Time to learn, Danger Ranger."

"Load up and let's roll."

Chapter Two

C ADE PORTER'S KNOWN residence was northwest of Boise city limits and smack in the middle of what Dot considered a living nightmare—suburbia. They drove past a lot of paved driveways with long lanes leading back to large homes set on acres of pasture ground at the base of the Boise National Forest. Dot noted a lot of horse farms and a few stating they were organic produce farms, but it was in part mostly a rich man's playground with golf courses and gated communities.

"If he's on bond, how the hell does he afford to live out here?" Dot asked as T.J. slowed the Suburban for a driveway bracketed by heavy metal gates left wide open.

"I don't think he owns any of this." T.J. stopped the SUV at a large sign greeting visitors at the lane's entrance and lowered his sunglasses. "Van Houten's horse farm. Boarding and breeding services."

"Wonder if he's a groom or something?"

He gave Dot a side eye and then pushed his reflective glasses into their rightful place. "Sure. We'll go with that."

He continued on down the immaculately kept lane bordered by equally immaculate white painted wooden fences. The pastures on Dot's side were empty, but she spotted a herd of ten mares with foals grazing in a field to T.J.'s left.

The lane ended at a circular drive before a huge barn. T.J. parked beside a small white building that looked more like a guard shack and cut the engine. They sat there, assessing what they could encounter once they exited the Suburban.

"Did you see a house?" he asked.

"Nope. It might be behind the barn."

"What day is it?"

Dot glanced at her partner. "Wednesday."

"And the time?"

She checked her watch. "Nearly four in the afternoon."

"Wouldn't there be people out here doing chores? Or boarders riding their horses?"

"One would assume yes, but we don't know their operating hours. It wasn't on the sign."

T.J. leaned forward and peered up through the windshield. "Nor was who is running it." He drew back and looked pointedly at Dot. "Gear up. My danger radar is going off."

Dot wouldn't tease him or rebut. T.J.'s track record for successful missions was legendary. Some of his guys might have come out with injuries, but no one died on his watch. That uncanny intuition had saved Dot's hide on more than a few occasions, past and present.

They exited the SUV and made short work of vesting up and arming themselves. Before approaching the barn, T.J. double-checked the small building.

"Office," he said as he pulled back from the lone window. He tried the door and found it unlocked. He poked his head in. "Hello?"

No answer. He stepped back, shutting the door.

He gave her a single hand motion to move forward. They made for a human-sized entry next to a closed large bay roll-up door.

"It's hotter than fucking Hades out here and they have all the barn doors shut," Dot said in a low voice.

"Maybe they have it air-conditioned." T.J. circled his hand around. "By the looks of the place, this Van Houten person has money."

Dot grunted. "If you put lipstick on a pig, does it still make it pretty?"

Ignoring her, he tried the side door, and it opened. He took point, Dot right on his heels after she did a quick check of their backsides.

The building, an enormous riding arena, was, indeed, cooler. Pampered horses could be beneficial to humans, after all. The ring—its flooring a mix of sand and dirt—took up most of the building. To their left was an alley where trucks and trailers could pull in, hence the large bay doors. Behind them, against the wall, a set of stairs led to a wide deck perched above their heads. Dot assumed it was a lookout or observation deck.

Otherwise, the arena was empty.

T.J. cautiously moved forward, his rifle pointed down, hand resting on the stock that was pressed to his chest for ready access. Dot lingered a few steps back, her trusty Colt 1911 gripped in her right hand and aimed over her left shoulder. She studied the staircase and slatted wood above their heads.

As he stepped past the edge of the observation deck, T.J. paused and squatted. "Got something."

Dot halted. Before she could ask him what he found, a dark blotch hit the back of his neck with a splat.

"What the fuck?" He cupped his neck and pulled his hand away.

Dot grimaced at a dark-red smear on his skin. She looked up. A large black stain covered two of the slats near the end of the observation deck. The slats were wedged tight, giving no clear view upstairs.

T.J. edged around a puddle in the sandy dirt and pointed his rifle upward. "I see a shoulder."

Dot broke away and darted up the stairs, slowing as she neared the upper deck. With the 1911 preceding her progress, she eased up one step at a time until she could peek over the lip of the deck. Except for the body of a male subject sprawled against the railing, the deck was empty.

Dot hurried up the last of the steps and over to the man. She hesitated when she got a look at what should have been his face.

"Got a DOA," she called down.

"Coming up," T.J. answered.

As he pounded up the steps, Dot scanned the area of the observation deck. A glass-enclosed room covered the whole western side of the deck. Or it had had glass windows at one time. Most of the panes were shattered, and jagged edges clung to the corners of the frames. Dot moved closer, spotting blood splatter on the pristine white wall near a door.

T.J. joined her as she eased up to an empty frame. They peered inside.

The hulking form of a man was draped over a broken armchair—dead if the huge pool of blood under his body was any indication.

"What the hell went on here?" T.J. muttered.

"Neither one of these guys is our target," Dot said as she entered the room through the shattered remains of the window. "We better see where that door goes."

They carefully stepped over upended furniture and glass shards as they crossed the floor toward the dead guy. Just to be certain, T.J. checked for a pulse and shook his head.

"Body's still warm," he said as he straightened. "This all went down recently."

Dot grabbed his shoulder before he opened the door. "We need to remember everything we touched here and tell law enforcement when we call this in."

He drew in a breath and let it out with a growl. "This is why you never say these jobs will be easy."

The door handle was smeared with blood and hadn't closed all the way. Using his rifle barrel, T.J. eased the door aside far enough to open it farther with his boot. Dot stepped through onto a landing. She checked the ground below and spotted a paved walkway and a rolling trash bin below. She didn't bother to wait for T.J. and hurried down the stairs, T.J. hot on her heels.

Laid out in a strategic manner were several more modest-sized barns with sectioned paddocks and between them a large pasture where another herd of horses milled about, their tails swishing.

"The horses are agitated," Dot remarked.

"I would be, too, if someone had been shooting the place

up and strange people were running around." T.J. pointed to a single-story house to the right of the barns. "That way."

Staying alert, they headed for the home. It was the only place on the property meant for humans.

"Get the sense Van Houten—whoever the hell that is—doesn't live here," Dot muttered as they walked onto the grassy yard.

"Got another body," T.J. said.

To the left of the house, half hidden by the small porch, lay another man. Dot winced at the sight of his mutilated body.

"Someone's using a shotgun," T.J. said. "Both barrels close range will do that kind of damage."

"Our Marine?" Dot asked.

"Maybe. And if that's the case, he's more than a shoot mortars kind of Marine." T.J. stepped in front of her. "Hello! The house!"

Silence greeted them.

"Cade Porter? I'm T.J. Roman, and this is my partner, Dot Ybarra. Your lawyer sent us to check on you."

More silence.

"We should call this in," Dot pressed.

He shook his head. "Not yet."

Dot didn't like the rigid lines in his face. He was mildly stubborn on a good day but a real horse's ass in situations where he was stressing out.

"Stay here," he ordered.

"Fuck you," she barked and marched past him.

"Dot ..."

She hopped onto the rail-less porch and approached the

open door with more caution than she planned. If T.J. was going to go all army ranger on her, then she would repay in kind.

Not calling in backup. WTF?

She glanced over her shoulder and found him missing. He'd better have gone around back, which he'd probably done.

Like T.J. had done inside the riding arena, Dot used the 1911's barrel to ease open the door enough for her to enter. The front hall walls were riddled with pockmarks. Sheetrock chunks and dust littered the floor. Dot made out tracks in the debris and followed it past a combo bathroom and a tiny den. She moved past a set of narrow stairs leading up to a loft area.

"Coming in," T.J. hollered from the back of the house.

Dot pulled up at the entry to the kitchen with a small dining table as T.J. stepped through the shattered screen door.

Two more bodies bracketed what remained of the table and lone chair. One of the victims sported a leg from the chair through his chest. Neither man was Cade Porter.

"What the ever-loving fuck?" T.J. groused.

Dot lowered her 1911. "Any signs outside he's still here?"

T.J. shook his head and let his rifle swing into his chest. "There was a spot back here where it looked like a vehicle had been parked. It's long gone."

Dot holstered her 1911. "Ready to call in the reserves?"

He dug out his cell phone. "Gotta call the troopers." He winced. "What the hell did Vivian get us into?"

Chapter Three

D URING HIS TIME in the army, T.J. Roman had seen
and experienced enough instances of violence to give
him a healthy awareness of when it was necessary and when
it was not. Between the total annihilation of villages brought
down by rivals over something as trivial as believing a
different way, the disputes over the poppy operations that
left both sides of the coin dead and rotting in the fields, and
walking into homes where defendants had succumbed to
their chosen poison, he was able to see the telltale signs of
amateur versus professional.

What had gone down here at Van Houten's horse farm
held the distinct signs of amateur thugs sent to deal with a
professional Marine. Cade Porter, five. Thugs, zero.

It'd taken a hot minute for the Idaho state troopers to
arrive with their investigative team. While he and Dot
waited, T.J. did a reconnaissance of the farm for more clues
on how their guy managed to kill five men and escape. T.J.
had located weapons on or near all five victims, so they'd
come with a plan. But what was the plan?

What had Cade Porter done or gotten involved with it
garnered such a violent outcome? By all indicators, this
looked necessary, like Cade was fighting for his life. Why

would he need to resort to killing? And where had he gone?

Dot had remained near the house. When he came out of the riding arena, she was on her phone. She ended the call as he joined her.

"Vivian is letting the judge know that Cade Porter is AWOL." Dot slid her phone into the front pocket of her Kevlar. "Once this spreads, every recovery agent in dire need of cash is going to be scrambling for his bond."

T.J. stared at her, letting her news sink in. "How big is the bond?"

Rigid lines deepened Dot's cheeks, making her high cheekbones more prominent. Her sharp, dark brown eyes narrowed.

"How big, Dot?"

"Half a mil."

T.J. staggered back a step. "For drug charges?"

She turned to the house and stared pointedly at the mutilated body gathering flies in the summer heat. "Vivian's associate failed to mention to Vivian that she knew nothing about this case or this client." Dot looked at him. "She's a junior associate in the firm. This whole fuckup was dumped on her by a senior lawyer."

"Obviously, his file would have the reason for a half-million bond. What was it?"

"Nobody knows. The bail bondsman of record doesn't exist."

"Sonofabitch! How is any of this fucking possible?" T.J. paced. "This favor Vivian owes us has compounded interest. By 100 percent."

A fleet of black-and-white-striped SUVs approached,

putting a halt to T.J.'s pacing. He and Dot watched the lead car park in the roundabout lane. The door opened, and a familiar figure emerged.

"Roman and Ybarra. Didn't think I'd see either of you this soon," Detective Sergeant Cassius Larrabee drawled.

"Larrabee," T.J. said and shook the Idaho state trooper's hand. "Believe me, I thought we wouldn't ever have to meet up again."

Nearly a year before, Larrabee had hired T.J. and his former partner for a private investigative gig. Things got out of hand, and Larrabee had to be brought into the chaos. Not only had T.J. lost a partner to retirement, and gained a new one in Dot, he'd also garnered much respect from Larrabee and a get-out-of-jail-free card if ever the need arose.

Larrabee smiled at Dot. "You a full-fledged bounty hunter yet?"

"Just about."

Larrabee sighed. "What craptastic episode of Bounty Hunters R Us have you gotten yourself into now?"

T.J. adjusted his sunglasses, swiping at a bead of sweat trickling down from his hairline. "I'm blaming Dot's cousin for this one." He pointed at the riding arena, then the house. "Between these two buildings, there are five DOAs. I checked the stables and no bodies. No sign of our person of interest either."

"Person of interest? More like suspect," Larrabee said.

T.J. crossed his arms. "Until we catch the guy and find out what happened, he's only a person of interest."

Larrabee gestured for his team to get to work. "*You* catch the guy? This one is going to fall within the purview of the police."

"Only until he leaves Idaho." T.J. shifted his weight to his right leg. "I'm not constrained by state lines."

Larrabee looked from T.J. to Dot. "You're in it for the money."

"No," Dot said. "It's more than that."

The three of them paused, listening to the sounds of crime scene techs, state troopers, and forensic personnel speaking in low tones and moving about the grounds.

"Normally, I would be warning anyone else to stay away from something like this and let the professionals handle it," Larrabee said. "But I've seen you two work." He moved past T.J. "Be careful and call me if you need help."

"You do realize he's a Marine?" T.J. asked.

Larrabee looked back. "Oh, I know. You two better be the ones to find him. We don't need any more bodies to clean up." He waved at them. "Leave your statements with my detective. I believe we have your fingerprints on file. Good luck," he called out as he stepped onto the porch.

T.J. turned to the woman wearing a black polo and khakis, her notepad out and ready. The detective looked like she'd just walked right out of the academy, all spit shined and new.

"Walk me through it," she said.

THE SUN DIPPED low in the sky by the time T.J. drove the Suburban into the parking lot behind their office. It was a small space rented out of what used to be a strip mall. The monthly rent on the place was going up, and rumors abounded that the owner was about to sell out to some big corporate conglomerate, which would circle around to a huge rent hike.

T.J. really needed to reconsider their location for something better suited to both his and Dot's needs. She was getting antsy to be closer to her mother, Angela, and the two adoptees, Ashley and Bethany Cooper, who were grafted onto the Ybarra family tree. If T.J. were honest with himself, he was feeling the same tug to set up shop in Euskadi.

He had procrastinated with uprooting Shadow Force Solutions, because much of their clientele—aka the bail bondsmen and women—were here in Boise. It had been the easiest and best choice to stay here to train Dot in the business. When she'd originally been approached with becoming part of the team, the plan had been to set up near her hometown and have Dot be the extension to the business here in Boise. Then the plan was shot all to hell, literally, when T.J.'s first partner, Sloane Cross, retired from the business.

It was a topic he didn't bother to bring up.

He parked the huge SUV beside his former truck—he'd signed over the vehicle to Dot after she came on as his partner—and killed the engine. Here they sat, neither willing to get out.

T.J. rested against the headrest, the fatigue from the day pressing down on him. What had started out as a good capture with Freddy flipped a full one-eighty with the Cade Porter situation. Damn, he needed a six-pack chilled on ice and juicy medium rare steak. If he were a cigar connoisseur like Dot, he'd be smoking a fat one right now. The problem was, there was no chilled beer and no steak waiting for him. Maybe a fifth of Wild Turkey was stashed somewhere in a desk drawer. God only knew how old that was. T.J. gave up liquor a year after his DD214 from the army went live. The final push to leave the harder stuff behind came when he had to participate in a funeral for one of his soldiers, a man too damn young to die but couldn't cope with his demons. There were just some things liquor would never solve.

"I'm going to my place," Dot said.

Her place was a little bungalow she rented on the edge of Boise. Far enough away from the bustle of city life but still not remote enough for her.

Dot was a mountain woman. Born and raised in the shadow of the Payette National Forest, she was left to run wild in the foothills and mountain ranges of the national park where she spent a lot of her time hunting and tracking. She preferred animals to humans and isolation to inclusion. She was a woman of dichotomy when one considered how long she'd been in the army herself, flying helicopters for men like him. Forward operating bases, or FOBS, were about as remote as one could get, but there were still more people per square mile there than where she'd grown up.

"We should probably revisit all of this in the morning," he said, reaching for the keys.

She grasped his forearm.

T.J. caught her gaze. He recognized that fierce gleam shimmering in her eyes.

Dot was filthy, smelled like a horse that had been worked heavy under saddle, and the bags under her eyes were dragging on her features. She had taken a beating today, but she wasn't about to give up.

He had to remind himself constantly that Dot had the drive of a cow dog. Give her a task and she'd work herself into a grave before she quit.

"I'm going home to clean up," she said. "You're going to do the same and then come to my place. We're going to figure this out tonight."

Anticipation knotted in his body, the friction of it creating sparks. Most of the time, going to her place ended in sexy time.

Neither of them had ever intended to pick up the torch from their days in the army. Neither of them wanted sex to interfere with the partnership. Yet, somehow, if they ended up together at night, at her place, it inevitably happened.

T.J. knew a few couples, dating or married, who did the recovery agent thing together. A lot of them hadn't planned to get to the point in their relationship, but you couldn't be together, alone, for long hours at a time before making a connection. Trust in your partner was hard to come by in this business. Couples trusted each other as well as soldiers on the battlefield.

"I'm calling Vivian," Dot went on. "We're having a confab with her about Cade Porter."

T.J. deflated. If Vivian was going to be there, then he had nothing to worry about.

Right?

"Fine." He turned the key. "You're cooking. Hope you have steak."

"I've got steak. Whaddya want, elk, bison, or beef?"

"You have bison?" he asked incredulously as she opened

the passenger-side door.

She slid out and turned to face him. "It pays to know people." She shut the door before he could ask more questions.

She stared at him through the window. He couldn't make out her expression because of the tint. He hit the automatic window control; the motor whirred as the pane slid down.

"What?" he asked.

If she'd had a cigar in hand, she'd take a long pull on it, let the smoke roll around in her mouth, and then slowly release it. This was her typical MO when she took the measure of someone or a situation. It unnerved T.J. at times.

This was one of them.

"Did you find anything out there you didn't mention to Larrabee?" she asked.

"I found jack squat. What I saw was what we'd already witnessed."

There was the look again. T.J. was about to roll the window up to get her to stop.

"You sure about this bounty?"

The question hung between them. He sensed what she didn't say. They weren't hurting for cash; they'd done a fine job in the last two months on bonds to cover their expenses for the next three months. Through his PI side of the business, he'd done a few legal document serves through the court, something Vivian and her firm liked to take advantage of from time to time.

So, what Dot wasn't saying, what T.J. was trying to avoid thinking on, were his reasons for wanting this bounty on Cade Porter.

They'd done what they were asked. They didn't have to take it any further. Let the big dogs run this guy down. Federal marshals were better equipped to handle someone like Cade Porter.

T.J. met Dot's steady gaze. A breeze filtered through the Suburban's cab, teasing the loose strands in Dot's braid.

"I really do think we understand him better than anyone else," he said.

"That's all I needed to hear." She headed for the truck.

She'd been through a hell of a lot in the last five years. Still, Dorothy Ybarra managed to find a way to the top.

Some days, T.J. wished he had half the strength she carried.

Chapter Four

THE SOUR STENCH of fear leached from the man. He paced the dusty path between the vehicles, coating the hem of his tailored suit pants and the once shiny Rockports.

A contrast to his own clothing, soaked in the blood of other men and smelling of manure and sweat.

"What do you expect me to do?" The other man stopped midway and stalked back to him. "They never told me this was a possibility." He balled a hand and jabbed a finger under his crooked nose. "You never told me. You came from this world. You should have warned me."

"I left that world eons ago," he said, his damaged vocal cords straining at the intensity of his statement. "You knew what you were signing on for."

Tailored Suit jammed the finger against his scarred chin. "I didn't sign on to anything. I was fed a line of bullshit to make this look legit." He wrenched his hand away and spun on his heel. "Fuck!"

The word echoed over the basin. It was their agreed upon meeting point to stay out of sight of prying eyes. A place so far out of city limits, it was considered wilderness. Tailored Suit wasn't keen on the spot, being too citified and pampered. But places like this were a safe haven for him.

He'd matured and thrived in desolate and dirty environments like these.

"You have one option," he said.

Tailored Suit stopped his angry march. "What the hell is that?"

He dipped his chin and leveled a hard stare. "Run."

Chapter Five

Attorney Vivian Montgomery, Esquire, had the fortune—or was it misfortune?—to be Dot Ybarra's cousin through Dot's grandmother's side. With that relation came a few perks. But here in the last year, those perks were being buried under the weight of the cons.

Before arriving at Dot's tiny bungalow, Vivian went to her apartment to change out of her court attire and into something more relaxing, like shorts, a tee, and a pair of canvas slip-on shoes. While the day's heat was not uncommon for Boise in August, it seemed to zap more out of Vivian than usual. It had to be the turn of events with Cade Porter.

For God's sake, why had she let Terri talk her into begging Dot and T.J.'s assistance on this mess?

Because she had a Wonder Woman complex, that's why.

Vivian's draw to the profession of an attorney came from her overwhelming desire to help the little man. She blamed Dot's Basque grandfather, Samo Ybarra, and his longwinded teachings on always doing right and fearing no man. Too many summers spent on the Ybarra sheep ranch bonding with her only cousin in the world had given Vivian a slightly skewed take on life.

Decades and one too many kicks of reality later, those views bore a decidedly strong shade of jade.

Camped out on the small deck at the back of Dot's bungalow, breathing in the tantalizing aroma of seared meat over a wood fire, Vivian nursed a melting peach margarita, watching her cigar-smoking cousin grill.

"Remind me again where the hell you got a taste for cigars?" Vivian asked, then took a long drag on the icy peach-flavored tequila.

Dot, decked out in jeans and a snug T-shirt the color of sagebrush, pushed a cast-iron skillet loaded with sliced potatoes to the far corner of the metal grate covering a firepit. She took a few pulls on the cigar before wedging it on an ashtray.

"I don't recall ever telling you," Dot said after blowing out the smoke.

The clap of the screen door announced T.J.'s arrival. "It probably happened about the same time she got a taste for dangerous men."

Keeping the margarita glass pressed to her cheek, Vivian eyed the broad-shouldered man wearing a formfitting dark-green tee and faded blue jeans as he ambled over to the only other chair on the deck. "It's amusing you think you're the first dangerous man she sank her teeth into."

T.J. halted before sitting in the chair and tipped up the brim of his ball cap to eye her. "I'll ignore that comment and consider you drunk."

"Joke's on you. This is my first, and I'm not even halfway through it."

He scowled then plopped down in the chair, the wood

frame creaking ominously under his bulk. "You have the file?"

Vivian bent over the side of her chair and grabbed up the black plastic expandable file folder. "This was not easy to come by." She held it up and fanned her face with the folder. "Nor was Terri's admission that Cade Porter's case was dumped on her last minute."

"Your law firm allows any senior member to just dump off on juniors?" T.J. asked, reaching out for the file.

Vivian passed it off and relaxed against her chair's smooth wood backrest. "No. Terri claims the lawyer in charge told her it was an easy case and the managing partners decided she would be better suited for the defendant's legal representation. Then he took off, leaving her with the fallout."

"Who was this senior associate who left Terri flapping in the wind on this one?" T.J. asked.

Vivian used her glass to gesture at the file. "That's all in there. But it was Hal Jones." She sipped her watery margarita, then asked, "Was it really that bad at the farm?"

Dot had given her only the bare minimum of what they had stumbled across. Vivian wasn't sure if it was out of Dot's need to shield her cousin or a natural inclination to say little because she was molded that way.

Dot was by no means a chatty woman, preferring to say exactly what needed said and not mincing her words. Angela, her mother, on the other hand, had no compunction whatsoever of chewing on your ear any chance she got, being the more sociable of the pair.

And now, neither Dot nor T.J. bothered to answer Vivian's question, choosing instead to glance at each other and then resume their current task, Dot squatting to stoke the fire and T.J. digging into the file folder. Vivian knew some unspoken message passed between them. They had been doing it for months every time she was with them.

Was it an army thing? Or just something these two had cooked up over the course of their acquaintance? Either way, Vivian's level of tolerance for it was beginning to tip into the nagging bitch phase, a side she rarely had to pull out. Vivian had perfected the fine art of getting her way.

"Fuck me," T.J. growled.

Dot ceased her fire poking and rotated on the balls of her feet. Vivian set aside her margarita glass and leaned toward T.J.

"What?" she asked.

He looked to Dot, who gave a nod, then to Vivian. "His full military history is in here."

"It's not unusual for us. If it calls for it, we can have access to your records. It's how I knew he was in the Marine Corps and what division. I don't see how it's a problem, considering his situation."

T.J. held a thin stack of papers and turned the front to her. "It is if they're redacted files."

Dot stood. Vivian noticed the shift in Dot's stance and the tight features to her sun-darkened face.

"I'm well aware of the significance of redacted files," Vivian said. "Bet you both have them on your records."

"We do," Dot said, her voice low and husky. She took the papers from T.J.

"What Dot is kind enough not to say is, records like

those could mean a helluva lot of things to us. Anything from he's been in and out of the court-martial process ..." T.J. said.

"Or he was something more lethal than a Marine in the artillery," Dot finished for him. "Doing shit we shouldn't know about."

"Which could explain why you two found the carnage you did at the horse farm," Vivian added.

Both bounty hunters looked at her with their own personal version of *duh!*

"How does someone even manage to get their hands on redacted files like this?" T.J. snarled. "If I'm reading this right, he hasn't been out of the Marines long. Three years. Shit, I bet he was going to be a lifer."

"His age and service time would suggest it," Dot said.

Vivian sat back and watched them process. She wasn't usually privileged to observe the two of them at work, having only been brought into their orbit after Dot begged for some information on a defendant they had been tracking three months before. The tradeoff for Vivian had been to ask for some pro-bono work.

Fascinated by their volley of words, Vivian sipped on the last of her now watered-down margarita and didn't hear anything they said. Beneath the low hum of their voices, she felt a slight vibration in her brain.

Was she drunk? On one margarita? No. Wasn't possible. Then, maybe it was. After all, she showed up to Dot's starving. When had she last eaten? Probably at her lunch break between court appearances, which would have consisted of a half hour walk on a treadmill and downing a protein shake. That was about eleven-ish. Right before her lunch and after walking out of her third hearing for the day, Terri had tracked her down and broken the news about this Cade Porter deal. Vivian had spent the rest of the day on that.

The drone of Dot's and T.J.'s voices had gone silent.

She blinked out of her mental lollygagging to see them staring at her. "What?"

"Where does this Halloway Jones live?" T.J. asked, his tone carrying a bit more irritation than Vivian liked.

"Hal lives south of Boise. Why?"

"Because …" Dot held out a plate with a steaming bison steak, juices swirling around the edges and mingling with the potatoes. "After we're done eating, we're going there."

"Who's *we*?" Vivian asked, taking the plate and fork.

"All three of us," T.J. said. "You're going to introduce us to Attorney Jones, Esquire. We have lots of questions to ask him."

"YOU DO REALIZE I don't have to be along for this little meet and greet," Vivian repeated for the fiftieth time from the Suburban's second-row seat.

And for the fiftieth time, T.J. ignored her. In the passenger seat, Dot looked up from her GPS, then pointed at a street shrouded in late evening shadows. The sun had slipped past the horizon and one by one the streetlights were kicking on.

Attorney Halloway Jones lived in the country club community of Boise. Swankier homes surrounded by walls of vegetation with curved driveways butting up to the street. Living here was just a perk of being near the top in a law firm.

"I'm seriously reconsidering my quid pro quo status with the both of you," Vivian grumped.

T.J. was feeling likewise. He peeked in the rearview mirror to see her glaring at him.

"There's our guy's house," Dot said.

He hit the turn signal and whipped into the bowed drive. He parked lengthwise in front of the garage, preventing any attempt at escape if it came to that.

"How do you want to play this?" Dot asked as she released her seat belt.

"Storm in and start demanding answers," Vivian snarked.

T.J. twisted around and pinned her with a hard stare. "You can package up the feminine outrage anytime now."

Vivian's two bird salute made Dot chuckle.

T.J. shook his head and exited the vehicle, turning back to Dot to say, "She's your cousin. Deal with her," and closed the door.

He and Dot had left off the normal suspect hunting gear of vests and guns, choosing the more personable approach of normal civilian clothing. Except T.J. wasn't about to walk into anyone's house without his sidearm. While he settled the appendix holster in a comfortable position under his jeans and tee, the two women hashed out their differences.

Though he didn't hear exactly what was said, he noticed Vivian carried the heavier load of the conversation. A minute later, the two seemed to come to a settlement, and both exited the suburban. Vivian imparted a particularly nasty scowl at him then stomped past.

He met Dot's gaze over the hood. She rolled her eyes and followed her cousin to the front door. T.J. noted that Dot had her Colt 1911 holstered to her leg. She, too, was not going into any situation unprepared.

They joined Vivian under the halo of the motion detection lights, bracketing her for protection and placing themselves in a way they could see the street and the edges of the house.

"I'm a lawyer," Vivian grumbled.

"And he's from your firm," Dot pressed. "Knock on the door and step to the side."

Vivian looked at her cousin. T.J. didn't have to see the expression to know what face she gave Dot. In defiance of her orders, Vivian forewent the knocking and punched the doorbell instead.

The *ding dong* echoed through the house. At least it still worked.

After a thirty-plus-second wait, Vivian hit the bell again. Another echoing call visitors had arrived. She let more than thirty seconds pass.

"Knock," Dot insisted.

Vivian did as ordered. "Hal, it's Vivian. You home?" she asked as she pounded the side of her fist against the white door.

There was a click and a creak, and the door inched inward.

T.J. grabbed Vivian's arm and thrust her behind him, at the same time drawing his pistol. Dot armed herself and sidled up to the junction of the doorframe and the portico wall.

Thankfully, Vivian had the good sense God gave her to shut up and stay where she had been positioned.

Without a word, T.J. held up a finger and pointed at himself. Dot nodded in agreement and inched away from the door, then swung around behind him, pushing her cousin farther to the back of the line.

Once his six was covered, T.J., using his boot, nudged the door open farther. A blast of cold air greeted him as the door came to a rest against the wall. Inside the dimly lit house, he made out a disorganized entryway; shoes of varying shapes, sizes, and colors lay where they had been kicked off haphazardly scattered along the opposite wall. Halloway Jones had a wife and teenagers if T.J. assessed the strewn shoes correctly. Coats hung uniformly above the shoes. Someone's backpack had been tossed to the floor at the end of the entryway.

He looked back at Vivian. "How many in his family?"

"Wife and two kids, teenage boys," she answered in a hushed voice.

He nodded, taking out his flashlight and clicking it on. "Hold the line, Dot."

She gave him a thumbs-up.

Flashlight beam proceeding him, T.J. stepped into the entryway, and careful to avoid tripping over the chaos, he made his way into the house. Ranch style, maybe only a single level, possibly a basement, looked like every other ranch style along this block. The hall opened into a combination living and dining room—nothing looked wrong with the setting. T.J. passed through the room and entered the kitchen, where a single light shone above the sink.

More chaos reigned here, but the typical kind with active boys who played football if the cleats dropped under the overhanging counter were any indication. A pair of duffel bags draped over a stool. Dirty dishes filled one side of the sink, and the dishwasher door stood open. With the hem of his T-shirt wrapped around his fingers, he opened the fridge and found the usual clutter of a family with growing boys—most of the food was labeled high protein and half-used.

Letting the door swing closed, he stepped back and spotted another hallway. T.J. followed it. Three bedrooms and a half bath lined the hall. The first two rooms proved to be the sons' rooms with the typical mess and stench, and the last bedroom was the master with an attached bathroom.

T.J. turned on the light and found what he'd been anticipating the moment the front door creaked open. Within the confines of Hal Jones's bedroom was frantic pandemonium—male and female clothing tossed over the bed, on the floor, and piled in front of the open closet. Discarded travel bags kicked aside, probably for something lighter and more compact. Dresser drawers left open, undergarments and jeans hanging over the lip. In the master bath was more of the same, missed bottles of cosmetics or toiletries scattered on the tiled floor.

T.J. backed out and headed down the hall toward the front. "All clear," he called to the two women.

Dot and Vivian followed him back inside and left the door open.

"I think Hal Jones packed up the family and ran," T.J.

said. "Looks like they took only the bare minimum."

"Why would he run?" Vivian asked, moving farther into the house.

"Probably has something to do with Cade Porter," Dot said.

"Shit," T.J. spat. "We've got someone else to track down."

Chapter Six

S TANDING KNEE-DEEP IN the Boise River in chest-high waders, Dot flicked her fishing rod and watched the lure sail out. Once the indicator settled on the bouncing waters, she reeled back the line a few times and waited.

This part of the Boise River was prime fishing for salmon and a beautiful spot to relax and think. So far, she'd done more relaxing than thinking. Her wicker basket already held one catch. She was allowed two per day, and she fully intended to reel in a second salmon for the freezer.

Dawn was fading into morning, and the sun was starting to peek through the trees. From her spot in the river, Dot heard the early risers making their way into the city for their daily grind. On the opposite bank, she spotted a herd of deer grazing on the lush river-fed grasses.

Dot chose to live in this part of Boise because of its access to Boise National Forest and the river with its prime fishing grounds. The first thing she did after getting her address was purchase a fishing license. If she got an itch to disappear into the foothills, she had access to more than a few trailheads. And if the urge hit to nock a few arrows and let them fly, there was an archery range northeast of her bungalow.

All this wilderness so close to a bustling city, but she still missed the wilds of the Ybarra ranch in the heart of the Payette National Forest. What she wouldn't give to saddle up, ride into the mountains, and camp out.

Adjusting her hold on the fishing rod, she eased out the travel mug she kept hooked on her catch basket and took a long pull of the coffee—a special brew roasted by a fellow veteran who talked her into being a shareholder in the company—and let the warmth seep through her. A breeze rolled down from the hills, teasing her face and hair. Today promised to be another scorcher. For now, Dot stayed cool standing in the churning river waters.

There was a hit to her line, and the indicator disappeared beneath the waters. With her mug hooked on the basket, she took hold of the rod and began reeling in her new catch. There was a struggle, and she worried she'd snagged debris instead of a salmon. The line came free, and she felt the drag on the fishing line. She had a big one.

She managed to reel the fighting salmon closer, take out her net, and scoop up the thrashing fish. Lifting the net, she admired the wriggling silver and yellow body.

Dot waded through the rushing waters back to the shore, where she deposited the net and rod on the sand and rock mixed ground. She made short work of freeing the salmon from the net and removing the hook, then held up the still fish. It was a good catch.

With the salmon laid to rest beside her earlier catch, Dot set the basket on the ground and sat next to her equipment. She enjoyed the last of her coffee as she watched the sun's rays dance on the water.

The rustle of boots through the dried grasses alerted her to his presence before he came to stand beside her.

"Knew you'd be out here," T.J. said, his voice low and rumbling.

She patted the empty ground next to her. He squatted, his knees sounding like popping corn, and then sat with a grunt. They sat there enjoying the morning.

"Catch anything?" T.J. asked after a bit.

"Two nice salmon."

"Those will taste good."

More companionable silence passed between them.

"Come up with a plan?" T.J. asked.

"Not a thing," she answered and tipped up her mug.

"Larrabee called me," he said, plucking the seed head from the grasses. "They've IDed some of the dead men at the horse farm. Low-level enforcers from Las Vegas."

"These wouldn't be the same types we tangled with before?"

"Larrabee says no. But there was a hitch in his voice when he said it."

Dot lowered her mug. In her short association with the lawman, he hadn't crossed her as one to wiggle on the hook when it came to doling out information.

"What are you thinking?" she asked T.J.

"I want to go through the lawyer's house. Vivian wrangled permission for us to be there."

"Shouldn't we bring the police in on that?"

T.J. made a scoffing sound low in his throat. "There was nothing there to prove foul play. Unless the law firm decides to call him a missing person, then the cops might get involved."

"And the law firm isn't because?"

"Because Halloway Jones put in for vacation time, starting yesterday."

AFTER CLEANING THE salmon and storing the meat in her freezer, Dot took a quick shower and dressed in tan cargo pants, a green tank top, and a lightweight white button-up she left unbuttoned. She laced up her boots and settled a dark-green ball cap over her damp head.

T.J. waited for her by the truck. Under the brim of his ball cap, his Aviators reflected. "Let's roll, Fly Girl."

She scowled at his old nickname for her and hopped into the driver's side.

The drive across Boise to the Jones's residency was about fifteen minutes. Dot kept the truck to a slow crawl down the street, watching for any kids—still out of school on summer break—to appear out of nowhere. She parked the truck lengthwise in the drive like T.J. had done the night before.

Before they exited the cab, they grabbed Nitrile gloves and armed themselves in case of unexpected visitors.

T.J. produced a key Vivian had procured for them. Once inside, he relocked the door and pocketed the key for safekeeping.

"We'll work our way from the back of the house forward. You take the master bed and bath; I'll handle the sons' rooms," he said as they wove through the clutter. "You're not going to want to deal with the boy stench in there."

"Can't be any smellier than a goat buck in rut." She

snapped on a glove.

"Trust me, it's worse."

They separated in the hallway.

With a finger, Dot pushed open the partially closed bed-room door and let it swing open. Before they had left last night, T.J. had returned any open doors back in the near exact position they had been as he did a reconnaissance of the house, except for the front door, that they had closed and locked. Neither they nor Vivian had moved or removed anything lying about. They didn't have to worry about fingerprints because they had worn gloves if they had to handle doors or locks.

The master bed looked as it had last night. Dot disregarded the scattered clothing and went to work searching the dresser drawers. Mr. and Mrs. Jones loved to work out if the unbelievable amount of spandex and moisture-wicking clothing was anything to go on. Dot was by no means an expert on clothing—if it didn't say Wrangler or Ariat or was handed to her by the US Army, she was clueless—but everything looked expensive.

On the drive over, she and T.J. had discussed what they should look for. They both came to the consensus it didn't have to be anything specific, just something that seemed way off to be in a family home. So far, the only thing Dot discovered off beat was the weird ass vibrating thing she assumed was a sex toy. To each their own.

She moved onto rummaging through the huge walk-in closet, scrounging through shoe boxes and garment bags. How did one woman have time to wear all of these clothes? Before working through what had to be Hal's side of the closet, Dot paused to stretch her back. Her tussle with Freddy yesterday had aggravated a few aches and pains leftover from the forest service helicopter crash she'd survived a few years ago.

Bent back as she was, she spotted the extra layer of shelves above. Something dark and leather dangled over the edge of the topmost shelf. Dot reached for it, but she wasn't tall enough. She stepped out of the closet and searched the room for something to stand on. Not spotting anything sturdy enough, she checked the closet and found a step ladder shoved behind five stuffed garment bags.

On the upper step of the short ladder, she was able to see over the edge of the shelf. The leather strap was connected to a long hand-tooled leather rifle case. Dot slid the case closer for inspection, finding it lighter than expected, and it tilted toward her. A silver medallion with a familiar leather crafts-man logo winked back at her.

"T.J.," she called out.

She stepped down, bringing the gun case with her, the lack of weight inside increasingly noticeable as she exited the closet.

T.J. entered the room, a black smudge on his cheek. "What?"

Dot pointed at her cheek. "You got something right there."

He wiped at his face, only making the smudge larger and darker. He peered at his gloved hand and grimaced. "Shit. That room is covered in black mold."

Now she was glad he'd taken it. She laid the case on the bed.

"Nice rifle case," T.J. muttered as he joined her.

She pulled back the heavy-duty zipper and let the case flop open. Empty. As she'd feared.

"Think Halloway has any other empty gun cases around here?" she asked T.J.

He ran his fingers over the tooled leather. "Where'd you find this?"

"Closet, upper shelf."

"See any gun safes?"

She swept her hand around the room. "Nope."

T.J. examined the carpeted floor. "If I were a betting man, I'd say our attorney has a floor or wall safe."

Together—Dot on hands and knees and T.J. moving artwork and mirrors—they scoured the room for any sign of a safe.

Dot was ducking under the bed to feel around when a loud clatter echoed through the house. She bolted upright, drawing her weapon as she moved. T.J. shifted away from the adjoining doorway to the master bath, his pistol pressed to his chest, barrel pointed down.

"I thought the house was locked up," Dot whispered, her voice strained.

T.J. shrugged and inched toward the bedroom door.

"I don't know who you think you are, but you better come out." The voice echoing down the hall was decidedly female and carried an undertone of fear. "I mean it. I have a gun. And I called the cops."

T.J. closed his eyes and let his head tip back as he mouthed *Fuck*.

Dot seconded his sentiment. The last thing they needed

was an adrenaline-fueled Stepford wife with a weapon.

T.J. pointed to the windows behind Dot, then made a circle motion. She looked over her shoulder and frowned.

"Why me?" she whispered.

"You're flexible and scrawny," he whispered back.

She flipped him the bird as she holstered her 1911. Every time. Every damn time. She was the one stationed as rear guard while he kicked in the doors. But after examining the window, she had to admit, his bulky frame would not fit through without making a ton of noise.

Slowly, she lifted the sash, happy it moved freely and quietly, then she pushed up the storm screen and lastly the screen.

"I know someone is in here!" the frightened Stepford wife hollered.

Dot glanced at T.J. "You better go defuse the situation," she whispered.

He waved her off and peered around the doorframe.

With a shake of her head, Dot made like an otter and slid through the gap, headfirst. She dropped to the ground on a flower bed, crushing delicate petals and stems. She was on her feet in a flash and stuck her head into the open window.

"Fat ass," she hissed at T.J., then bolted before he could respond.

Dot left the 1911 in its holster and headed for a neat patio jutting into the backyard. The whole yard was encased by a dark-stained wooden fence, its boards evenly spaced with hair-width gap between each board. The lone gate dividing the Jones's yard from the neighbors' gapped open. So,

Stepford wife was a nosy neighbor.

As Dot reached the patio, she heard T.J. inside the house.

"Ma'am, I'm a fugitive recovery agent here on official business. Would you please put that gun down?"

Dot slipped across the patio's cement pad to the open French doors. Nosy Neighbor had a key?

"The cops are on their way," the woman's voice wobbled.

"That was not necessary," T.J. said.

Dot peered in through the window bracketing the doorway and spotted the neighbor standing at the edge of the tiled kitchen, trembling arms pointing a too-heavy pistol in the direction of the hallway. Dot noticed some of the football gear left on the chairs in the kitchen had been dumped to the floor, probably the clatter they heard before the woman announced herself.

"Ma'am, if you'd just let me show you some ID—"

"No! Keep your hands where I can see them."

Dot crept inside the house, careful to avoid the scattered gear, and keep out of the woman's line of sight. The best method was to approach her from behind and disarm her before she could fire a shot. It was going to be tricky, because this incompetent female had her finger on the trigger.

Dot spotted T.J. as she cleared the table. Ever the professional, he didn't flick his gaze her way.

"Ma'am, I need you to set that gun down before you end up doing something you'll live to regret."

"I'm not falling for that." She jerked the gun at him.

T.J. ducked. "Ma'am, I'm serious. You don't know what

you're doing."

"I do too!"

Dot acted. With one hand, she gripped the pistol's slide and with the other the woman's right wrist. The gun went off as Dot pinched hard on the wrist nerves, making the woman screech. Dot disarmed her and forced her onto her knees by twisting her wrist. Once she had the woman subdued, Dot ejected the clip and the spent cartridge.

"You good?" she called out to T.J. over the ringing in her ears.

"Good," he answered.

Dot chucked the pistol with its slide racked and the clip onto the kitchen table. From her cowering position on the floor, the woman tried to glare at Dot.

"Next time you try to play hero," Dot said, leaning closer to the woman, "don't. If we'd been real criminals you'd be dead."

She looked between Dot and T.J. "I called the cops," she croaked.

Before Dot could say anything, T.J. had his phone out. "I'm on it," he said.

"Who are you?"

"Well, Nosy Neighbor, we're fugitive recovery agents, as my partner told you we were." Dot untucked her badge from behind her vest and let it dangle about her neck. "We're here per the request of Mr. Jones's law firm."

"Yeah, Bukowski, it's Roman. Did you get a call for a unit to respond to a B and E?" T.J. rattled off the address to the LEO, then waited.

Dot stared down at the woman who had the good sense

God gave her to remain in the position with her hands up.

"That's what I thought. Hey, can you call the car off? It's just me and Dot here on request of the owner's place of employment." T.J. waited again. "Oh, that? That was nothing." He met Dot's gaze and winced. "Well, the alarmist decided to play heroine with a loaded gun ... Yeah, she fired a shot, but it hit a wall. No one's hurt ... No, that's not ... Okay, fine. I'll let the law firm know. Thanks." T.J. ended the call. "For nothing. Squad car is almost here. Someone else just called in shots fired at this location."

His withering look dropped to the woman kneeling on the floor. "Who the hell are you?"

Nosy Neighbor pointed a trembling finger at the back-yard. "I live next door."

"And just happen to have a key to the place?" Dot asked.

"Yes. I'm the HOA president." Her voice rose. "Every owner on this block has to give a copy for emergencies."

Dot made a face, the one she gave when she didn't believe whatever lie vomit was coming out of someone's mouth. He shook his head and rolled his eyes.

"Pretty certain a lawyer is not going to give over a copy of his key to some rando no matter how much perceived authority she gives off," Dot said as she circled the kneeling woman. "So many violations in the span of a few minutes."

"I have not broken any laws." She pointed between Dot and T.J. "You are the ones who broke in."

T.J. walked past, dangling the key and the authorized letter of permission from the law firm. "Yeah, no."

Nosy Neighbor must have realized her mistake and went for the next best defense. She clutched her wrist. "You broke my wrist."

Dot gave her a canine-bearing smile. "The nerves might bother you for a few hours, but nothing was broken." She leaned forward. "You, on the other hand, wielded a firearm. By the way you were brandishing it, I'd say you have no idea how to use it, and you have no legal right to do so." Dot cocked her head. "Is it your husband's? Maybe the pool boy's?"

The woman's features turned red and blotchy.

"Squad car is here," T.J. said and exited the house.

Dot straightened to her full height and went over to the table to check over the gun. It was a nice weapon, a Desert Eagle, a pistol primarily used for target shooting and hunting. But not by a five-foot-four-inch trophy wife.

Dot corrected the slide, having interrupted its ability to recycle the next round after she'd grabbed the slide and jammed it. Dot reached for the clip.

"Oh my God," the woman croaked.

The fear had returned to her voice. Dot looked out the open French door.

Two figures emerged from the open gate and were coming this way. Dot grabbed the clip and rammed it into the pistol grip as one of the men lifted a firearm, aiming it her way.

"Get the fuck down," Dot barked and leveled the Desert Eagle out the door.

Chapter Seven

D OT FIRED TWICE. One of the windows exploded from the .44 caliber bullet. She had only a second to glimpse the men in the yard as she took cover. One of the men wheeled about as if hit, and the other was moving.

Nosy Neighbor screamed as she ran for the front door.

"Fuck!"

Dot didn't have a chance to stop her before a barrage of fully automatic gunfire hit the house. Over the chaos bullets breaking glass and splintering wood, the woman stopped screaming.

From her position behind a love seat, Dot saw the woman lying facedown on the floor, blood blooming on her back.

"Shit-shit-shit."

"Dot!" T.J. yelled from outside.

"Stay out!"

There was a pause in the gunfire before another burst blasted through the house. The shooter must have changed magazines.

Staying low to the floor and using furniture to protect her, Dot belly crawled to the neighbor's body. "Don't you fucking be dead," she growled.

"Police!"

The gunfire was redirected away from Dot's area. The sound of return fire and then silence.

Dot reached the bleeding woman. She'd taken a bullet to her right shoulder, and she was still breathing.

T.J. came in through the front door, low and armed. "Dot?"

"I'm fine. She's been hit."

He reached back into the entryway and returned with a towel. "Here."

Dot took the soiled thing and pressed it to the woman's shoulder.

One of the responding officers ran into the house. "We got the shooter. There's another man down."

"Call for an ambulance," T.J. told him. "We've got an injured bystander."

The officer grasped his radio and hailed his dispatch for medical services.

Dot met T.J.'s heated gaze.

"You're sure you're not hit?"

"I'm fine," she barked. "I think I hit the other one."

He sighed. "Damn it. What the ever-lovin' fuck was that all about?"

"I don't know, but how much you want to bet they were here for Hal?"

The police officer returned. "Bus is en route."

Dot beckoned him with a bloodstained hand. "You hold this here and take care of her."

"Where you going?" the LEO asked, pressing down on the towel as she started for the back of the house.

"To see who just tried to kill me."

"Ma'am, I'd advise you to stay where you are," he said, his young face a misdirect with the level of authority he carried in his voice.

Dot gave T.J. a half-hearted smile. "Getting younger every day."

He grunted his response and walked outside.

Dot winked at the officer. "Just worry about our madam president." She didn't wait for his comeback.

The other officer had found his way inside the fenced-in yard and stood over the deceased gunmen beside T.J. Dot joined them.

"Thanks for the assist," Dot said to the older patrolman.

He touched his forehead as a salute. "Your partner says you got that one." He pointed at the man Dot had hit with the Desert Eagle.

"Yeah, it was a lucky shot. I didn't think I'd hit anything but glass." Dot held out the Desert Eagle, grip pointed at the officer. "This is the weapon. Not mine. Our injured bystander thought to threaten us with it."

The police officer frowned. "Is it emptied?"

"It is."

"I don't have any evidence bags. Would you just leave it on the table or something until scene techs can get here?"

Dot shrugged and placed the firearm and its clip on the patio table. "Guess I can."

She moved to squat next to the body of the second gunman.

"Please don't touch the body," the LEO said.

"Hadn't planned on it."

She studied the dead man's clothing—a black blazer over

a green button-up discolored by his blood and black slacks—and the weapon, an MP5, Heckler and Koch submachine gun with a curved elongated clip and a nylon strap wrapped around the man's arm. This was some serious firepower for suburbia. This man wore clothing better suited for the office, not tracking down people to shoot and kill.

"Do you see it, Dot?" T.J. asked.

"See what?" she asked, squinting up at him.

"His neck. Behind the collar of his shirt."

Dot didn't see much from her angle and stood. On doing so, she saw what T.J. was trying to point out to her. "What is that?"

The police officer leaned over. "I have no idea."

"Would you mind if we got a better look at it?" T.J. asked.

The officer seemed to hem and haw in his head before shrugging. "I guess. Just don't change anything."

"Got it." T.J. removed a folding knife and popped out the blade. With the tip, he moved the shirt collar aside.

The lower half of the tattoo looked like the base of a tulip with three rounded protrusions sticking upright out of the center. An open eye stared back at them from the middle of the tattoo, and below that was a symbol with a single upright line with a swoop at the top and an upside-down swoop on the bottom. Embellishments of different sorts filled the open spaces.

Dot took photos with her phone. "It's some kind of emblem." She turned her phone to T.J. "Ever seen it before?"

He squinted at the photo. "It looks vaguely familiar. Can't place where I've seen it before."

"Wonder if our other guy has one."

They moved over to the other body and scanned him without touching. This dead man wore similarly styled clothing as the other and had been carrying a Nighthawk pistol with a suppressor.

"Where the hell does this dude get the kind of money to own one of those?" Dot grumbled.

"What?" The LEO sounded genuinely confused.

"The gun. That's a Nighthawk 1911. Those are custom made and expensive as hell."

"Aren't you carrying a 1911?" the officer asked.

"A Colt 1911, and I inherited mine." From her *ai-tonatxo*, Samo Ybarra. He had carried it with him during World War II and had passed it down to Dot when she'd become skilled enough to handle the weapon. Dot was never without it, except during her time in the army, where they expected her to carry the weapons assigned to her.

"He was a killer, intent on ending a civilian's life. What do you bet he stole this off one of his previous victims?" T.J. asked as he crouched beside the body.

"The likelihood is high," Dot conceded.

Using the blade of his knife, T.J. shifted the shirt collar aside. "I don't see a tattoo."

"Probably hidden under his clothing," the LEO said.

Dot stared at the photo. "Man, I swear I've seen something like this before."

The piercing wail of the ambulance coming down the block broke up their little confab. Not far behind the bus came a slew of squad cars with their sirens blaring.

"Bookmark this for later," T.J. said. "We've got another round of interrogations to get through."

LIKE THE DAY before, a good chunk of their day was chewed up by questioning and leading the techs and detectives through their movements in the house. By the time the lead detective gave them permission to leave, Dot and T.J. were exhausted, starving, and irritated.

Seeing Detective Sergeant Cassius Larrabee waiting for them beside the truck soured Dot's gut.

"You two." Larrabee shook his head. "Are you magnets for chaos?"

"What are you doing here?" T.J. snapped.

"The lead on this called me in. He heard about my case from yesterday and asked me to join him to see if we have any overlap other than the two of you."

Dot and T.J. looked at each other.

"We can tell you what the overlap is," Dot said. "This is the lawyer for our missing bounty from yesterday."

Larrabee flicked his Stetson up and settled it back farther on his head. "Who was the injured party? Not a single soul would tell me."

"The next-door neighbor," T.J. said. "The lawyer and his family are missing. We were here looking for something to give us a clue where they went."

"Wherever they ran off to, they went armed," Dot added.

Larrabee digested what they'd told him.

"Have they done the autopsies on the guys we found yesterday?" Dot asked when a thought popped into her head.

"No, they'll do them tomorrow," Larrabee said. His contemplative look changed to curiosity. "What are you looking for?"

Dot pulled out her phone and brought up the image of the tattoo. She showed it to him. "Recognize it?"

He stared at it a moment then shook his head. "Want me to ask the ME to look for something like it on the other guys?"

"Yeah." Dot turned the phone back to her and studied the image.

"If they find one, I'll let you know." The Idaho state investigator started for the house.

"Larrabee," T.J. said, bringing the Black man to a stop. "Would you mind if we comb over the scene at the horse farm?"

Larrabee frowned. "Didn't you already do that before I arrived yesterday?"

"That was before I knew what I know now."

Dot joined Larrabee's frown. What was T.J. thinking? Frankly, what did he think he was going to find that Larrabee's team hadn't already discovered?

Larrabee considered T.J.'s request—hard, it looked like—then shrugged. "Sure, why not? Just don't remove anything without consulting with me first."

What kind of kinship did these two have that a normally by-the-books cop like Larrabee would allow someone like T.J. to just tramp all over his crime scene?

"By the way, did you ever reach the owner of the farm?" T.J. asked.

Larrabee shook his head. "The name on the farm is a leftover from its previous owner. The current one is under some corporation, and no one seems to know who the owner of that is either. We're running in a million different directions, and no one has time to figure it all out."

"We'll do it," T.J. offered.

Dot gave him the side-eye but kept her own counsel.

Larrabee shrugged. "Suit yourself. You find something, let me know." He glanced at his watch. "I need to take care of this and get." He pointed at Dot. "Don't let him sweet-talk you into committing a crime."

Dot gave him a sly smile. "Don't worry. Sweet talking never worked on me anyway. I'll just kick his ass."

"That's my girl."

Chapter Eight

"WONDER WHO'S TAKING care of the horses."

T.J. glanced at Dot as she navigated the truck along the lane leading to the back of the barns. His head and body still hadn't recovered from the shooting at the Jones's place. While the firefight went down, he kept flashing back to the last time he and his previous partner, Sloane, had been caught in a crossfire. Sloane had been severely wounded and barely survived the ordeal.

T.J. kept reminding himself that Dot was a different breed of woman. She'd survived a helicopter crash, for God's sake. With nothing more than a bow and arrows and a pistol for backup, she'd systematically picked off a squad of killers to rescue a child and walked away from it with minor injuries. Dot was beyond capable of handling situations like a pair of shooters.

But it still didn't stop T.J.'s heart from racing.

"You okay?" she asked.

"Fine. Just thinking," he replied, then pointed at the small parking area beside the house. "Don't park right in the spot."

Without a word, she stopped the truck in the two-tire track that served as the drive and killed the engine.

He sensed her staring at him. She most likely had that deep assessing thing going on that she was damn good at doing. T.J. wasn't sticking around to find out. He bailed from the truck.

The sun hung halfway in the western sky. It amazed him how much of the day had been chewed up by so few events. The hours-long interviews with the Boise police had pushed them into midafternoon. He was starving, but his stomach would have to wait.

Without waiting for Dot to join him, he marched to the house. Other than the bloodstained grass at the edge of the porch, there was no sign of the carnage that had taken place here the day before. He mounted the steps and headed for the doorway blocked by red DO NOT CROSS tape and yellow CRIME SCENE tape.

He pulled away the edges surrounding the door.

"God, it stinks in here," Dot said as they entered the house.

"Decomp," he said in passing and moved to the short flight of stairs leading to a loft area.

The one place he hadn't explored yesterday.

"T.J.," Dot said, her tone low and commanding.

He hadn't heard her use her officer voice since the day she'd told him and Larrabee that she would be the one to have a comin' to Jesus moment with a murdering rapist.

He stopped at the base of the stairs and turned to her. Neither of them spoke.

T.J. remembered the first time he met Dot. Gussied up in her flight suit and carrying her pilot's helmet, she met him and his squad before they left the base for a mission into the

Afghan mountains to give them the checklist of how the upcoming flight was to go. By this point in her career as an army helicopter pilot, Dot had served two tours and flown fifteen times into the field, gotten into two firefights with Taliban fighters, and brought back every man under her watch. The men T.J. commanded—himself included—tried to push her buttons. One of his lower ranked guys went so far as to insult her choice of music. Like the alpha female in a wolf pack, she flipped his ass to the ground and locked him into submission. No one from his squad ever gave her shit again.

"You're back there," she said softly.

The shift in her voice hurtled him through time and space back to the present. By nature, Dot was not a soft woman. She generally saved her gentle nature for Bethany— the young girl Dot had rescued—and animals.

"I'm right here," he ground out.

"Don't fuck with me, T.J. You were remembering something. I'd bet my best hat you were back in Afghanistan."

He jabbed a finger her direction. "I ain't hearing no lectures from you about memories." He faced the steps once more.

"What do you have on Larrabee that he'd be willing to let you just trample all over his crime scene?"

Apparently, he wasn't going up those steps anytime soon. Dot had something on her mind, and it usually meant she was about to unleash hell. God, sometimes he forgot she was a woman with female tendencies.

"I don't have anything on him. Before you ask, he's got nothing on me. We're two dudes who had a moment out in the mountains and lived to tell about it. That's it."

Dot stared at him, those normally twinkling eyes hard as stone. Without a word, she stalked toward the kitchen.

Guess they were now at the intermission part of this interrogation.

T.J. mounted the steps to the loft, bothered by his sudden trips down memory lane and how perceptive Dot was getting about those trips. That she was trying to force him to talk about it was disturbing. This was not Dot.

She suffered from her own versions of PTSD and had found a way to handle the flashbacks while refusing to talk about them herself. She was not one to delve into someone's brain. Nor was she ever one to hold their hand and talk them through it.

He, on the other hand, had gotten counseling for his PTSD. Once he found ways to cope, he stopped going. He'd taken the path of therapy because a few of his men had sought to end their pain and suffering by suicide. T.J. never wanted to resort to such measures. Bounty hunting had become his therapy.

Topping the stairs, he surveyed the small loft, stuffing down his wayward thoughts. A single bed jutted out in the middle of the room, the bedding tucked in tight and smoothed to perfection, not a single wrinkle in the fabric. A faded green heavy-duty footlocker was stationed at the end of the bed. Positioned under the lone window was a small desk and chair. Leatherbound journals, stacked three high, sat on the left-hand side of the desk, and a chipped mug with USMC scrolled across the width held a handful of pens and pencils. Marine to the bitter end.

T.J. decided to start with the footlocker.

A bang from downstairs halted him.

"You good?" he called out.

"Fine" was Dot's response.

By her tone, he didn't think so, but he wasn't about to contradict her.

The footlocker wasn't locked. He popped the clasps and lifted the sturdy top. A pungent waft of desert dirt with an undertone of male sweat hit him. T.J. reeled back as the odor flung him across two continents and landed him in the middle of a FOB that didn't exist any longer.

"No." He growled and shook free of the flashback.

The top layer consisted of civilian clothing—T.J. took a wild guess and figured they were Porter's since this was his supposed residence—a few articles were not long for this world due to how worn and tattered as they looked. The next layer was a dark-green wool blanket, probably one Porter had *inherited*, as those in the military were ought to do with items being phased out. The blanket had spots of smudged dirt, and T.J. could feel the grains of sand clinging to the wool hairs. Why wouldn't Porter wash this out?

T.J. rolled the blanket aside, revealing a stack of folded desert combat uniforms. Lifting out each crisply folded set, he noted that none of them had name or rank tapes, each one a blank set but almost threadbare from constant wear. After he placed the last pair aside, he came to a black vinyl garment bag.

He pulled back the zipper and found Porter's dress blues. He shoved aside the edge of the garment bag to expose the left breast of the jacket. The dimension of the ribbon holder amounted to the size of T.J.'s hand. He recognized a few as universal awards given to anyone who'd served overseas. A good chunk of the ribbons were Marine Corps specific, and he had no clue what they meant. As with the combat uniforms, the dress blues lacked a nameplate and rank.

Why the hell would Porter not have his name on any of his uniforms? The rank, TJ could understand. A trick they'd learned from Vietnam, the men on missions or in the field would not wear anything to indicate rank to avoid having their NCOs or officers killed by the enemy. But Porter not having a rank of any kind on his dress blues made no sense.

T.J. rezipped the bag, placed it on the floor, and turned back to the footlocker.

A pair of bloodied boots sealed in a clear plastic bag and an equally bloodstained uniform in a sealed bag lined the bottom of the box. There were no patches—not even the American flag—on this uniform, and it looked like someone had taken a butcher knife to the material.

Breathing hard, T.J. rocked back on his heels and looked at anything but the items at the bottom of the box. Bile clawed its way up his esophagus, burning a path as it went.

The smell reached him, sharp and metallic. On its heels was the ringing in his ears. He squeezed his eyes shut and shook his head, hard.

He would not do this again. It had been a long time since he relived that day. This was not a setback.

He gathered up the articles strewn about him and shoved them haphazardly into the footlocker, then slammed the lid shut, forcing it down when the clothing pile refused to allow it to close properly. T.J. climbed to his feet and backed away.

The desk and its neat stack of journals called to him. He picked up the top one and flipped through it.

The handwriting was cramped and small, the style a mix between print and cursive. This edition was about the daily work on the horse farm, notating horse rations and which mare foaled and when; it was half-used, the remainder of the journal's pages left blank. The second one was more personal and confirmed these journals and the items in the room belonged to Porter.

T.J. stopped on a page and read Porter's entry dated four months prior.

EACH DAY GETS EASIER, BUT IT DOESN'T STOP THE PAIN. IT SHOULD HAVE BEEN ME.

"T.J., I found something."

Startled, he spun. Dot stood at the top of the stairs.

Her gaze flicked down to the brown leather book in his hands, then up at his face. She looked over at the footlocker.

"You found something?" he asked, his voice sounding rough.

She dragged her attention back to him and held up a blue glass jar with a swing top lid. A half-used compressed cake sat on the top of crumbled pieces at the bottom of the jar. He'd seen stuff like this in large blocks wrapped in yards of plastic in Afghanistan. It was popular in Europe, but not here in the States.

"Is it?" he asked.

Dot popped the jar open and held it out to him. "What you think it is."

He set the journal down and took the jar from her. One sniff told him exactly what it was. "Hashish." He flipped the lid over and snapped down the metal clasps.

She took back the jar, held it up, and examined the contents. "I don't know why the crime techs left it here."

"Where'd you find it?" he asked.

"In a cabinet with other home-canned goods, clear at the back."

"They probably didn't see it." He picked up the journal. "I don't know why they passed these over. They're sitting out here in the open."

"What's in them?" Dot asked, setting the jar of hash on the bed.

"Daily journals for the horses. And personal ones about his time in the Corps."

Behind him, he heard Dot lift the footlocker lid.

T.J. flipped through the journal and the next one. More of the same entries. A decidedly guilty conscience on Cade Porter's part. Not once did he mention the circumstances to what led him to this point.

Her stoic presence at his side pulled T.J. from his reading.

"You need to stop," she said, her voice iron-hard.

Slowly, he closed the journal and set it on the desk, fighting the urge to snap back at her.

Dot took hold of his arm and tugged him toward the stairs. Before they started down, he put the brakes on and whipped her around. Dot slammed into his chest and glared at him.

T.J. tried to force the words into his mouth. Tell her how damn scared he was. Explain how much this bounty was beginning to fester in his brain. Reveal how bothered he was by these circumstances. None of it would come.

Their stare down ended when Dot freed herself and walked down the steps.

T.J. smothered his mouth with one hand, then moved it to the back of his neck to cup it, giving himself a hard squeeze.

At the bottom of the steps, Dot looked up, then exited the house.

Oh, he'd fucked up bad.

Chapter Nine

H E'D BEEN DOING reconnaissance on the horse farm for a good chunk of the day. He wanted to get in, grab his gear, and bolt but didn't want the cops to arrive unannounced and catch him.

His spot was positioned less than a mile out from the main house and barns. Its secluded area with an unobstructed view of most of the farm was perfect for a blind. On the downside, he had no clear line of sight on the main entrance.

When he'd been certain he was in the clear, he had gathered his aching body off the ground, then the big dark-gray truck rolled in. He'd abandoned his plan to get in and out and watched the unknown man and woman enter the house. While he waited, he scoped intel from the truck's license plate. Except his position out among the trees and hills gave him no stable connection, forcing him to access a direct link to a satellite.

On a small notepad and with the stub of a pencil, sharpened by a knife blade, he jotted down the information he was able to pull up on the owner of the truck, the woman. And the previous owner, the man. It was amazing the things one could find with a simple search. What he couldn't find was their lives beyond anything most recent. He wasn't able to locate where they lived, but he did find the location of their business.

Bounty hunters. Both of them. Here? Had Tailored Suit sent them on his trail? Or had he done what he was told to do and now Tailored Suit's associates were behind these two coming here? They could prove to be problematic.

Close to an hour later, they exited the house, first the woman then the man. By their stiff, agitated movements, he got the sense the two were on the outs. Neither delayed in getting in the truck or leaving, so whatever bee was up their bonnets wasn't worth sitting around discussing. Once they'd gone, he made his move.

His trek down was halted twice as the blinding pain in his head took hold. The second time, he accepted defeat and popped the pills. Gave himself a ten-minute break to allow the drugs to work before resuming his march forward.

He bypassed the kitchen and its bloodstained floor. In the small room that served as the living area, he paused before climbing the short flight of steps to the loft. Standing in the house that had begun to feel like a home for the first time in his life, he surveyed the damage wrought on the little place by yesterday's fight. The scent of decaying blood lingered in the air. A smell so familiar to him, it had taken permanent residence in his sinuses and now and again it would pay an unannounced visit.

Those visits would bring with them memories. The echoes of laughter and the rattle of gunfire. Dust and heat, decay and rot.

He slapped his face, pulling him back from the precipice. There was no time for regrets or recriminations.

In the loft, he went straight to the footlocker. It had been rifled through, which was to be expected. What was not—all his gear had been left behind. He avoided digging farther than taking the top layer of clothing out of the locker. Once he had them stuffed in a duffel pulled out from under the bed, he slapped the lid shut.

He spotted the jar of hash lying on his bed. How had that gotten up here?

He picked up the glass jar and let the weight of it seep into his hands. This was the last of it. He'd needed to get with his dealer before it completely ran out or he'd be fucked. After a quick scan of the room, he shoved the jar in between his clothing to cushion it.

The journals whispered ugly words from across the room. He stared at them; the top two books had been shifted aside. All were there. If he took them, even one, it would be noticed. Someone had made a point to look through them. Why the cops had left them behind was a head scratcher. Maybe they'd figure it out later and come for them. He'd rather they not. The journals were not meant for them. The LEOs would not understand the cryptic messages coded within the leather binding.

Nothing he could do about it now. The person they belonged to would have to find a way to get them. It was no longer his worry.

He turned for the stairs, then stopped and looked to his right. The concealed panel looked undisturbed.

Slinging the duffel strap over his shoulder, he moved to the wall. He drew out the fixed blade knife from its leather holster strapped to his left leg. With the tip wedged into the seam, he wiggled it deeper, then popped the panel free. He set the piece of wood on the floor and returned the knife to its holster.

From within the hallowed compartment, he pulled out a battered metal child's lunchbox. He flipped back the aged clasp and lifted the lid. Shifting aside the rubber-banded stacks of hundreds, he found the desert-colored M9 Beretta, a full magazine, and an extra box of ammo. He removed the pistol and slid the magazine into its slot in the grip, then replaced the useless .22 he had lifted off one of the dead men from the previous day's firefight. He stashed the extra ammo in his duffel along with the cash.

He stared at the old dinged-up lunchbox. A lone reminder of a fleeting moment when he'd been happy. It had survived the years bouncing from one place to another, then through the rigors of training and multiple trips into hostile areas. He ran a calloused thumb over the raised words and the character images of a long-forgotten children's cartoon, the color smudged out from decades of wear.

He set it inside the space and picked up the panel. He gave the lunchbox one last longing look, then replaced the panel. With the side of his fist, he sealed it in place. It was time to put away childish dreams.

At the bottom of the steps, he paused to check his perimeter through the single pane of glass in the door. Still clear.

Time to disappear.

He was halfway to the secluded spot where he'd left the old truck when a notification pinged on his phone. He dragged it out from the right pocket of his pants. It was an encrypted message.

Before he lost service connection, he accessed the encryption decoder and opened the message.

Where the hell are you?

A shipment is coming in and you're needed at the drop-off.

And what the fuck is going on at the farm?

The sender would see he'd opened and read the messages. That would be all they'd get.

In order to sever the ties here, everything had to go.

He found a decent-sized rock and set the phone on top. With the butt of his knife, he smashed the cell. Then sorted out the electronic fragments and gave them an extra grinding until they were dust. The phone completely disabled, he took each individual piece and threw them in different directions, then brushed the rest into the grass.

Life would be lived off-grid from here on out.

Chapter Ten

DESPITE THE LIGHTS of Boise, Dot was able to see the stars from the deck of her rented bungalow.

Dot had foregone the usual cigar tonight and went straight for the joint. Being shot at had rattled her but hadn't left her incapacitated like she'd been around explosions or fireworks.

No, being shot at wasn't what drove her to the calming effects of the marijuana tonight. That fell on T.J.'s shoulders.

Damn it, one joint wasn't doing the trick.

She stared up at the sky, listening for that familiar voice. One she hadn't heard in months since starting this new venture with T.J. After the helicopter crash, her *aitona*, Samo, would pay her a ghostly visit when she was in need of his guidance. She missed him fiercely.

Samo Ybarra had passed away while Dot was training to be a pilot. Her last real conversation with him was the day she left for basic. *Aitona* had driven her to the airport, alone. Fit to be tied over her daughter's insistence on following through on this venture, Angela refused to come. It wasn't until this past winter that Dot learned why her mother had been furiously against the army; Dot's biological father had left a pregnant Angela behind and died serving overseas.

Dot had remained quiet the majority of the drive, but as they came closer to Boise airport, Samo broke the silence.

"Do not let your ama*'s anger turn you from her. She, like your* amona*, has a fierce loyalty. She loves you,* nire gudaria.*"*

My warrior. Samo had called her that for as long as she could remember.

Angela's father had done his due diligence in never revealing to his granddaughter his own daughter's deepest grief. He had always insisted it was a truth Angela would have to discuss when the time was right. Who knew it would be more than thirty years before she'd be able to talk about it.

Before she passed through the security line, Dot hugged her grandfather with a desperation she hadn't understood at the time. She begged him to tell Angela she loved her and she would write as soon as she could. He vowed he would.

With a kiss to each cheek, he waved her off into the unknown.

It was the last time she saw him alive.

Dot closed her eyes and expelled a long breath. The churning turmoil going through her. Difficult memories coming to the surface. The peace and ease she sought from the marijuana was not there.

Resisting the urge to go into the house and roll another joint, she picked up her phone and scrolled through the contacts to the right one. Once she tapped the call icon, she pressed the cell to her ear and waited.

"Dorothy" was the greeting from the other end. The only person in the world allowed to call her by her given name.

She smiled at the sound of her mother's voice. In the

background, she made out the chatter of a young girl.

"*Ama*, how does it go this fine summer's evening?" she asked. Maybe a cigar would be best to keep her on the straight and narrow.

"It goes well," Angela Ybarra said. "And you, *alaba*?"

Dot rose from the deck chair and meandered into the house to pick her cigar for the night. "Your daughter has had a few taxing days."

"Which explains the phone call at this hour." Angela tried to chide her, but Dot knew *Ama* was glad she called.

Tucking the cell between her head and her shoulder, she opened her humidor and selected her cigar. "It's not that late."

As she prepped the cigar for lighting, she heard a commotion from her mother's end of the line. "Is that Dot?"

She smiled as a small girl's voice demanded to speak to her favorite *izebak*. When had Bethany Cooper, the young girl Dot rescued on more than one occasion, taken to calling her aunt?

"Dot!"

She winced at the now-seven-year-old's exuberance. "*Kaixo, txiki.*"

"Are you coming home?" Bethany asked.

"Not sure. T.J. and I have been real busy lately."

Bethany's groan was one of those Dot had heard come from girls a few years older than Bethany. The girl wasn't ready for those years. She was a child, for God's sake.

"You need to tell T.J. to suck it up and bring you home."

Dot nearly dropped her phone as she burst out laughing.

Bethany's early life with men had been traumatic to say

the least, and she was apt to avoid them any chance she got, except for T.J. Maybe it was because he was close to Dot. Or maybe because he had found a way to bond with her.

"I'll see what I can do, *txiki*."

"Good, because you need to come see what *Amona* has taught me. Oh! Mommy let me bake my first cake too."

"Was it good?" Dot lit the end of her cigar and drew on it to get the flame established.

"Ehh, okay. Mommy thinks we added too much flour."

The flame took hold, and the end of the cigar glowed. "Keep practicing. Soon you'll be able to do it without your *ama*."

"I know." Dot could hear the smile in the girl's voice. "*Amona* wants to talk to you. *Gabon, izeba.*"

"Night, small one."

Bethany had picked up quickly on their Basque language, which thrilled Angela to no end. It warmed a spot in Dot's heart to hear the girl speak the tongue of Samo Ybarra's people.

"She's coming along nicely," Angela said when she was back on the line.

Dot, cigar in hand, wandered back out to her deck chair. "She's got the perfect teacher."

"I have my limits." Angela sighed. "She wants to learn how to use a bow. That's your field of expertise."

Easing down onto the wooden seat, Dot grinned. "Get her hand-eye coordination up to snuff, and I'll be out to work with her."

A pregnant pause over the line made Dot tense.

"Dorothy, what is on your mind?" her mother asked.

Dot stared at the burning end of her cigar, watching the embers flare red and settle into an orange glow. "We're caught up in something I think is going to go bad very quickly."

"Is it an impossible scenario?" Angela asked.

"At this stage, it's hard to say."

Another drawn-out pause.

"You are your mother's daughter."

Dot smiled.

"You are more than capable of handling any conflict or horror thrown your way. You are a Ybarra."

The statement, one her grandfather said over and over again when she was growing up, loosened the tension in Dot's body.

"*Eskerrik asko, ama.*"

"Sleep. Tomorrow is on the horizon, and things will become clearer."

They ended the call with their traditional goodbyes. Dot set her cell on the wide armrest and continued to stare at the starry sky while she smoked.

Halfway through the cigar, she picked her phone up, pulled up the photo of the tattoo, and studied it. The symbol burned into her brain.

Where had she seen this before?

A flicker of light. A memory of blood-smeared skin. The acrid odor of burned flesh.

Dot blinked at the images.

Wailing. Screams.

Twisted metal and powdered concrete.

Abbey Gate.

The memory flooded her senses. She had crawled out of the cockpit and stumbled toward the horror.

The first body she'd come across was a man, ripped in two by the blast, his ghutra thrown back to reveal the marking on his neck.

The same tattoo she'd seen on the shooter. On her phone.

Dot snuffed out her cigar and left the deck chair. There would be no sleep tonight.

THE AGED WOMAN T.J. rented an attic apartment from said he hadn't come around yet. Dot accessed their shared GPS locator and headed for his current location.

As predictable as she, T.J. found comfort in an outdoor shooting range. Where she preferred bow and arrows, he chose rifle and ammo.

The owner of the range waved at her when she entered the shop. He directed her to the lone outdoor range in use. Dot checked the time, noting it was coming on closing for the range. The owner assured her that he'd stick around as long as it took. The man being retired military himself, he recognized a troubled spirit when it walked onto his facility.

Echoing gunfire and the low lighting guided her to the range where T.J. had set up.

She called out to him, alerting to her approach. After he secured the range, he let her know it was safe to come.

T.J.'s setup was as she expected; his Mossberg with a night scope nestled on a tripod and a sandbag settled under the spot where he'd placed his elbows. He'd been prone versus sitting to shoot. His ear protection set pushed up to cradle his forehead, the ball cap turned backward. His beard was coated in dust, and grime smudged his tanned cheeks. He'd been at this a long while.

"How much did you win?" she asked.

When he got into a grump, T.J. liked to bet with the other shooters on the range on who could do what kind of shot and how close to a designated target they could get. He did this only with the guys and gals he'd shot against in the past, never with a newbie or a stranger. Everyone who bet with him knew his history and knew when he was in a mood.

T.J. had a tendency to lose more than he won. But it was never high stakes.

"A hundred," he answered as he began stripping the gun down. "Thought you were going home to sleep."

"You know that wasn't going to happen." She grabbed his hand to cease his work. "Look at me."

He set down the items in hand and faced her. Seeing him like this, covered in dirt and kitted out for a firefight, reminded her of those days back on the FOB after she'd picked up him and his squad outside the wire. Years and a few pounds heavier around the midsection, he still looked like he could kick some serious terrorist ass.

"You got whatever was bothering you today out of your system?" she asked, nodding at the range and the rifle.

"Some," he rumbled.

"I'll take what I can get," she groused. "I remembered where I've seen that tattoo." This was going to hurt coming out of her. "It was on a ... man who was killed ... at Abbey Gate."

"A refugee?"

"Maybe." Dot bowed her head and blew out a breath. "God ... there had been so many."

T.J. took her by the shoulders and pulled her into his arms.

What a pair they were. Pieces of them broken beyond repair.

That reason had to be why T.J. was suddenly so gung-ho on finding Cade Porter. The far-off looks. Slipping into a blank state that was clearly his brain dredging up memories. T.J. had more instances of war's trauma than Dot herself. There was something to the cockpit giving the pilot a sense of disconnect when it came to the horrors of combat.

They stood like this for a moment. She breathing in the scent of male musk, spent gunpowder, and dirt. He with his head bowed into her shoulder, his ear guards pressing painfully into her cheek.

T.J. lifted his head and shifted to look at her while keeping his arms around her. "If you want out of this case, we'll leave it to someone else to handle."

Dot stared at him. "What did you find in those journals? I want the truth of what you read between the lines, not what was written."

T.J.'s delayed response was a good sign he was sorting out his thoughts, a typical maneuver on his part she had come to trust.

"Something bad went down while he was in the Corps. So bad he saved a bloodstained uniform and boots. Were they his? I don't know. But we weren't given the whole read in on his dossier."

"You think his guilt is leading him down a bad path?" Dot asked, unable to bring herself to say that ugly word, *suicide*. Though he rarely talked about it, and didn't elaborate much on it when he did bring it up, Dot was aware of his history with fellow soldiers who had crossed the line and were no longer with them. "Then we stick it out. We were the right ones to pick up this case."

"Not if it's going to get us killed. That isn't why I got into the bounty business. And it sure as hell wasn't the reason I asked you to join me."

She frowned, analyzing what he said versus what he wasn't saying. "Is this about Sloane?"

His former partner and her long ago childhood friend, Sloane Cross had taken a bullet while on Dot's family ranch and nearly died from it. She had retired from the PI and bounty hunting business and was helping one of their other childhood friends run her bed-and-breakfast business.

T.J. made a noise as if to refuse, stopped, and sighed. "Maybe a little."

"At least you're being honest."

He leaned back a fraction and reached up to take her ball cap and turned it around. With the ball cap set backward on her head, he let his hand trail down the side of her face and settled it on the juncture of her neck and shoulder.

"If you're sure?" he asked.

"We see this to the end. No matter what comes our way." She held up a finger and whapped his nose. "And this pretending you're not having flashbacks ends."

He huffed. "Practice what you preach, Ybarra."

She wanted to kiss him. Sensed he wanted the same. But kissing and fucking hadn't solved any of their issues in the past. Tonight, she wouldn't go down this path.

She slipped free of his embrace and adjusted her ball cap brim forward. "Clean up here. We've got work to do."

Chapter Eleven

V IVIAN STALKED THROUGH the offices of McLaughlin, Pryor, Grainger, and Associates, scowling at the wide-eyed stares from fellow lawyers and paralegals. The sharp *click* of her heels sounded a lot like the crack of gunfire.

Despite the interior decorators' best intentions for ease and comfort, the entire place had a clinical feel to it with its light-gray walls, muted blue carpeting, and white and silver furnishings. When Vivian had become part of the law firm, she'd expected dark colors and dark woods, with an overall sense of power and sexism. This was far from the case for the two lower levels.

She marched up the wide staircase to the third floor. Up here, the décor was more masculine in color and taste—dark wood trimmed walls painted gunmetal gray sporting trophy heads of elk, deer, and antelope. At the top of the steps, she turned left and made a beeline for the main office dominating the left wing where a taxidermy grizzly stood sentry beside a dark cherry wood door.

An empty secretary's desk was stationed kitty-corner to the grizzly. Loren McLaughlin's administrative assistant had retired more than a year ago, and he'd never bothered to hire her replacement. Rumors whispered by those who'd been around the longest said the reason for the delay was because Loren was about to cash out himself.

Vivian's rapid-fire knock rattled the cherry wood.

"I'm busy" came the response to her summons.

Scowling at the door, she knocked again, harder.

"What?"

Plastering a fake smile on her face, she opened the door and breezed inside. "Loren."

"Vivian," Loren McLaughlin groused. "What brings you storming up to the third floor and banging on my door at this god-awful hour?"

God-awful hour was subjective. It was nine a.m.

The man behind the huge cherry wood desk didn't bother to get up. Loren wore a tan Western-cut blazer over a light-blue button-down. The gradual progression of light skin to dark in his face indicated much time out in the sun under a wide-brimmed hat. Said hat—a fawn-colored Stetson—lay crown down on a shelf behind the aged lawyer's gray head. Loren came from one of the oldest and largest Idaho ranching families and still had a hand in the operation. Word was his youngest son actually ran the outfit.

"What is going on with Hal Jones?" Vivian blurted, the irritation in her voice punctuating each word.

Loren scowled. "I have no idea what you're talking about. Not one iota."

"Really? So, it hasn't reached you that one of Hal's troublesome clients got dumped off onto a lower-tier lawyer? A client who ended up an FTA in court, and when recovery agents went to retrieve him, they found a massacre at his residence and said defendant was missing. Then when we went to talk with Hal, we found he and his family gone. Poof! Vanished into thin air."

Loren's features morphed from perturbed to disbelief.

"And the final straw came yesterday when my cousin and her partner, the recovery agents sent to retrieve the FTA, were ambushed and fired on at Hal Jones's home."

Loren threw up a hand and cut her off. "What fresh hell is this?"

"Just as you said, fresh hell."

Shaking his head, he closed his open case files and tucked them in a corner. "Okay, start from the beginning, and let's not summarize it."

As Vivian relayed the Cade Porter and Halloway Jones situation in more detail, Loren listened intently. Once she finished, he nodded.

"Better, Counselor." He sat back in his large leather chair and placed intertwined hands on his chest. "Sit down, Vivian, you're making me antsy."

"I'd rather not."

He leveled a stern frown on her. Squaring her shoulders, Vivian did as the old lawyer ordered and took one of the two chairs positioned before his desk. Once she was seated, he leaned forward and placed his hands on the desktop.

"First, I have no notion of where Hal has gone off to. Luke handles all the time-off nonsense."

Luke was the head of the HR department. Time-off nonsense was Loren's way of saying he didn't like people taking a leave of absence for any reason. Probably why he was three divorces deep and estranged from most of the children produced from said marriages.

"Secondly, you said *we* went to Hal's home. We being you, your cousin, and another man, T.J. Roman did you say?"

"Yes. I went because … well, they made me. But it made sense to have me along since Hal is a colleague."

"Vivian, you're a lawyer, not law enforcement. Why would you ever—"

"Loren, no offense intended here but cut the crap."

"This is not crap, Counselor. By your mere presence in Jones's home, you put yourself at risk for countless infractions, highest among them putting your life in peril."

"We had no way of knowing there was going to be serious trouble when we went to Hal's place. If something had gone south, I was in the most capable hands I would ever want to be in."

"Being your cousin—what was her name again? And this T.J. Roman?"

"Yes, my cousin, Dot Ybarra."

Loren mulled over this information. "What makes her so special that you'd trust her with your very life? Aside from her being your cousin, that is."

Vivian gave him a wry grin. "Aside from being my cousin, she's hell on wheels and one of the most accurate shots I've ever seen."

"Ybarra? This wouldn't have been the same woman who put the screws to that whackadoodle kiddie rapist months back? Made national news?" Loren asked.

"One and the same," Vivian said.

"Be that as it may, it still doesn't give you immunity from the blowback created if a serious incident with you involved had occurred. Bad press for you and this firm."

Vivian returned Loren's hard stare with one of her own. She'd faced hardened criminals and smug defendants with a penchant for sexist remarks that would make most women resign on the spot. Loren's sourpuss attitude was a minor inconvenience.

"Are you quite finished scolding me?"

"Are you sufficiently reprimanded?" he asked.

"Were you under any illusion I was going to take your verbal ruler to the hand to heart and change my evil ways?"

He sat back in his chair with a huff. "One can always hope."

"Now that we've circled the room a few times, let's get back to why I'm here. Do you have any idea of what Hal got himself caught up in that would scare him into hiding?" Vivian leaned toward the desk. "Do you have any clue as to where Hal might have gone to ground?"

Loren sighed. "Vivian, I'm sorry, I don't. For the last year, I've stayed out of the firm's daily grind. As I'm certain you've heard the rumors, I plan to retire by the end of this year. I've left most of the day-to-day to Meredith."

Meredith Pryor, the Pryor portion of the firm's managers. And the instigator of the horrible décor on the lower levels.

"I would get with her and discuss this whole matter," Loren continued, this time standing.

Vivian popped onto her feet. "You don't have any inkling on Hal's life outside of the firm?"

"Hal was close to Charley; in fact, I think they spent weekends fly fishing or golfing or whatnot. I'd ask him. But check with Meredith first." Loren rounded his desk and showed Vivian to the door. "Might I add, if this is as dangerous as you're making it sound, you should consider not involving yourself any further. Having one missing lawyer is too much."

"I'll be fine, Loren."

He opened his door and paused to study her. "You're a damn fine lawyer. Extremely intelligent. Don't let your cousin and her partner drag you into anything."

She gave him a half-hearted smile. "You're thirty years too late for that warning." She nodded to Loren as she exited his office.

As she passed the secretary's desk, she heard the door click shut behind her. Vivian halted and looked back. Was Loren serious about not having a clue on what was going on?

Or had he just put on the best acting performance of his life?

Whatever the case might be, she'd have a one-on-one with Meredith and see what the she-dragon had to say.

Vivian was about to take the steps down when a hiss followed by her name halted her. She turned and followed the beckoning hand into the older case files room. Once she'd entered the room, Charley Ash, a fellow attorney and apparently best buds to Hal Jones, closed the door and locked it.

Vivian gave him a glare that could peel paint. "If you plan to molest me in some way, I'll—"

"Whoa, chill, Vivian," he said as he passed her, holding his hands up as if surrendering. "Come with me."

The room they were in was situated like a library graveyard. Ancient law books and aging white banker's boxes covered in dust on tall bookshelves made narrow pathways to the far wall lined with old metal filing cabinets. Vivian swore she'd felt a spider swing past her face.

Charley stopped and faced her, peering past her shoulder. "Good," he said in a low voice. "Don't speak too loud."

"Why?" she asked in a whisper.

He pointed to his ear and then circled the room. Vivian looked around, didn't see anything that looked like a listening device or even a video recorder. She made a pinched face at Charley.

"Not like that," he said quietly. "This is about Hal and that defendant of his."

"Cade Porter," Vivian supplied when Charley faltered.

"Yeah, him." He turned to a light silver filing cabinet and unlocked the top drawer.

"Where'd you get a key for that?"

"I've always had it." He opened the third drawer and pulled it out as far as it would go.

The drawer was crammed with old case files. Vivian noted some of the dates on the folder tabs going back to the seventies. At the back of the drawer, sitting in a five-inch gap between the last file and the drawer's panel, was a black leather portfolio. Charley picked it up and held it out to Vivian.

"We were never in here. I did not give this to you. And you say nothing to anyone about this or what is in it. Understood?"

She took hold of the portfolio, but Charley held fast.

"Understood?"

"Yes, I understand."

He released his grip on the portfolio. "Find a way to get this out of here and the building without anyone noticing it."

"How do you expect me to do that? I didn't exactly walk up here with a huge bag to stuff things into."

He looked about and grabbed up an old banker's box. He yanked the lid off and peeked inside. "Empty." He thrust it out to her. "Grab some of those books and pretend you needed to look up an outdated law or something."

He'd lost his damn mind. "No one is going to believe that."

"Then come up with your own lie. Either way, you have to get this somewhere safe."

She went to open the leather covers. "What's in here that makes you act like—"

Charley clapped his hand on hers and smacked the portfolio shut. "Don't read it here. I'm serious, Vivian. Take it and leave. Go through it somewhere else."

Scowling at him, she yanked the aged carton from him and shoved the leather binder inside. "I should box your ears."

"I'm serious about this. There's a reason Hal's gone to ground."

"Do you know where he went? Loren said you and Garret hung out with him a lot."

Charley shrugged. "Have no clue. We go fishing and golfing now and then, but we're guys, we don't have deep conversations."

She paused grabbing a few books from a shelf. "Do you

know what's in the portfolio?"

Charley shook his head. "I made a point not to know. Hal warned me not to read it."

"The two of you have a lot of nerve dumping this off onto Terri if this is as bad as you're making it out to be."

"Terri just got a dummy case file to take to court."

Vivian set the box down and moved closer to Charley. "Come again?"

He held up his hands defensively. "She was never in harm's way. All she had to do was show up to court, let the judge make his ruling, and that was it."

"What kind of dumbass nonsense was that? Whatever is hunting Hal could have gotten wind of Terri's involvement. They've already made a try on Hal's home and got dead."

Charley paled. "I swear I didn't realize how bad this was."

Vivian grabbed up the box once more and glared at him. "Well, now you do. I'd be real careful yourself from here on out." She slapped on the lid and left the filing room.

Before stepping into the hall, she double-checked her surroundings. Finding the way clear, she made a beeline for the backway exit that led to the employee parking lot behind the building.

There was no way she was going to review any of this alone.

She reached the main floor with no intervention. As she crossed the parking lot, she pulled out her cell.

"Dot," she said when her cousin picked up. "I got handed what might amount to the golden egg in this whole messy Cade Porter affair."

Chapter Twelve

B Y MIDMORNING, DOT was on her tenth cup of coffee and no closer to learning why a strange symbol had been tattooed on the shooter. Larrabee had called them and reported that the second shooter from the Jones's home had the same tattoo, as did three of the dead men from the horse farm. Common thread initiated.

She and T.J. had managed to scrounge up from deep searches interesting tidbits that gave some insight into what they were dealing with. The symbol tattooed on the men was a creative re-creation of the Hamsa, aka Hand of Fatima. The original Hamsa was well-known and well loved among those of the Berber Jewish and Muslim cultures. Its more common meaning for those who wore it was protection against the "evil eye." This re-creation must have a different meaning for the dead men bearing it. Whatever its meaning for them had been, luck was not on their side.

Further research on T.J.'s part brought up a thirty-year-old photo of a well-known Israeli-American mobster in Las Vegas with the very edge of the tattoo peeking out from under the sleeve of his jacket. That find took him down a rabbit hole of long-ago Jewish mafia organizations running with and against most Italian or Irish mobsters. Their misdeeds mimicked those of their partners or counterparts in booze, sex, and drugs. For the majority of Las Vegas's heyday, the Jewish-American mob ran the show. They had long since gone to ground and were now aligned with the Russians or an Israeli crime family that had moved in about twenty years prior.

One gold nugget of information came from T.J.'s rabbit trails. He'd learned the identity of the name on the horse farm—Meyer Follman, a casino owner in Las Vegas with deep pockets and deeper connections. T.J. continued to gather as much information on the man he could.

Dot's male victim of the Abbey Gate bombings didn't bring up any connections to what they'd learned so far. She believed him to be a mere bystander caught in the blast while trying to flee the country like thousands of others. Hundreds to thousands of men, women, and children of all walks of life had filtered into Afghanistan during America's occupation. He could have been from any of the Middle Eastern and Northern African countries and there would be no way of knowing.

"So, we've slammed face-first into a brick wall," Dot said as she pushed away from her desk in their small office.

T.J. had just ended a call declining a bond jumper job and was staring at the wall decorated with their business name and logo. Shadow Force Solutions was being very shadowy at the moment.

He sighed. "None of it will make sense at first. You've got to remember that."

"Doesn't stop me from being frustrated about it."

He chuckled. "You're just exhausted and hyped up on caffeine."

Vivian's number flashed up on Dot's cell and she answered.

"We're at the office. Bring food," she ordered after a moment, then she ended the call. "Vivian claims she was handed the golden egg on Cade Porter."

"I'll believe it when I see it." He rose from his seat and arched his back. "I need air," he said and headed for the door.

Dot pushed to her feet. She needed to get out in the open too. They'd been cooped up in this small space way too long.

They stepped out into the sun's bright onslaught. Dot tilted her face to the midmorning rays and soaked them in. Normally, they would not spend so much time in the office. On a typical day, they were either on the hunt, parked somewhere on surveillance, or chasing down leads or cosigners. All of that meant time in vehicles or on foot. Neither she nor T.J. were wired to be chained to a desk and a computer, pressed in by four walls.

The horseshoe-shaped strip mall where the Shadow Force Solutions office was situated held a nail salon, a combination Mexican eatery and grocery store, a certified accountant's office, and a payday loan store. The Flores and Lopez families, the owners of the Mexican store, were a young family, a brother and sister who ran the place after their parents retired. When not in school, their kids rode bikes or played soccer in the parking lot.

Today, the five cousins sat on the sidewalk drinking Jarritos from the bottle. They spotted Dot and T.J. and waved.

Seeing the three boys and the two girls lined up in a row,

oldest to youngest, struck Dot in the feels. After last night's brief conversation with Bethany, she was getting homesick.

Leaving T.J. to his own devices, Dot strolled across the lot toward the kids.

"Dot," all five cried out in unison, holding up their arms. "*Kaixo, mutilak.*"

The Basque's native homeland bordered northern Spain and southwestern France, bracketing the western end of the Pyrenees mountains. Their language, unique in its own right, had been borrowed in some cases by their Spanish and French neighbors. Though they didn't understand her, the Flores and Lopez cousins giggled.

The eldest boy and girl scooted over, and the girl patted the empty spot she'd made. Dot settled down between the kids. She'd no sooner made herself comfortable than an opened bottle of bright orange Jarritos was thrust into her hand.

"*Eskerrik asko*," she said before taking a gulp of the mandarin-flavored soda. "What are you up to today?"

"Trouble," the youngest boy, a known smartass, remarked.

Dot chuckled. "Looks like you're taking a break from it."

"We're gearing up," the youngest girl added. She, too, was known to throw out the quips.

"More like sugaring up," said the eldest girl.

Dot noticed the twinkle in her dark eyes. She was usually the more reserved one of the bunch and kept her lone sibling and three cousins in line.

"Hey." The single middle child elbowed Dot. He was about Bethany's age and the hellion of the group. "Did you know you had a visitor this morning?"

Dot frowned. "We did?" She looked around. "What time?"

"Over an hour ago," the elder boy said. "He was hanging around the door, and when I yelled at him, he spooked."

Dot looked at him. "Why did you yell at him?"

"He looked like one of those punks from out of town." Eldest boy flushed red when Dot gave him her half-lidded scowl. "Okay, he looked out of place. Wore a black hoodie with the hood up. It's summer, and it's hot. Who wears a black hoodie?"

Someone who doesn't want to be recognized.

"Was there anything on the hoodie?" Dot asked. "What kind of pants did he wear?"

The rest of the group let the older boy talk. "The back of the hoodie had some design. It was white, but I couldn't see what it looked like. And his pants were those kind with all the pockets."

"Cargo?" Dot supplied.

"Yeah, those. Kinda brown colored." His eyes flared wide. "And he walked funny."

"Funny how?" Dot asked.

"Like this," said the middle boy, who hopped onto his feet and mimicked an odd gait.

After he stopped, Dot asked him to do it again and studied how the boy slung out his left leg. He might be exaggerating the walk, but Dot recognized it. She'd seen it too many times in her life after leaving the army.

She downed more of the soda. "Was there anything else about our strange visitor?"

"Yeah," the eldest girl said. She pointed to her right hip and leg. "He had a bulge right here." Her dark intelligent eyes locked with Dot's. "He was carrying a gun."

And all five of them had been out here. A tightness strained Dot's chest as she looked at each child.

"Tell me you went inside with your parents after he ran off?"

The oldest boy's face scrunched into disgust. "Why would we do that? He left."

His female cousin whacked him. "Because, *estúpido*, he had a gun." She looked at Dot. "We did. I made them all wait until a little while ago to come outside."

Dot squeezed her shoulder. "Good." She drained the Jarritos and handed the bottle to the middle boy. "If you see him again, do not approach, do not talk to him. Do you understand?"

All five nodded.

She leveled a heavy stare on the eldest boy. "Stay out of trouble."

He blushed again and nodded.

"If he comes back when we're not here, make notes. When we get back, and he's not here, come tell us. Okay?"

More nods.

Dot stood. "Thanks for the soda and the information." She gave them a wink and then crossed the parking lot to the music of their chatter. God, how she missed Bethany.

T.J. was sprawled in the back of the Suburban with the hatch up and his boots pointed toward the front of the vehicle and his head under the shade of the hatch's tinted window. Dot hopped inside beside him and let her legs dangle over the edge.

"I think Cade Porter knows about us."

T.J.'s eyes popped open, and he squinted at her. "How so?"

"The kids saw him loitering outside our office over an hour ago."

He bolted up into a seated position. "How do you know it was him? It could've been an associate of the men who shot at us yesterday."

She looked him dead in the eye. "I doubt they would have run off when a kid caught them. Those guys cross me as the type to start shooting and never ask questions."

"Shit," he muttered.

Vivian's sporty blue Outback pulled into the lot and parked beside the truck. She emerged, carrying a huge plastic bag loaded with cardboard containers and a drink holder.

Dot hopped down from the Suburban and helped her cousin. Once Vivian had handed off the food and drinks, she got into the back seat and pulled out an ancient banker's box.

"Inside," she ordered.

THEY SETTLED AROUND Dot's desk with containers of Italian goodness in hand.

Vivian brought out a black leather portfolio and set it down on the desk with a *thunk*. "Here you go. I haven't looked in it yet."

T.J. paused in stuffing his mouth with pasta covered in a

spicy marinara sauce. "Why?"

Vivian settled in the last remaining chair in the cramped office and picked up the mug of coffee she'd poured for herself. "I was warned not to do so until I was far from the firm and where no one would see me read it."

Dot and T.J. glanced at each other, then Dot snagged the portfolio before he could. She pushed back from the desk and set the leather binder in her lap. The thing was thick, and the binding looked worn. She turned back the top and let it fall against her leg.

The first thing glaring back at her was a stained and tattered file folder with CONFIDENTIAL stamped in huge red letters across the front.

T.J. scooted around the corner. "Shit. That looks like it came from the DOD."

The Department of Defense, the proverbial boogeyman for all special operations teams. By far and large, T.J. had seen more of these confidential or classified folders than Dot. Although there were a few floating around in the Pentagon that she'd laid her eyes on for special missions she'd flown or had herself been heavily involved in.

"How did someone in your office get their hands on something like this?" T.J. asked Vivian.

She shrugged and shook her head. "All I know is what I was told. Hal had one of his fellow lawyers hide it away in a random filing cabinet and gave orders to never open it. I think Charley, the lawyer who passed this off to me, figured with Hal missing and me involved, I was the best person to bequeath it to."

Dot opened the confidential file and found Cade Porter's

service record. Except, the name in the file wasn't Cade Porter. And he was never an artillery man. "Well, that explains how we can't find a damn thing about this guy." She turned the file to T.J. "His real name is Caleb Podolsky."

He grabbed the confidential file out of her hands and began reading through it.

Left the remainder of the portfolio, Dot skimmed through the information. It was a living history of a troubled youth, orphaned at a young age, got messed up in drugs, theft, and a few B and Es. One of those breaking and entering charges he had nearly killed the homeowner who'd surprised him on being home.

All of the reports and files were stamped by Las Vegas law enforcement and legal system.

"None of this matches up to the file you gave us earlier."

Dot looked up at T.J.'s statement.

"What do you mean it doesn't match up?" Vivian demanded, shifting forward in her chair.

He got up from his seat and went to the cabinet where he'd filed the packet she had given them days before.

"Exactly what I mean." He pulled out the file and brought it to the desk, where he dropped it, wide open. "This is a dummy file with just enough of the truth to throw someone off." He stabbed a finger at the confidential file. "That is the real one."

While Vivian took both files in hand, Dot met T.J.'s troubled gaze. That haunted look was back. The one warning her he was revisiting places best left unvisited.

"Cade Porter is an alias. Caleb Podolsky has been out of

the Marines longer than three years, and he's older than what is in that other file," he relayed to her.

She picked up the report she had been reading. "He's also got a criminal record going back to his early teens."

"He's disabled?" Vivian's incredulous comment halted their back-and-forth. "He lost his left leg in an RPG attack in …" She looked up. "It just says the Middle East. No specific place."

T.J. took the confidential file back and was reading through it.

"It would explain the bloody uniform and boots you found," Dot said, setting the portfolio on the desk. "Maybe it is his."

"Doesn't explain his journals," T.J. said.

"What journals?" Vivian asked.

Dot settled deep into her chair, letting it rock back. The tired metal squeaked under her weight. "At the horse farm. He had a stack of journals."

"I read some of the entries," T.J. admitted and sank into his chair. "Most of them are daily updates on the horses at the farm. Others were personal. He blames himself for someone's death. Kept saying it should have been him but never mentioned who this person was. It might be related to the RPG attack."

"Why didn't the state police take them into evidence?" Vivian asked.

"Have no idea. That's a question better directed at Larrabee," T.J. said.

Dot continued to flip through the criminal records. "I think I'm getting a picture here." She looked at the dynamic duo across from her. "It ain't a good one."

"I don't like the look on your face," Vivian said.

Dot grinned. "Where'd we learn Follman was from?" she asked T.J.

"Wait, who's Follman?" Vivian asked.

T.J. ignored her and answered Dot. "Las Vegas."

She held up the criminal records. "These are all from Las Vegas."

Her partner's scowl faded, and he shook his head. "Damn it. We're going on a trip."

Chapter Thirteen

AFTER SENDING VIVIAN on her way with a warning to watch her back, T.J. and Dot prepared to leave. Both of them had left extra clothing in the office and had bug-out bags ready in their vehicles.

"Las Vegas?" Larrabee asked incredulously over the phone.

"Yes, Las Vegas," T.J. answered, watching Dot strip down to her underwear and bra.

The woman had no modesty with him. He figured it stemmed from their occasional sack hopping. He'd seen her naked, so what did she care if she changed clothes in front of him?

"Am I to assume that you're giving me this courtesy call to tell me you're headed down there to interrogate the man?" Larrabee's question dragged T.J. back to the conversation at hand.

"Look at you, being the sharp smartass detective you are."

"Fuck you, Roman."

T.J. threw a couple of tees into his duffle. "It's going to take you too long to wade through the red tape and jurisdictional dick measuring before you can even talk to the guy.

Easier for Dot and me to do it."

"A simple phone call usually works," Larrabee reminded him.

"Not this guy."

There was a moment of dead air, then Larrabee said, "How connected is he?"

His ability to click into the moment without asking extraneous questions was why T.J. liked Cassius Larrabee. A good man to have on his six when trouble was brewing.

T.J. chuckled. "So damn connected, the governor of Nevada is suspected of visiting his bed every time she visits Las Vegas, which is a lot."

"Shit, man. You better let Dot lead on this one."

Dot paused in braiding her hair and gave him the stink eye. She wore a pair of well-loved Wranglers, a light-blue sleeveless shirt, and had slipped on scuffed boots—her traveling clothes.

"I think I better handle it. She's liable to make him a eunuch and hang his castrated balls out for the birds."

A sly grin lifted one corner of Dot's mouth.

"You might be right," Larrabee conceded.

"Hey, one other thing. There was a stack of journals left on a desk in the loft at Porter's place," T.J. told Larrabee.

"There were?" Larrabee's tone warned that whomever dropped the ball in that area was about to get a strip down.

"Yeah, seemed off to me too. Anyway, you might want to go collect those. I don't know if they'll be of any good to you or not."

"Why do you sound like you read through them?" Larrabee asked. "You know what, never mind. I don't want to know. I'll take care of it myself. Just be careful down there and keep me posted. You run into any red tape yourself, let me know."

"Ten-four." T.J. ended the call and set his phone on top of his packed duffel. "Ready?"

Dot flicked the completed braid over her shoulder. "Let's roll, Danger Ranger."

They'd decided to fly. Too much of a time lag between leaving Boise and driving to Las Vegas for word to get to their target. But they wouldn't take a commercial flight—while faster, it was much harder to get their weapons through.

Dot had connected with a charter helicopter company that worked out of Boise airport. The service typically took people up for aerial tours of the mountains. For Dot, they gave her the chance to get back in the cockpit and keep her skills fresh and sharp.

Personally, T.J. liked the ability to get somewhere quicker than driving. He trusted no one better than Dot at the stick. Secretly, it was nice to see her get past any trepidations that had crept into her mind after she had to crash-land a forest service helo two years before. Her love of flying eventually had overpowered her anxieties.

T.J. drove to the airport in the Suburban due to its hidden gun safe in the cargo area. They had both decided they would take what they could justify with them. No reason they should get caught naked while facing off against potential mobsters.

At the airport, he took the back entrance where the charter service had their office and hangar, and they were greeted by a security guard. Once cleared, T.J. navigated the Suburban to the parking spot for short term.

Dot went to check in with the manager. T.J. unloaded their gear. She returned shortly with a clipboard in hand. A white and black single engine Bell 206 helo sat on the landing pad, waiting for them.

"They got her fueled up and the clearance to fly out," she told him.

While she was busy with her preflight check, he loaded up their gear and stored the gun cases where they'd be out of the way. T.J. was settled in the passenger seat with headset on and mic cued when Dot climbed into the cockpit. He'd flown with her enough in the past to know he couldn't and wouldn't interrupt her process.

After getting her headset on and mic placed next to her mouth, she started flipping switches. The turbine engine began its high-pitched whine as it fired up. As the blades started turning, Dot was checking gauges and flight instruments and talking to the airport tower.

Once the blades picked up speed, the music started piping through the headset. The *donging* of a huge bell preceded one of AC/DC's infamous guitar riffs. T.J. grinned and relaxed in his seat.

Dot was notorious for blaring some of the band's more famous songs while she flew. Rumor had it, on the FOB during the flight that put her in consideration for a Distinguished Flying Cross medal she had been playing "Shoot to Thrill" while she took out an RPG bunker and a squad of insurgents hell-bent on shooting her down. The men she was there to evac were watching the whole event from their pinned-down position. Her injured copilot left Dot to her own devices, and she singlehandedly ended the standoff and got all those men out. T.J. never learned if she ever was awarded the medal, as Dot wasn't apt to talk about her accomplishments or accept accolades.

By the time "Hells Bells" ended, she was giving the helicopter a boost, and the machine lifted from the landing pad. Moments later, they were skyborne and zipping out of the airport heading south.

"We might hit some crosswinds when we get to the mountains," she warned him over the intercom.

He stretched his legs as far as they could go, crossed his arms, and settled in for a nap. "I trust you."

He peeked out of the corner of his eye and spotted her making a face and shaking her head. Closing his eyes, T.J. drifted off to the sound of "Thunderstruck."

T.J. JERKED OUT of his dream at a sudden dip. He scrambled upright and fought the grogginess numbing his brain.

Dot was handling the stick like the pro she was; a slight lift of the corner of her mouth peeking over the top of the mic.

"Good morning, sunshine," she quipped.

"Not one bit funny," he growled.

"Neither was your snoring. You might want to get that checked out."

"Fuck you, Ybarra."

She glanced up at the overhead instruments. "You already do that."

Damn it. She was dialed in. There'd be no getting one over her—she'd have a quick comeback.

"Where are we?"

"Five miles outside of Las Vegas."

He scowled. He'd slept the entire two and half hours?

Dot had switched channels and was in communication with the Las Vegas airport. He left her be so she could get them in and landed without incident. While she was focused on her task, he got to work on his phone.

Before they'd left, he'd secured an SUV the size of their Suburban and a hotel room that didn't break the bank. They were here at their own expense. T.J. highly doubted Vivian's law firm would reimburse them for this trip. If they caught Cade Porter, aka Caleb Podolsky, and got his bounty, it would more than cover what they spent on the helicopter and vehicle rentals and their stay here, however long that might take.

"Two klicks out," Dot reported.

He gave her a thumbs-up. God, it felt like the old days.

Back on his phone, he tapped out a text to his contact here in Las Vegas. He hadn't told Dot about the contact, nor had he told the contact about Dot. Would he pay for his duplicity when the two met up? Oh, hell yeah. Could he live with the consequences? That one he wasn't so certain on.

Soon enough, they were landing on the helo pad. They made the switch between helicopter and SUV quickly and were out of the airport in no time.

It was early evening, and traffic was getting heavier. Heat haze shimmered above the roadway, distorting the view before them. Dot turned on the SUV's satellite radio, and a Frank Sinatra song blared out of the speakers. Whoever rented the car last liked the Rat Pack. She turned the volume down and was reaching to switch the station.

"Don't you dare," T.J. growled and swatted her hand away.

"I will dare," she came back. "We're not listening to this."

"We are, and you'll grit your teeth and bear it."

T.J. sensed her withering glare and ignored it. "Driver's right. You got your flying soundtrack. I get my Vegas one."

"For fuck's sake," Dot muttered and slouched in her seat.

Triumphant that he won this skirmish, T.J. turned the volume up. He directed the SUV south and tried to avoid the Strip as much as he could.

When he turned on a street that wasn't part of the original route to the hotel, Dot straightened from her slouch.

"Why are we going this way?"

"We're meeting up with someone. There's a fifties-themed diner that has some of the best damn burgers in this whole city."

Dot turned to pin him with a hard stare. "Who are we meeting?"

"You'll see when we get there."

"Titus Jethro."

Aw, shit. She used his birth name. Only his momma did that.

"Cool your jets, Ybarra."

"My jet is cooling back on the tarmac. You better start crowing. *Orain.*" The Basque came out like a whip crack.

110

He brought the SUV to a stop behind a long line of cars at a red light. Glancing over at Dot, he saw the perturbed creases in her face. He'd better tell her.

Drumming his fingers on the steering wheel, he weighed the best way to say it.

"It's Stevo."

The light turned green, and the line of cars rolled forward. They had gone a hundred yards before she spoke.

"How is he still alive?"

T.J. smiled. Good ole Stevo, aka Steven Arturo Bautista, was one of his sergeants who took every opportunity to flirt with anything that had tits. The only woman he never tried to woo was Dot, but it didn't stop him from antagonizing her. Steve's likable personality made it difficult to hate him. American on his mother's side and Filipino on his father's side, he was a walking, talking contradiction. While he acted like the biggest man slut, one couldn't find a more intelligent or resourceful man. There was a reason Steve was T.J.'s second. He trusted Steve's intuition in many a difficult situation during missions.

Today, he ran his own PI and security consulting business out of Las Vegas. And T.J. was one of the lucky few to be present at Stevo's wedding.

The man-whore had tied the knot with one helluva woman.

"He's got a nice business set up here, and I've asked for his help."

Dot twisted in her seat to face him. "But how is he still alive? I figured by now he'd screwed the wrong woman, and her husband put him in the ground."

T.J. chuckled. "Actually, he's married."

She tried. She really did. But her attempt at not being shocked won over the scowl. "How is that even possible?"

"Oh, you'll see when you meet her. She runs the financial side of things for both his business and her boutique."

"A boutique of what?"

He bobbed his eyebrows at her. "Kink."

"Oh, for fuck's sake." She groaned. "I should have known."

Damn, she was too easy to mess with today.

"I'm kidding," he countered. "She's a forensic accountant."

"I'm too fucking tired to be playing mind games with you, Roman," she snarled.

He spotted the diner and made the appropriate lane change and turn. "Get some food in you, and we'll head to the hotel, after we give Stevo the lowdown."

The diner was running brisk business tonight, but it was far from packed. T.J. found Steve's bald head sitting at the back of the diner, high above the rest of the patrons. Not only was the man tall, he was built like a brick house, maintaining what could only be considered a heavyweight boxer's physique.

Steve stood as they approached, a huge grin on his gray-bearded face. "My God, Ybarra, you look like hell." His deep voice could rattle the windows.

"Same to you," Dot countered.

Steve moved around the table and wrapped T.J. in a man hug, all backslapping and fist bumping. "Good to see you, man," he said with a final hard whack to T.J.'s shoulder.

"Thanks for meeting us."

A plump brunette with piercing brown eyes and a noticeable bulge in her midsection hovered nearby.

T.J. joined her and placed a chaste kiss on her cheek. "You look beautiful, Dana. When will the spawn of Satan be born?"

Dana snorted and gave him a hard pinch on the cheek. "Not soon enough. This kid kicks like her father." She turned and held out her hand to Dot. "You're the infamous Dorothy Ybarra. The only woman Stevo could never seduce."

Dot gave a bemused grin as she took the shorter woman's hand. "Because I gave him a ball twisting he never forgot."

"Not true," Steve objected.

"Sit," Dana said and pointed at the round table. "With three veterans, I figured the safest bet was round."

A round table gave all three of the army vets a chance to keep their back to a wall and watch for danger.

Once they were seated, a cheery waitress in an old-school fifties diner uniform of a blue dress with a starched white collar and a jaunty creased cap pinned to her dark-brown hair arrived. She took their drink orders, and before she could scurry off, Steve told her to bring their drinks and three plates of their All-American burger and fries and a Cobb salad for his wife, all at the same time.

"Little presumptuous there, Stevo," Dot said as the waitress hurried off.

"Face it, we all know that's what we'd order. Save her the hassle of running back and forth. And it gives us a chance not to be interrupted as much." He shifted so he could get a bead on T.J. and Dot. "What's the intel?"

T.J. explained their current case and its predicament. Dot filled in gaps when he missed something. By the time they'd wrapped it up, their meals and drinks were delivered.

Before digging into his meal, Steve studied T.J. and then Dot, nodding as he did. "Yeah, I know your man, Meyer Follman. When I first set up shop here in Vegas, he approached me asking for my expertise on security. Hell, he even wanted me to head up the whole shebang in all three of his businesses." He winked at his wife. "It's how I met Dana."

T.J. zeroed in on Dana. "Did you work for Follman?"

She gave him a sly smile. "Hell no. I was tasked by the Vegas DA at the time to investigate Follman's books. A little undercover work." She wiggled her fingers near her face. "Would this innocent face shout out that she's an investigator?"

Dot pointed a fry at Steve. "How the hell did she fall for you?"

He grinned, flashing brilliant teeth. "She loved my boyish charm."

Dot groaned.

"Anyway," Steve continued. "Dana roped me into the DA's investigation, I told Follman what he needed to do and accepted his offer to be head honcho. Six months later, Dana had what she needed and got out. I wasn't far behind."

"Problems for the DA started kicking in about then. The governor heard about the investigation, and she came down hard on him. He lost his job, we managed to stay unknown to the powers that be, and in what we consider an act of self-

BAIT THE DEVIL

preservation, Follman closed up shop on two of his businesses. Now all he has is the casino. With the money he saved shutting the two other places down, he invested in horses."

"Racehorses to be exact. Everything from Thoroughbreds to Quarter Horses," Dana added. "He's got farms as far north as Idaho and as far south as Arizona. Word is, he's wanting to branch into the California racing scene, but it's slow going because that's old money and they close ranks out there."

"Casino and horse racing go hand in hand," T.J. said. "Makes sense he'd keep to what he knows. What were the two places he shut down?"

"An entertainment venue and a restaurant," Dana replied. "In a city like Vegas, those are a dime a dozen. If you aren't unique enough or attract the right celebs, you're sunk. But that wasn't Follman's issue."

"The issue was his behind-the-scenes shenanigans that got the former DA sniffing around in the first place," Steve continued. "Pretty certain the mayor and the governor told him to close up shop."

"Probably because they had their fingers in the pies, too, and didn't want his stain to show up on them," Dana added before eating another forkful of her salad.

"Follman's ego isn't one to trifle with. He might have ended the other two places, but that casino of his makes bank."

"What were ... or is it *are* those shenanigans?" T.J. asked.

"High-end drugs and prostitutes," Stevo said bluntly.

Dana made a disapproving noise.

Steve rolled his eyes. "Excuse me, escorts. And the *escorts* had a special flavor to them, if you get my drift."

Dot had downed most of her meal. She reclined in her chair, holding her glass of half-drank tea. "He could still be doing the same thing out of his casino."

"Oh, he is, but he would have had to scale it down. One would think illicit activities would be easy to launder through a casino, but they're not. The regulations by gaming commissions in each state leaves no wiggle room for any hanky-panky. Vegas is stricter yet. With the advent of online gaming, the rules got harder to break," Dana explained.

T.J. braced his elbows on the table and leaned into them. He was starting to formulate a plan, but Steve had given him a huge hitch in that plan.

"You said you set up the security for Follman's casino. Is he still operating it the same way?" he asked.

Steve made eye contact with his wife, then turned to T.J. "I trained his current head of security. The guy is no joke. He might have tweaked some things, but I doubt he's deviated much from my model."

There'd be no going at this on the sly. T.J. looked to Dot, and she tilted her head as if asking, *What are you getting at?*

"What about the horses?" T.J. asked.

Steve and Dana glanced at each other again. She shrugged.

"That one might be more up your alley, since the two of you are the horse people," Steve said. "Follman does have a couple of horse farms near the city."

"We're not the racehorse type of people," Dot pointed out.

"But you know horse flesh. You'd be able to get in." Steve leaned toward them, eagerness glowing on his bald head. "In fact, acting like potential buyers would be your perfect cover." He gave Dot a sly grin. "You're gonna need to dress up, Ybarra. In a skirt."

"The army never could get me to wear a skirt. There's not a chance in hell I'll start now."

"You might wanna sing a different tune this time," Steve said, sitting back in his seat.

T.J. cut off what potentially would be a brutal tongue-lashing from Dot. "We're going in through the back door. That's how we're going to learn anything about Caleb Podolsky."

Chapter Fourteen

VIVIAN ENTERED HER darkened apartment, flicked on the lights, and let out a startled yelp.

The figure seated at the table pulled back the hood covering his face. "Don't scream," he said in a rough-hewn voice that grated the eardrums.

She didn't scream; she did what Dot and T.J. had drilled into her for months. She lifted the Glock 19 and leveled it at his chest. "Who the hell are you, and how the fuck did you get into my home?"

He lifted his hands in surrender, also revealing he was unarmed. "I think you know full well who I am." He tilted his head to the opened balcony door. "Smart to be on the third floor."

Dot had warned Vivian, over and over, that when faced with a situation where she had to pull her weapon, she would feel panicked. She had to strangle those emotions and be calm and levelheaded.

Easier said than done.

Vivian ground her teeth and willed her hands and arms to remain steady.

Her unwelcome visitor slowly lowered his hands, resting them on the tabletop.

"I'm not here to hurt you," he said, his voice sounding like he gargled with gravel.

In flipbook style, her brain flicked through the information she knew about Caleb Podolsky and stopped on the page with the answer. Not only had he lost a leg in the RPG attack, he'd also sustained damage to his face and upper chest. He looked like a reincarnation of Freddy Krueger.

"There are a lot of people looking for you," she said.

"I'm aware." He made invisible circles on the glossy surface. "Where did they go?"

She gaped at him. "Where did who go?"

"The bounty hunters. The ones your firm sent after me." He stopped making the circles and stared at her with cold, calculating eyes. "Where did they go?"

Sweat pooled in her pits. Still, she held her ground with the pistol leveled on him.

"Where's Hal Jones?" she countered.

The scars on his faces pulled into a macabre form of a smile. Vivian detected a spiteful amusement behind the expression.

"Counselor, I did not come here to play games with you." Slowly and stiffly, he rose, making sure to keep his full weight on the flesh and bone leg. "None of you realize what you've gotten yourselves caught up in."

"So, enlighten me … Marine." She was gambling with her life, of that she was certain. If she had read between the lines in his actual files, he was not a man to allow such a cavalier attitude to be thrown at him.

"What else do you know about me, *lawyer*." Her title sounded dirty coming from his mouth.

"Only what Hal allowed to be known." The lie was convincing.

A dark veil came down over his eyes. Vivian realized then that she was baiting the devil.

"I see coming to you was a mistake." He sidestepped away from the chair.

"Where the hell do you think you're going?"

Those cold eyes penetrated her skin and pierced her soul. Vivian couldn't stop the shudder.

"I'd advise you, Counselor, to stop digging around in things better left alone. If you value your life, stop. Now."

He stalked toward her. For a man with a prosthetic leg, he moved remarkably well, enough to disguise the slight hitch in his gait.

Vivian sidled away from him, smacking her backside into the wall, and then scooted to the side, not once lowering the Glock.

He walked right up to the door, acting as if he owned the place. After opening the door, he paused and looked back at her.

"I'd get a security system if I were you." With that parting advice, he flipped up the hood and left.

She rushed to the door and threw the dead bolt. Before she let herself relax, she hurried to the balcony door and slammed it home and locked it. She drew the curtains and then sank into the chair he'd vacated.

There she sat, regaining control of her nerves and running through a hundred different scenarios where the outcome of this encounter would have left her dead.

Finally feeling like her normal self, she left the Glock on

the table, went to her leather satchel, and dug out her phone. She debated, hard, on calling Dot to let her know. Vivian knew the right answer would be to warn both her and T.J. But she also knew the first response from Dot would be to abandon their current mission and come rushing back to Idaho.

What kind of fool would she be to unleash Dot's righteous indignation over something she had warned Vivian to do? Of course, Vivian enjoyed playing second fiddle to Dot's Red Sonja. She was quite capable of handling herself, thank you very much.

Instead, she called the only person she could trust to help her out and who Dot and T.J. would approve of her calling in a pinch.

He picked up on the second ring. "Counselor, to what do I owe the pleasure?"

"Sergeant Larrabee, we need to talk."

Chapter Fifteen

B Y NATURE, DOT was not a flashy woman. She found no logic in makeup, dresses, high heels that destroyed her feet, or hair products that attracted flying pests. Practicality and function was the name of her game. She had not been lying when she told Steve she'd never worn the uniform skirt issued to her by the army at the start of her career. They offered her trousers and that was what she wore.

Somehow, she'd let Dana Bautista talk her into an airy light-peach-colored cap-sleeve blouse and a turquoise bracelet and necklace set to brighten her up, as Dana put it. Dot drew the line at the blouse and jewelry, but she did purchase a new pair of dark-blue Wranglers. A good washing and the jeans lost most of their stiffness.

Last-minute add—a silicon ring. Her and T.J.'s cover story was a married couple.

When she emerged from the hotel bathroom in her new getup, T.J. grinned and gave her a wink. He, too, had fancied up, buckling under pressure to trim his unruly beard. In prime Oklahoman cowboy fashion, he'd paired up new jeans with a white button-down under a lightweight tan blazer. They were both going to get sweaty in this Nevada heat, but it wasn't anything they hadn't dealt with most of their lives.

"Damn, Ybarra."

"Fuck you, Roman." She settled a yellow straw Stetson on her head and headed for the door.

It was about a twenty-minute drive to one of Follman's horse farms from their hotel. The entire facility was trapped by residential housing on all sides in the thick of the city limits. And no one cared.

Both Steve and Dana confirmed that Follman loved to be on-site during the weekends to confer with his managers and watch the goings-on. He was especially hands-on when potential buyers or interested parties would visit. Normally, he was holed up inside his casino, safe and sound from the prying eyes of law enforcement.

Through his network, Steve learned that Follman was hosting a horse auction today. It was the opportune time for Dot and T.J. to show up and mingle. If a chance opened for one or both of them to snoop around unnoticed, they'd take it.

T.J. followed the signs into the farm's main entrance and parked between two similar black SUVs. Dot exited their vehicle and immediately felt naked without her gun.

T.J. insisted they not give anyone a chance to focus on them. They were regular people interested in horses. Packing weapons posed a risk he wasn't willing to take.

They merged as they strode across the parking lot, joining a group of six strolling through the open doors of a grand alley. Dot studied the wide path and its arching shelter, all constructed in stone and brick, noting the cool air drifting along the alley.

The couples ahead of them chatted about the potential of going all in on one of the yearlings they had heard good things about. Dot rolled her eyes when T.J. met her gaze. He shrugged, keeping his own comments to himself.

As the alley ended, a blast of chilled air greeted them as they entered into a large indoor arena. The design was exactly the same as the indoor arena at the Idaho farm where Caleb, aka Cade, had worked. Men in light-colored trousers and pastel shirts and women in dresses of varying lengths mingled with glasses of their preferred drink. Their chatter, while low, was amplified by the sheer number of people and the open space of the arena.

A white jacketed male in his early twenties, lifting a tray of fluted glasses holding what must have been mimosas, split their group with an offer of a drink. The party of six nearly wiped out the contents of the tray. T.J. and Dot shook their heads and separated from the group.

Along the back side of the arena—placed under the large deck above them—sat a long row of tables laden with silver food warmers. Posted behind the tables were more of the white-jacketed servers.

"Coffee station," T.J. said, his voice low and rough. He glanced around. "Stay here. I'll grab us some. You see if you can spot Follman."

She gave him a nod, and he walked away.

The heavy tread of steps above drew her attention upward. How many people were up there? If she was a betting woman—how could she not be in a place like Las Vegas—the upper level was for the priority guests. That's where Follman would be.

But just in case he decided the unwashed masses below were his schtick, Dot studied the crowd better.

In the center of the actual riding ring, a stage with a long table draped in purple cloth and adorned with microphones took up most of the platform. Four people stood in a circle going over papers in their hands. No one else was inside the ring. Buyers and onlookers took position around the railing.

Dot spotted the stairs on the far-right wall. A few people stood on the steps, and there were others coming down or going up behind the step vultures. Three of the people she noticed going up wore a special badge dangling from a lanyard around their neck.

T.J. returned with two cups with lids. "It's decent."

Dot took her cup and rotated to face the back wall. "Badges going up and down the steps."

"Has to be security," T.J. said, then drank his coffee.

"High rollers up above. Follman will be mingling with them." Dot tried the coffee. Her partner was right; it was decent, just not as good as her preferred brew. "Lots of bidding paddles floating around here." She turned back to the stage in the center of the ring. "I doubt we'll have any chance to sneak around the place. Especially if there's security."

T.J. grinned. "Wanna buy a horse?"

Dot gave him the side-eye and drank her coffee.

Standing there among the milling crowd, Dot sensed someone's attention. She scanned the group. As she turned to check behind her, she was jostled forward, nearly losing her hold on her cup.

Righting herself before T.J. could touch her, she shifted

to confront the rude person, but the culprit had not lingered to apologize. She studied the people around her, noticing a brunette in a lavender pantsuit striding toward the exit. The woman glanced over her shoulder, and Dot locked eyes with her. The brunette turned away and disappeared through the archway.

"You good?" T.J. asked.

"Be right back," she said and thrust her cup into his hand.

Dot squeezed through a gap and warily darted into the alley. The purple-suited woman was passing through a set of doors halfway down the stone path. Dot nodded to a pair of men coming up the path as she approached them and trailed the woman through the doors.

She'd entered what was a hall leading to a stable. The woman paused at a stall and placed something on the stall door. She looked back at Dot, then turned on her heel and strode away, leaving the object behind.

Checking to make sure she wasn't being observed, Dot headed to the stall. The stable was empty, but the smell of horse permeated the air. This must have been where the animals had been housed. They were probably moved to another staging area until they would be paraded before the bidding crowd.

The object left on the door was a small phone. Again, Dot did a sweep of her sector, then picked up the phone. It came to life with a text message.

Keep. I'll contact soon.

Scowling, she looked toward the spot where the woman had disappeared. Pocketing the phone, she headed in that direction. No one was loitering around here, not even security.

Dot rounded the stall and stepped into an empty, sunny courtyard. Bracketing the yard were two more stable entrances and a wall of glass doors on what appeared to be living quarters. Through the tinted panes, Dot could make out movement.

A sound behind her stopped her from moving forward.

T.J. emerged from the stables. "What are you doing?" he asked, looking around.

Dot patted the pocketed phone, but before she could show him what she had, there was a flicker of movement behind him. A man clad in the typical getup of one who thought security meant military emerged from around the corner. She closed the gap between herself and T.J.

"Folks, you shouldn't be back here," the security man said in a gruff tone.

It sounded forced to Dot.

T.J. scowled at her before shifting his features into a look of confusion as he turned. "Sorry about that. My wife here was looking for a restroom." He half cupped his mouth. "It's that time of the month," he said in a loud whisper.

He was going to pay for that archaic and stupid ploy.

Even so, it worked. The man blanched at the mention of a woman's menstruation and backed away like he was avoiding a contagious disease. Some men.

"Uh, those are in the arena. We have restrooms toward the back of the main level. Behind the food service tables." He jabbed a finger to direct them back to the arena.

"Thanks, man," T.J. said as they followed the security

man's directive.

Dot made a face at him as she passed and feinted forward. He jolted and jerked back a step.

"For fuck's sake," she snarled under her breath.

"The bleeding woman trick strikes again," T.J. said when they were out of earshot.

"Next time, I'm going to use the weak prostate approach. Or better yet, explosive diarrhea."

"Wow, angry much?" T.J. quipped as they entered the arena once more.

"Use a better lie next time." She glared at him. "Or just shut your yap."

A pounding gavel brought the noise level down to a whisper. All bodies turned to the three men and one woman standing on the stage.

"Welcome to the fifth annual Smokin' Hearts auction. If everyone with bid numbers could please find a spot where our auctioneers can see you, we'd greatly appreciate it."

Dot glanced back to see the traumatized security guy lingering in the doorway, watching her. With a roll of her eyes, she gripped T.J.'s arm and pinched.

"Ow, what?"

"Now I have to make good on that whole finding the restroom."

He peeked past her hat and then jerked his head. "We're not splitting up this time."

They threaded their way through the press of bodies as the bidders moved closer to the railing. Once clear, Dot peered back over the heads and noticed she couldn't see the doorway or the guard. Free of his scrutiny, she bumped T.J.'s elbow and pointed toward another set of doors where people were coming and going.

Outside, under shade trees, a series of roped-off pens showcased the horses going through the auction. Each animal was handled by a groom and had a bright white square with a number secured to their left hip. Potential buyers lingered before each pen to study the horse inside and ask the groom questions.

T.J. found an out-of-the-way position to observe the action. "Why were you in the stable?"

Dot showed him the phone, keeping it tucked in her palm, then returned it to her pocket. "Someone is trying to reach out to us."

"Cade?"

"Maybe. Though it was a woman who led me on a merry chase to get it."

T.J. looked up; Dot followed his gaze, noting the guards at the bottom of the steps, sweating in the Vegas heat. No one lingered on the steps or the landing above.

"No chance of us getting upstairs," she groused.

Some of the potential buyers went inside the arena, thinning the crowd. The first horse, a sleek bay Thoroughbred, was led in through a sliding door.

"I'm recalling a few entrances at the back of the other arena," T.J. said.

They both ceased their people-watching and peered toward the back of the building. Tall orange caution stands with white cord strung between them and placards dangling from the cord cut off the pathway behind the building. The area was restricted.

"Thing One and Thing Two will probably sound the alarm if we go that direction," Dot said. "This was a waste of time and brain space."

"Stevo's never failed me before," T.J. said.

"We should have gone the direct approach with Follman."

T.J. tilted his reflective aviators down and eyed her from under the brim of his Stetson. "Patience and timing have always been your strong traits."

She shook off his pointed comment. "Your paranoia is rubbing off."

"I'm not paranoid." He slid his sunglasses up. "Besides, it's not a total failure. You got the phone."

"How do you suppose this mystery person knew we were going to be here?"

He shook his head. "That one I haven't worked out. Let's move—this sun is hot."

They wandered toward the last of the rope pens, nodding to the groom and his bored horse who had taken advantage of the shade covering half the pen. Dot and T.J. settled on the opposite side of the handler and horse. A waist-high table placed under the tree was the catch-all for discarded drinkware.

Their new position gave Dot a clear view of the backside of the arena. T.J. had been right in his theory of another set of stairs, which began from a large deck. Again, more security guards on watch, but this pair were able to linger in the shade of the deck.

Avoiding the chance she'd be noticed for studying the layout, Dot angled her body to survey the rest of the farm and still be able to keep an eye on the guards.

"The arena might be the same," she said. "The rest of this place is considerably different than the Idaho farm."

"This outfit is meant to showcase the sellable horses." T.J. leaned on the paddock fencing behind them. "The other one was a broodmare facility."

"Breed them up north, then bring them down here where all the high roller money is." Dot crossed her arms. "So, what are the functions of the other farms in Arizona?"

T.J. looked over his shoulder. "Probably more of the same like here. More people. More money."

A commotion from the rope pens kicked up. There was a shout, and horses squealed. More shouts of surprise. Someone yelled, "Look out!"

Anyone lingering outside scattered as a snorting and bucking sorrel broke through the melee. His handler struggled to keep hold of the horse and avoid his flying hooves. People scattered to keep out of the way.

Dot knew what was coming next and tore away the rope creating the pen. Through the buzz in her head, she heard T.J.'s voice but not what he said.

The sorrel jerked his head a final time, ripping the last of the leather lead from the handler's precarious hold. The second the horse realized he was free was the same moment Dot told the groom to give up his horse. Wide-eyed, the man held out the line.

The sorrel squealed and took off, barreling for the open paddocks. Nostrils flared and attention fixated on the path before him, he flew past, the lead on his halter trailing behind him.

Dot took hold of the stud's lead, grabbed a handful of mane near his withers, and in long practiced moves, swung up onto his back. The horse jolted with a snort. Dot slapped his neck and heeled him into motion. Sensing her urgency, the stallion broke from the pen like he was leaving the starting gate. The momentum flipped Dot's hat from her head, and it flew behind them.

They flashed past T.J., racing after the fleeing horse. If that sorrel made it the end of the paddocks he would have nothing but a low riding fence separating him from a road filled with heavy traffic. Dot leaned into the stud's neck like a jockey and urged him faster.

Ahead, the sorrel gathered himself and jumped the first paddock fence. Dot gritted her teeth and hoped like hell this horse knew how to do that too. The stallion's huge brain seemed to click into place, and Dot felt his muscles bunch and his stride alter for the jump. She, too, prepared herself for his upward motion. All energy shifted to his hindquarters, and as they were about to crash through the fencing, his front feet left the earth, and they hurdled the wood fence.

Dot was thrown off-balance on the landing but managed to readjust her seat as the stud hit a new gear and tore after the fleeing sorrel. She could see the gap shrinking fast, but the far pasture fence was coming faster. Just past it was a narrow path and opposite that the fence and the roadway.

"Come on, big guy," she urged.

With a grunt, the stud kicked into another gear. Dot clung to his slick back with nothing but her sheer leg strength. The sorrel's lead was gone as the stud's nose passed his hip, then came in line with the sorrel's back. Dot was mere inches from catching the floating lead line.

She nudged the stud for more power.

The fence was dangerously close. The sorrel backed off his speed, preparing for another jump. The stud came in line with him, and Dot was able to grasp the leather lead.

She pulled the stud's head away from the sorrel and brought the two horses around sharply, away from the fence. The stud, having spent all his energy, slowed to a canter. The sorrel jerked on the lead line but followed the other horse. Dot guided the two animals back to the pasture fencing where a line of people stood.

As she neared, she heard the cheering and clapping. T.J. stood front and center of the grouping, and just to his left was a man in an impeccable light-blue suit.

Meyer Follman had decided to emerge from his hidey-hole.

Chapter Sixteen

"**Y**OU'RE QUITE THE horsewoman."

Dot paused in her perusal of Meyer Follman's digs. A grand suite taking up the entirety of the top floor on one wing of his casino. He had the suite decorated in retro fifties furniture and a color scheme of mint, pinks, and sandstone, like he wanted to relive the Rat Pack heyday. At the overburdened bar, Follman poured a glass of dark-amber liquid.

"I have only been at this horse business for a short time. But you ..." He lifted the crystal decanter in offering. "You are exceptional. Whiskey?"

"Don't drink," Dot and T.J. said as one.

Follman frowned.

"We're low class," T.J. said. "Beer is more our thing."

Understanding lit up Follman's surgically fine-tuned features. "That puts your skills into perspective."

The remainder of the horse auction had gone on without a hitch. Follman himself had pulled the stud Dot commandeered and gifted it to Dot for her selfless act. Despite her repeated attempts to dissuade Follman in his quest to give her the horse, she found herself the new owner of an Arabian cross stallion.

She hadn't figured out how she was going to one, get the horse back to Idaho and delivered to the ranch without blowing their cover. And two, tell *Ama* what in the hell to do with a stallion meant to be a show piece and a love machine instead of a mountain horse.

T.J. had offered to have the stud sent to his family ranch in Oklahoma. But he wasn't sure his sister would know what to do with the horse either as they, too, ran a working cattle ranch and needed ranch-trained horses.

Follman set the decanter aside and took possession of his glass, then wandered over to them. "What brought you to my little horse auction today?"

His gaze centered on Dot as he sipped his whiskey, then his gaze flitted away. The quickness at which he'd avoided trying to meet Dot's eyes gave her pause. He'd gushed all over her in front of a crowd, practically draping himself over her, prevented from actually doing it by T.J.'s hulking presence. Here, in his private quarters, he struggled to maintain the Jekyll persona.

Instead of looking at her, Follman focused on some point past her and T.J.'s shoulders.

"We flew in to visit some friends, and they told us about it," T.J. said. Not a lie. Just missing the full details. "Thought we'd check it out."

A frowning Follman, seemingly put out that he had been pulled from whatever thoughts he'd been pondering, forced an interested expression before engaging T.J. "Flew in? It would explain why I'm not familiar with the pair of you. I know most of the people who run in the horse circles around this area." He turned from them and meandered toward a circle of love seats. "Where you from?"

"Idaho," T.J. answered.

Follman rotated and then sank onto one of the love seats. "Idaho? And you flew down in a jet?"

"A helicopter actually."

Dot stepped away from T.J. and found a wall to prop up, next to the beefy bodyguard, who eyed her. This was T.J.'s schtick, and she'd let him run with it. She hadn't joined him in the bounty hunting business for her gabbing abilities. She was his partner for her tracking and hunting skills. He was the one who could easily slip in and out of whatever persona needed for the job.

"A helicopter?" Follman tilted his head and smiled brightly at T.J. "You don't cross me as a helicopter pilot."

"I'm not." T.J. jabbed a thumb her direction. "That's her gig."

Follman blinked at T.J., then turned his owl eyes at her. "You're the pilot?"

Dot wiggled her fingers and gave him her less-than-enthused smile.

"Is there anything you can't do?" he blurted out.

Shoot you, she wanted to say. She gave a nonchalant shrug.

"Now do you understand why taking your horse is a problem?" T.J. said, regaining the conversation and bringing this whole thing back to their excuse to be alone with Follman. "We have no good way to transport a horse up there and to find a home for it."

Follman pointed a finger at the ceiling. "Ah, there I can help. I have a place in Idaho you can board that gorgeous stallion. I can have one of my guys haul him up there. In fact, I've got two farms up there. Take your pick of whichever is closest to you."

The bodyguard cleared his throat, fairly violently. Follman shot him an irritated look. The bodyguard made a cutoff motion with his hand and then held up a single finger. Dot studied the interaction closely, waiting for the ax to drop on whatever was going on between them. Follman's eyes widened, and he put on a lopsided smile.

"Actually, I forgot," he said quickly. "Only one farm is open for taking boarders. The other I've recently purchased, and it's not up to standards yet."

"Mr. Follman, neither of us—" T.J. started.

"You know," Follman interjected, lifting his whiskey glass and circling it between Dot and T.J. "You both give off an air of ... oh, what is it I'm thinking?"

"Military," his bodyguard rumbled.

Follman lit up and pointed with his non-glass-bearing hand. "That's it!"

Dot peeked over her shoulder at the bodyguard and gave him her own version of salacious eyeballing. He blinked and turned a slight shade of pink, then took a slight step to his right, away from her.

Oh, yeah, handi-mandia, *I'll eat you alive.*

"What is it you two do? If you don't mind me asking," Follman said. "Other than be married, that is."

Despite Dot's attempt at common sense, T.J. kept up the façade of the married couple. Again, his mission. However, he had relented to her other rebuttal.

"We search for people." T.J. crossed his sizable arms.

There was a half beat of deathly silence in the room. Follman's smile faded, and he lowered his whiskey glass to the center of his lap. The bodyguard tensed, and she prepared herself to pounce if the need arose.

"You search for people?" Follman's voice was lower. "What are you? Cops?"

T.J. snorted. "Far from it."

Follman glanced at Dot, then his bodyguard, then back to T.J. "If you ain't cops—"

"We ain't feds either," T.J. cut in. "We're bounty hunters."

A scoffing laugh burst out of Follman. "What? Like that dude from TV?"

"Not even close," Dot grumbled.

Follman seemed to digest what T.J. revealed. He downed the last of his whiskey and set the glass aside. Then draping both arms over the love seat's back, he crossed one foot over the opposite knee, revealing a bare ankle popping with blue veins.

"Bounty hunters? No shit?" Follman flicked a finger at them. "Who are you looking for?"

T.J. slid a sidelong look at Dot. She lifted her shoulder slightly and resumed her sentry duty on the bodyguard. She was leaving it up to him which version of Caleb he'd reveal. If he went with it.

"There's a bench warrant out on a man who's suspected of being under your employment," T.J. said.

Follman pursed his mouth and bobbed his head. "Is that so? Who is this man?"

"Does the name Halloway Jones ring any bells?"

Dot had to refrain from twitching. He'd gone with Hal Jones? What was T.J. playing at here?

The casino man mulled over that name, glanced at his bodyguard, who shrugged, then shook his head. "Can't say that it does. What's he done that he's got bounty hunters on his tail?"

"A bench warrant," T.J. said, "Just means he failed to appear in court."

Follman wagged his hand. "Yeah, yeah, yeah, I know all about those. But what got him in trouble in the first place?"

For supposedly not hearing of Hal, Follman seemed too damn interested in the man's story.

"We're not at liberty to speak about the defendant's case," T.J. stated.

Making a noise, Follman decided to examine his fingernails instead of looking at T.J. "Sorry I can't be of more help, but I just don't know the guy." He pressed his forefinger and thumb together and swung his gaze back to T.J. "Though, I am wondering why you went to all this subterfuge to meet with me." A slick smile appeared. "A phone call would have done quite nicely."

"And miss all the fun and games to see my woman save one of your prized horses?"

Between the period ploy and now calling her "my woman," T.J. was going to feel the burn of a thousand solar flares.

Follman's steely gaze slid to Dot.

He looked her up and down, then flung himself forward and upright from the love seat. "She is an intriguing woman. I'll give you that."

Yet, the man did not seem one bit captivated by her. Dot

noted he spent more time keeping his attention on T.J. or the bodyguard. Either Follman didn't really like or respect strong women—which didn't explain his attachment to the governor of Nevada—or all of it was a ruse and his interests lay elsewhere.

Follman picked up his empty whiskey glass and returned to the bar. "You know, her ability to fly a helicopter might be of some interest to me," he said as he poured another fifth into the glass. "Do either of you pick up odd jobs outside of your normal bounty hunting gig?"

T.J.'s shoulders shifted under his blazer. Dot went on alert.

Before T.J. answered, Follman went on. "Since I declared that fine stallion off the auction block and gave him to you, I think it only fair that I ensure his safety and ownership be rightfully passed into your hands." He sipped his whiskey and rotated to face them. "You see, I'm shifting my business with the horses to focus solely on Thoroughbreds, and I can't keep him. If you would allow me to arrange transportation to my boarding facility in Idaho, I would waive any and all fees, in exchange for a favor."

His gaze flicked back and forth between Dot and T.J. "What do you say?"

Dot pushed away from the wall, jolting the bodyguard out of his stupor. "We don't do *favors*."

"Let's talk money then," Follman countered.

"We're listening," T.J. said, his voice dipping lower and rougher.

The one he would use on taciturn defendants they were trying to haul into lockup.

Dot looked at him sharply. "No. We're not listening."

The glare he leveled on her made Dot's blood pressure rise. This had ceased to be a recovery job. It had ended being a search-and-rescue mission as well. Had T.J. lost his damn mind?

"Do the two of you need to have a marriage counseling session first?" Follman asked, amusement dancing in his voice.

His bodyguard snickered.

T.J. gripped Dot's arm, pressing his forefinger into her bicep. "We're just fine," he said to Follman.

Oh, they weren't fine. They were nowhere near fine. Fine wasn't even in the next galaxy.

T.J.'s eyes widened, and Dot caught the pleading look in them. The *please trust me on this* one that she always had a hard time refusing. If she relented to this stupid ass line of thought from Follman, T.J. would owe her. God, would he owe her.

She better not regret this.

He released his hold on her and gave Follman his full attention. "What's the deal?"

Follman lifted both his glass-wielding hand and the empty one in a dramatic gesture and gave a sly smile as he looked pointedly at Dot. "How good of a helicopter pilot are you?"

This was how the ass wanted to play this game?

Dot closed the gap between them, forcing Follman to take an unexpected step back. The bodyguard went to intercept her, but T.J. intervened.

"You think my skills as a horsewoman are exceptional." She leaned in, close enough to catch the sour odor of

Follman's breath. "I threaded a Black Hawk through one of the tightest mountain passes in Afghanistan, hauling about two thousand kilos of equipment and fully kitted-out men into hostile territory while eating a fucking sandwich."

T.J. snorted. He was fully aware she'd never eaten on a mission, and the army sure as hell wouldn't have allowed her to do it. God forbid she get crumbs all over the highly sensitive equipment. Fuck the fact sand and dirt got into everything and never came out.

Follman gave himself more space between them. "Impressive." He threw back the last of his whiskey. "All the more reason to give you this job."

"What job?" she snarled.

"The kind of job that will give you an adrenaline rush the likes of which you can never obtain riding a stallion at breakneck speed without a saddle and bridle." Follman walked over to the bar and set the glass down with a *thunk*, then whipped around. "The kind of job that can make you both a shit ton of money you'd never see in ten bounties."

"Sounds like the kind of job we don't cater to," Dot countered.

"You just need to give it a chance." Follman's smile grew.

"Difficult to do that when you're not giving us details," T.J. growled.

"All you had to do was say so." Follman held out a hand and gestured as if trying to calm a rabid dog. "I had a guy in Idaho who was supposed to take care of a shipment of goods for me, then he went all psycho and bailed. We can't find hide nor hair of him. The shipment arrives tomorrow, and I have no one to handle it. If you both would pick it up, keep watch over it, and then fly it here, I'd give you each a hundred K cut."

The guy he was referring to had to be Caleb. How the hell was he supposed to have handled this shipment if they wanted it flown in? Caleb was not a trained pilot, one, and two, he was a wounded veteran with a prosthetic leg.

"Where the hell is this shipment coming from?" T.J. asked.

"Canada."

Dot stared hard at the man and then crossed her arms. What could he possibly have routed through Canada into the US? Through Idaho of all places.

"What would we be protecting and shipping to you?" she asked.

"It's a don't ask, don't tell kind of deal. Once it arrives here, I make the necessary arrangements, that's it."

"Two hundred K ain't enough for that kind of risk," T.J. said and shifted to leave.

"A quarter of a mil," Follman threw out.

Dot scowled. "What's your take in this? Seeing as you're the one not taking the risks."

In the moments of weighted silence, Follman studied them while he fiddled with a gold band on his right hand. The wheels were grinding hard inside his brain.

With an exasperated sigh, he held out his hands in supplication. Yet, somehow Dot didn't believe for one minute that he was at all being supple.

"My cut is five million. It's small potatoes, but with enough of these shipments, you can make a lot more. Do this one time, we can talk a more permanent partnership."

"We'll think about it," T.J. said. Now he was talking sense.

As one, they both moved to the door.

"Don't call us," Dot threw back over her shoulder. "We'll call you."

Chapter Seventeen

"THE BALLS ON this woman," Stevo crowed.

T.J. grinned as Dot slapped the back of Stevo's head as she passed his seat. "I wouldn't provoke the she-wolf any more than she's been," he warned his old second-in-command.

"No, let him dig. He can help you make your grave, then join you," Dot said then sank into a chair placed next to him, a burning cigar pinched between her fingers.

The three of them were seated in a hexagonal-shaped shaded arbor with huge paddle fans stirring a fair amount of cooled air down on them. Each of the five sides were draped with blackened netting that kept flying pests out and shaded them from the slanting sunrays.

Dana was inside her and Steve's home, finalizing details on a case she'd been assigned. Leaving the three old army chums to themselves.

After leaving Follman's casino suite, Dot hadn't said a word the entire drive to Stevo's place. She was pissed with him for changing the mission parameters and practically selling her skills without her permission. Give her enough time, and T.J. knew she'd come around and allow him to explain his reasons.

Her continued silence might be an indication she was plotting through this—or plotting his demise. T.J. couldn't blame her for wanting to leave him twisting in the wind on this one. If he admitted to her his actual reasons for letting Follman offer them this job, she'd probably end this partnership, tell him to fuck off, and return to her previous life at the Ybarra ranch.

Sad part was T.J. himself couldn't grasp a solid reason for running down this path half-cocked and less informed. Every time he thought about Caleb's situation, the harder the pull to find this guy became. Trying to explain it to Dot was difficult still, because each reason sounded weak and stupid. Like he was making excuses to justify his needs.

Why was it so damn hard to admit that he should never have involved them in this at all? She'd been right last night when she'd tried to talk him out of even going to Follman's horse auction. This was not bounty hunting. This wasn't even PI work. This was a personal agenda for T.J.

He glanced at her as she removed the sweet-scented cigar from her lips and blew out a thick cloud of smoke. They'd both switched out of their finery and were back in their usual get-up of worn-in jeans and tees. Stevo and Dana had prepared them all a hefty meal and now they were letting it digest. Hopefully the wind down was easing her into a rational plan.

It certainly wasn't doing him any favors.

"You know, Ybarra, I always knew you should have been placed in a combat unit." Steve tilted his beer bottle toward her.

Dot drew on her cigar and said nothing. It was a common topic of discussion from the past. One that never really went anywhere, just gave them all something to talk about. Dot's path in life had put her where she was best suited, and they all knew it.

"What's your next step?" Steve asked after they stewed in their own thoughts.

"See how desperate Follman gets," T.J. said and finished his beer.

"Actually, I'm more interested in knowing who wanted me to have this," Dot said as she pulled out the phone T.J. had completely forgotten about. She set it down on the stone ledge of the unused firepit centered between them.

Steve leaned forward and studied the black phone. "A burner? How'd you get this?"

"Before all the hoopla started, some woman led me out of the arena into a stable and left it on a stall door," Dot explained.

Steve resumed his previous lounging position. "Remember what the woman looked like?"

Dot sat in silence, smoking her cigar and squinting her eyes. Steve went to say something; T.J. held up a hand and cut him off. With a nod, Steve closed his mouth and waited.

T.J. had been around Dot long enough to read her features to know which mode she was in and to not pull her out of it. That serious contemplative face said she was in memory recall. When the crow's feet in the corners of her eyes relaxed and she lowered her cigar, T.J. knew she was ready.

She didn't get a chance to say a thing.

The mysterious phone rang.

How fucking convenient.

Dot reached for it, but T.J. took the phone. The number crawled across the screen; no name joined it. He answered the call and put it on speaker, then sat it down on the firepit ledge. No one spoke.

"Ms. Ybarra, for a minute there, I figured you would ignore the call." The voice from the other end was higher pitched than T.J. expected, but male.

Dot removed the cigar from between her teeth. "If I'd known I was dealing with a paper pusher, I would have. And Ms. Ybarra is my mother."

"Apologies, Dorothy."

T.J. had to bite his tongue to stop the chuckle. This knucklehead was pushing the wrong buttons left and right.

"Only two people ever called me Dorothy, and one of them is dead," she said.

"I'm really at a loss here. What am I supposed to call you?"

Dot took two puffs on her cigar with a wide grin. She released the smoke in a small cloud from her mouth. "Just plain Ybarra will do. Or you can call me Al."

Steve lost it and roared with laughter.

"Are we quite through with the childish games?" the voice on the line demanded as Steve died down.

"You opened yourself to the sport when you decided to play spy with me today," Dot said.

"My tactics were the cleanest and easiest way to get in contact with you without blowing this whole operation. You and Mr. Roman have already fouled it all up."

T.J. bent forward, catching Dot's stream of cigar smoke full in the face.

"We fouled up nothing," he said, pulling out his NCO voice, the roughened, battle-worn one that always put ass-kissing, rank-climbing officers up against a wall. "By the way things are playing out, I'm going to take a stab in the dark and say we're dealing with one of the thousands of alphabet soup agencies run by bureaucrats who have no fucking clue how the real world works. Either you take a different tone of voice with us or go find someone else to fuck in the ass."

In the subsequent silence, Dot slowly ground out the last of her cigar in an Elvis-shaped ashtray.

"Again. Apologies," the man said with a tone of contrition. "I'll start over. I'm Kurt Eriksson. I lead a multiagency taskforce through the DOJ. And I'm Cade Porter's handler."

"What the shit?" Steve muttered. "What did you two get caught up in?"

"I'll assume the voice I'm hearing is Steven Arturo Bautista. He needs to step away from this conversation. If not, then we're through conversing."

Steve was about to say something, but T.J. signaled for him to shut up. He circled his finger and Steve nodded then vacated the arbor. As he passed T.J., he tapped his ear and jerked his head toward the house. T.J. smiled and winked.

"Now that he's gone ..." Eriksson said after enough time passed to let Steve get inside the house.

"You can stop with the magic tricks," Dot said. "What do you want?"

"Were you able to get an in with Meyer Follman?" Eriksson asked.

"What are the mission parameters of this taskforce?" Dot countered.

There was a moment of silence. T.J. met Dot's calculating gaze. She had Eriksson's ticket, and she was going to punch every last one of those holes. The woman didn't give herself enough credit when it came to verbal warfare with clients and defendants.

"Fair enough. If you're going to cause me more of a headache, *Dot*, then I think we're officially through speaking."

"You gave me the phone."

Eriksson made a sound on the other end. "That was not how the handoff was supposed to happen. My agent decided on the best course of action and you were the one to take the bait."

Dot sat upright and leaned toward the phone. "Are you saying that your agent meant to give T.J. the phone?"

"He is the one with the clandestine mission experience, is he not?"

"You have to be fucking kidding me."

T.J. reached over and grasped her arm. She glared at him, then relaxed against the seat. Damn it, she was more pissed off than he expected. It took a lot to get her this far gone, and obviously today's events had taken her right to the edge. Eriksson's remarks had just pushed her over. In his years working with Sloane, they had never butted heads like he and Dot were doing now. Then again, he and Sloane hadn't ever had sex and always kept their partnership business only.

"We're a packaged deal," he told Eriksson.

"I'm well aware," Eriksson said. "I needed to speak to both of you."

"Then speak," T.J. said.

"What do you know about the Israeli mafia?" Eriksson's question sliced through the arbor's quiet.

Dot gestured to T.J., passing the torch in this case.

"They have a tenuous foothold here in Vegas. Mostly low-key. Drugs and gambling are typically their thing."

"That's what you know about them in Las Vegas, and it doesn't even scratch the surface," Eriksson said. "Meyer Follman has allied himself to one of the most powerful crime families in Israel. This family has ties in Morocco and Mexico with a slim thread leading into Afghanistan."

T.J. latched on to the Afghanistan part. "Opiates."

"Yes. In fact, ecstasy with heroin as the base. They like it as pure as they can get it, making these drugs worth billions. It's what put them on our radar. And it's where Cade comes in."

"You mean Caleb."

"Cade is his name as far as this conversation is concerned," Eriksson shot back. "I know you have the real files on him."

"How the hell ..." Dot started.

"It doesn't matter how I know. What matters is, not only have you put yourselves in danger, you've included your cousin. The shooting at the lawyer's house is just one of many ways for them to get to you. Yes, they were going after the Jones family and got you instead; by now they have become aware of you. They're seeking you out. And so is Cade," Eriksson said.

"If your intent is to scare us off, it's not working," T.J. replied.

"Not in the least. I've done my research on you two, and I like what I read. I'm even impressed by Bautista's record, but I can't bring him into this any more than you two have already done." Eriksson sighed. "Here's where my initial question comes in. Have you managed to get inside Follman's operation?"

Dot eyed him. Follman made the request for both of them, but he really wanted Dot's skills as a helicopter pilot. T.J. was probably just the dressing on this salad.

"We have been given an offer," she said. "Told Follman we'd think about it."

"What was the offer?" Eriksson asked.

"A shipment coming in from Canada into Idaho. No details on what this shipment is, only that it's soon and it comes with a huge price tag," Dot said.

"Canada? That's new." There was the sound of shuffled papers. "We had the intel that a new shipment was inbound. Thought it was coming through the usual channels, up through Mexico into Nevada and then dispersed accordingly."

"How do those shipments come?" T.J. asked.

"By the trailer load. Our intel pointed to them using the horses as cover. Get some buyers in another place, load up the horses, and haul them out. No one, until Cade, was able to get close enough to learn how they did it."

T.J. looked at Dot. "Would explain why Follman was so anxious to give you that horse and haul him up to Idaho for free."

"Until you told him I flew a helicopter. He jumped all over the idea of using a helicopter to move the shipment," she said.

"He wanted to use a helicopter?" Eriksson asked.

"Wanted to fly it out of the horse farm in Idaho down here. If they're transporting trailer loads of drugs, what I fly isn't the way to go," Dot said.

"Unless this shipment is smaller than the usual fare," Eriksson added.

"Follman was cagey about what this shipment was," T.J. pointed out. "Do you think they've changed up the goods and kept him out of the loop?"

"No, he's read in on every transaction. If he was cagey, it was to keep you two in the dark as long as possible. But it still doesn't explain the attack on Cade." Eriksson sounded absentminded. "The family Follman has gone into business with aren't trifled with. Intel has placed a former Mossad agent in their ranks."

"Back the fucking truck up," T.J. spat. "Mossad?"

"No way any of those men Cade and I killed were Mossad," Dot pointed out.

"They wouldn't be," Eriksson said. "More likely they were low-hanging fruit looking for way up the ladder. We made Cade out to be a broken-down veteran who was scared of his own shadow. He was supposed to be an easy mark."

"Joke's on them," Dot muttered.

"With you eliminating more of their men, they're out too many foot soldiers. The next step is the militants, and these guys won't be so easy to kill."

"Why turn on Cade? Right before a new shipment is coming in?" T.J. asked.

"Only Cade knows that. With him off-grid, we're never going to find out." What Eriksson said rang false.

He knew. He damn well knew what it was that drove Cade or Caleb, whatever he called himself, to doing an undercover job as a wounded and disabled man.

"We need to find him," T.J. said to Dot.

"No," Eriksson broke in. "He can handle himself. When he's ready to return, we'll get the message. The problem is the here and now. Work with me and take Follman's offer. We'll never get another chance like this. If this is bigger than drugs, I need to know."

"What do we get out of this for being dragged into the middle of a national taskforce?" T.J. demanded.

"You'll be generously compensated for your work and time," Eriksson said.

"Like we haven't heard that line of bullshit before," Dot said, reaching for the cigar butt.

"We're not the army, Ybarra."

"I stand by my statement." She stuck the dead cigar between her lips, looking very Winston Churchill with a perpetual scowl as she stared at T.J.

She was leaving this up to him. He'd already dragged them further into this mess than she would have liked. Between dealing with repressed memories, people trying to kill them, and an uncooperative partner with his own agenda, Dot was doing a damnable job of not throttling him for this shitshow.

While he watched her gnaw on the cigar tip, he recalled the tattoos. "Eriksson, this Israeli family, do they have any special rituals or markings?"

Dot frowned and removed the cigar butt, then understanding dawned on her.

"Yes. I'm aware you two found the tattoos. Anyone associated or part of the family gets one. It's their universal mark to prove their loyalty."

"Would that loyalty extend into Afghanistan?"

"If they have ties to the family and the operations, yes, yes it would."

"No fucking way," Dot muttered.

T.J. didn't give her chance to back out. If he could make it connect with Abbey Gate, she'd be further invested. And maybe her drive to resolve this would be the piece of the puzzle he was seeking to fit in place for his own reasons. He still got a kick in the gut when he remembered the look on her face when she told him about the dead refugee with the tattoo.

It had to be about saving a fellow veteran. It *had* to be.

"We're in," T.J. said. "We'll tell Follman tonight. You just provide us with the backup we're going to need."

Chapter Eighteen

E RIKSSON'S PEOPLE WERE watching the woman lawyer.
They did a decent job of staying unnoticed, but they weren't as good as Armand Revach's men. He was having damn difficult time trying to locate them himself, and he knew they were following Eriksson's men.

Caleb Podolsky had been undercover with Follman for more than a year before he had his first encounter with Revach and his right-hand man, Yonatan Hassin. Both men paid Caleb, a lowly farm manager, no mind. They had visited the Idaho horse facility as a favor to Follman, or that was the reason given to Caleb at the time.

Next came Follman's lawyer. A man so puffed up with himself, he paid Caleb a tip to move his car. Then the constant flow of horse trailers began. And the steady stream of new faces driving those trailers. Eventually, Caleb was banned from certain areas of the farm. His cover as a drug addict made those people coming and going disregard him. Even fooled Follman.

Until it didn't. And Caleb got caught where he wasn't supposed to be.

Now here he sat, in a beater truck, staked out not far from Tailored Suit's, aka Hal Jones, law firm. The same law firm where Vivian Montgomery worked. Here Caleb watched and waited for Revach's men to make a move.

Caleb should have never involved Hal Jones in his whole scheme. Shoulda, coulda, woulda.

He'd gone outside of the parameters of Eriksson's task force mission by making Hal's role in this whole thing bigger than it already was. Hal reluctantly went along with the behind-the-scenes changes after Caleb revealed there was a rat in his law firm. A giant one at that.

Those secrets and Caleb's own personal mission had put him in this spot.

Caleb checked his watch. It was midmorning. Vivian Montgomery had entered the building a few hours earlier. If Revach's men were going to make a move, it wasn't going to be during the daytime hours.

A few people walked along the sidewalk, but most did not linger or dawdle. The heat drove people inside. Caleb didn't mind it. It was comforting. A reminder of his childhood and his years spent in the Corps during his multiple tours.

The female jogger caught his attention. No one jogged this time of the day.

Caleb pressed his binoculars to his face and zeroed on the jogger. She'd done an admirable job of blending in with the Western woman's ideals of what she should wear to run in this heat. Big red flag was the slight *hamsa* tattoo on her right shoulder, exposed because of the revealing tank top she wore.

Caleb tossed the binoculars onto the seat next to him and started the truck. He'd leave Vivian Montgomery's security to Eriksson's men. Caleb had bigger fish to fry.

He trailed the jogger for several blocks. She met up with male in a manbun and a substantial beard who was wearing a folksy artist getup, a white tee smeared with charcoal, khakis held up by black suspenders, and flip-flops. He was set up by a café with an eye-rolling cutesy name, his easel loaded with a huge sketch pad.

Caleb parked his old beater on the opposite side of the street, among the sleek and shiny of Boise's upper echelons. From the side-view and rearview mirrors, he observed the brief exchange between jogger and artist.

Information exchanged, the jogger went on her way—no doubt circling back to stake out from the opposite side of Montgomery's law firm, wearing a whole new disguise. It's what Caleb would have done.

The artist closed his sketch pad and broke down the easel. Once he had his gear stowed, he went inside the café. Caleb admired the genius of this location for criminal activity. Nothing about it screamed dark, scary, and deadly. The café was quaint, the neighborhood trendy, and the people ignorant. A far cry different than the places most criminal organizations liked to set up shop.

A good place to ply a bit of the trade.

The beauty of these old pickups was the room inside the cab for the driver. Caleb exchanged his hoodie for the faded and dirty army jacket that smelled of two-month-old body odor. In the mirror, he did a bang-up job of disheveling his long hair and beard and smudged dirt from the truck floorboard across his face, hands, and in his hair. A wad of chewing tobacco tucked in his mouth to scum up his teeth and gums pulled off the last touch. Satisfied with looking like a broken-down homeless vet, he grabbed up the ratty duffel he kept for such purposes.

Armed with the Beretta, he eased out of the pickup and locked it. He pocketed the keys and hiked along the sidewalk opposite the café. As he passed people walking along, he played the panhandler. As predicted, most wrinkled their noses at his stench and ignored him. One guy decided to be a self-described savior and urged Caleb to come with him to a place where he could get his life turned around. Caleb was finally able to wash his hands clean of the dick by hacking up the tobacco wad on his white canvas shoes. Disgusted, the man stormed off.

Free to get back to his mission, Caleb made his way through the light traffic to the same side of the street as the café. He was about three blocks down and sufficiently distanced from his truck. He kept up the panhandling gig, keeping on alert for any outlying watchers for Revach's or Hassin's people.

Reaching the café, he did what every good panhandler in need of a drink did, and using the duffel as a seat, he set up shop near the entrance under the shade of the canvas awning. Each new customer that came through, he begged for some change. With each attempt, he got wide-eyed and disgusted expressions.

He'd been there maybe fifteen minutes when he noticed the blurry edges to his vision. He squeezed his eyes shut and tucked his chin to his chest to stave off the inevitable black-out. After a few seconds, he tested his efforts with a peek. No blurriness, no headache. Good.

The café door opened and this time an employee stepped outside.

"Dude, you need to pack up and move on," the young guy said.

Caleb peered up in a drunken manner. "Huh?"

The kid moved closer. "You need to leave. We have customers complaining."

"Fuck," Caleb moaned. "I just needed a rest."

"Do it somewhere else." The sour expression on the kid's face was priceless, and he backed away.

Old BO for the win.

"Could I get a bottled water? It's hot out here."

"You gonna pay for it?" the kid demanded from a distance.

Caleb frowned and glanced down at himself, then at the disgusted employee. "It's water, man."

"Just leave."

Caleb groaned. "Fine." He exaggerated his struggle to stand and kicked out his bum leg for effect as he reached down awkwardly to pick up his duffel.

The playacting did soften the kid's features, but it did nothing to make him rethink punting Caleb to the curb. He hobbled back the way he came, peeking over his shoulder to catch the kid watching him. Once Caleb rounded the primly trimmed bushes boarding the edge of the café's property, he stopped, gave it a few seconds, then checked. The kid was gone, back inside the café.

Caleb pushed the leaves aside and spotted a courtyard with unoccupied tables. Too hot for the patrons to sit outside. And no windows along the building wall to see in or out. Perfect place to sneak in and do a bit of recon.

He slipped through a break in the bushes, dumped his duffel and the stinky jacket on the ground between the shrubbery, and entered the courtyard. Staying low and cautious, he circumvented the bricked patio and headed for the alley between the building and line of shrubs. The alley led to a narrow back street wide enough for just one vehicle to come down, be it a garbage truck or a delivery van. Jutting out from the back of the business was a set of stairs with pipe-style railing and a slight docking area. The swing-style doors were closed, keeping the hot summer air out. The rest of the back alley was clear.

Caleb doubled back to check his blind spots, found himself still in the clear, and then quietly climbed the steps, keeping his attention on the doors. He made the dock without incident.

The doors were not fully closed. Drawing his Beretta, he inched up to the door. He paused every few steps and strained to listen.

The RPG blast had not only taken half a leg and left him riddled with scars and shrapnel, it had also ruined his hearing. Being a whole man made him a fucking top-notch Marine, but he had other skills that had appealed to the Corps. His uncanny intuition had saved his ass in more situations than he cared to count. His fellow Marines had always teased him about being too jumpy or having weird Spidey-like senses. Caleb chalked it up to being a product of the life he'd been dealt. One had to be aware when an abusive foster parent was about to throw a slap or a punch.

It had failed him once. And once was one too many.

He eased up to the door left ajar and listened inside. Quiet. Slowly, he pushed the door inward and followed it. Inside, he eased the door shut to the near exact position it had been in when he entered.

The café's cool storage was dimly lit and rife with freshly roasted coffee beans. It took Caleb's vision far too long to adjust to the dimness. Retinal damage in both eyes from the blast had left him with a form of night blindness. He would have to be careful. To this day, he still marveled at how well he'd faked his physical for Eriksson's task force. Long overdue justice had a way of fueling your needs.

Slowly, Caleb made his way through the shelves of dried goods and burlap bags of coffee beans, heading for a large square of light ahead. The source of that light came through large viewing windows in a pair of swinging doors dividing the main dining area from the storage.

The hiss of an espresso machine mingled with light jazz and the chatter of patrons. He could not let things go south with innocents nearby. Caleb came to the end of the shelves and followed another pool of light to a single door.

The door swung open. Caleb darted behind a pile of empty burlap sacks and crouched down. Manbun emerged from the room, turned off the light, and headed for the doors to the café. There was a burst of light as he pushed into the café, then it was gone as the doors slapped shut.

Caleb waited a few seconds for his eyes to readjust from the dramatic change in light, but the spots wouldn't fade, and the darkness encroached. Through the haze, he heard the amplified beating of his pulse. *Damn it, not now.*

He took deep breaths, felt his equilibrium return, and

then left the safety of the pile. Before he left, he would see what was in the back room. Follman had risked a lot to have Caleb taken out by sending in low-level thugs to do what Yonatan Hassin was better trained to do, because Caleb had discovered Follman's off-the-books activities. If he was marked to die for Eriksson's stupid-ass operation, then he damn well deserved to have the smoking gun to bust open this whole dirty scheme. Caleb would see to the end of Follman's existence. It was the lifelong vow he would cash in.

He inched closer to the backroom, keeping an eye on the door into the café, and trying to find a better hiding spot. This close to the front of the business, there was no cramped hole for him to crawl into. If someone came through the café doors, he would be exposed.

Another wave of spots crossed his vision. The wave turned into a flood of darkness, and Caleb stumbled. He bumped a shelf, froze at the slight rattle of stainless-steel utensils. He couldn't see a blasted thing and now his head was pounding. He had to get out of here before he passed out.

There was a break in the dark cloud, and he turned to get out. He was passing the café door when it flew open and slammed into his face. Jolted by the force, he staggered back, losing his balance on his prosthetic leg. His good leg buckled, and Caleb hit the floor hard.

He hadn't even gotten his bearings when he was hauled upward and flung into the brick interior wall. The force of his head hitting the wall sent sparks flying across his vision. He tried to get his arms up to defend himself, but his assailant slammed his head into the wall again, and again, and again.

The sparks fizzled out. Caleb stopped feeling.

Darkness engulfed him.

Chapter Nineteen

DESPITE LARRABEE'S WARNING and advisement, Vivian came to the office. She'd spent the prior day holed up working at her apartment, mulling over Cade Porter's—or should she be calling him Caleb Podolsky?—reasons for breaking into her apartment and where Hal Jones might have run off to.

She'd also taken a deep dive into Caleb's actual file that Dot and T.J. had left in her care. The man Caleb Podolsky was had been heavily influenced by the child Caleb's life, but there were reports missing, like his actual foster care history. Vivian made a few calls to some people she knew in Las Vegas and was able to access Caleb's full juvenile records. Except the Las Vegas courts would only allow the records to be sent to her office.

As for Hal, without knowing enough about the other lawyer, Vivian's ideas petered out. She'd need an insider into Hal's personal life in order to give Larrabee a better understanding on how to find the man. Vivian knew the perfect person to get her that information. Charley Ash. But for some reason, the man was nowhere to be found.

His paralegal informed Vivian he hadn't seen or spoken to Charley since the day before. The same day he'd passed off the files on Cade Porter/Caleb Podolsky to Vivian. She pressed the paralegal about Charley's routine and whether it was usual for him to be unaccounted for during an extended period of time when he wasn't in the middle of a trial. The para told her it was, in fact, customary, because he and Hal Jones loved to play hooky now and again to visit a local golf course.

Except this time, Hal Jones was purposely hiding. Charley had no reason to be out. Far as Vivian was aware, no one outside of herself, Dot, and T.J. knew about Charley's involvement with the Cade Porter and Hal Jones situation.

Vivian tried to focus on a few of her upcoming cases and wait to see if the man showed up. She struggled to remain on task. Cade Porter's unexpected visit to her apartment and his menacing presence had left her more rattled than she cared to admit. Another reason to not be in her apartment. If the man could sneak in despite all her security measures, she was doomed if someone with more ill intent were to try.

At half past ten, Loren dropped by her office unannounced.

"Vivian, this was left for you, and Meredith gave it to me," he said as he entered her office with a thick file in hand. "Are you doing okay?"

She took the file, glanced at it, saw the words *Las Vegas*, and then returned her attention to Loren. "I'm fine. Why do you ask?"

"Well, you didn't come in yesterday. Got me a bit worried, what with all this hoopla going on with Hal and whatnot."

"Loren, I'm fully capable of handling things if they get

hairy. You don't need to worry about me. I was just taking a day for myself, which I haven't done in I can't remember when."

His gaze flicked down to the file lying on her desk. "What's that all about?"

She gave him a placating smile. "Just some light reading I need to do for another case." She tilted her head. "Why did Meredith give it to you? And how did she get it?"

"Common procedure. If a file from an out-of-state court gets sent here, Meredith is the one to process it so we can keep track. I don't know why she gave it to me."

A little voice in the back of Vivian's head whispered to her. Something about Loren's reasoning was not right. Even if he'd read through Caleb's juvenile records, he'd have no idea what it was all about.

"Well." Loren clapped his hands. "If you're sure you're doing just fine?"

"I'm fine."

"Then, I'll leave you to your *light* reading."

"Thank you for bringing it to me."

He gave her a wide shit-eating grin. "My pleasure."

Once he'd gone, Vivian stared at the closed door. Something was off with him. As long as she'd been a lawyer in this firm, she'd not once seen Loren just visit any of the nonpartnered attorneys. He kept to his domain, and all conversations were done in his office. And he'd *never* deliver a case file—that was beneath him. It was legwork for paralegals and secretaries.

Whatever. She had better things to do than pick apart Loren McLaughlin.

Vivian began her methodic research on Caleb Podolsky's childhood.

By half past eleven, she gave up waiting on Charley. She'd pay him a visit. First, she stopped Charley's paralegal again on the way out.

"Which golf course did Charley and Hal go to?" she asked.

The para removed his fashionably red reading glasses, tapped the curved part of an earpiece against his lips, and *hmmmed.* "I think they went to all of them in the city. But Charley had too many trials coming up to take time to play golf. I doubt he's on the course today."

"Would he be at home?"

The para shrugged. "Maybe. I do know he ritually goes to the YMCA to swim every morning. He and Hal were jocks back in the day and like to keep up the image."

Vivian eyed the man. "Why does that not surprise me?"

Shrugging again, the para put on his glasses and resumed his work. Vivian left the firm with Charley's address in hand.

The drive to his place was a short one. He didn't live far from the firm.

Charley's townhouse was a prime bachelor paradise. No families here. Her persistent knocking and hailing his Ring camera went unanswered.

Her summoning did bring forth the next-door neighbor. One very pissed off, very disheveled blonde in a skimpy blue silk nightie and matching robe.

"Do you mind," she grumbled. "Some of us are trying to sleep."

"Sorry." *Not really.* "I'm a colleague of Charley's and I

need to speak to him. Would you happen to know if he's home?"

The blonde squinted at Vivian. "What *kind* of colleague?"

"The lawyer kind. Do you happen to know if he's home or not?"

A noncommittal one-shoulder shrug was the answer. The blonde crossed her arms, pushing up her breasts, and tilted her head in that way unsecure women did when they sensed competition to their territory.

Charley, I hope to God you didn't sleep with this woman. Or maybe he hadn't and that was the issue.

Vivian put on her best compromising lawyer smile. "Do you know Charley well?"

"As well as a neighbor should."

"If you're trying to sleep during the day, what is it that you do, ma'am? If you don't mind me asking."

"I do mind, and it's none of your business."

Vivian nodded. "Then I'll leave you to get back to your sleep." She stepped down from the small portico.

"Like that's going to happen."

Vivian ignored the parting shot and made her way along the sidewalk back to her parked car.

"He was here early this morning."

Vivian stopped and turned. The blonde had moved to the edge of her own portico and gripped the support post for the angled roof.

"I passed him going into my place as he was leaving. I think he likes to go to the Y and swim."

"What time was this?" Vivian asked.

The blonde bobbed her head back and forth. "Between five and six. He doesn't usually come back after his swim. I think he goes to the office afterward."

How the neighbor knew this, Vivian wasn't about to ask. Her suspicion that something had transpired between Charley and his neighbor was further confirmed when the blonde hugged herself.

"Did something happen to him?" she asked, then proceeded to gnaw on her lips.

"Why would you ask that?"

"Because you're, like, the third person to come looking for him."

A niggling of alarm shot through Vivian. She walked back to the blonde and mounted the single step onto the portico.

"Two other people were here?"

"Yeah. Two men. Different times. He doesn't get male visitors. If you know what I mean?"

Vivian got the gist. "What times were these men here?"

"One guy last night, before I left for work. Charley was home and let the guy in. They must have known each other."

"What did this guy look like?" Vivian pressed.

The blonde shrugged. "It was dark, and Charley didn't have any lights on. They were going inside as I was coming out. He was a big guy, I do remember that. Dressed kinda nice too. Sorry, I couldn't tell you what he looked like exactly."

"That's okay. What about the second guy?"

"He was yesterday afternoon. Charley wasn't here."

And he wasn't at work either. So where had he gone?

"Did you see this guy?"

The neighbor nodded. "I'm usually up around four, and I heard the guy banging on Charley's door. I was going to confront him about being so loud until I saw what he looked like. I stayed inside and waited for him to leave."

"And he looked like?"

"Like someone put him through a woodchipper. Scars all over his face, and he wore a black hoodie. Who wears a hoodie in the summer?"

Caleb? Vivian recalled her own revulsion at the sight of Caleb's damaged face. Maybe it was him. Maybe it wasn't.

"People are strange. I'll give you that," Vivian told the blonde. "Thank you for telling me this."

"Seriously? Is Charley in trouble?"

"Not that I'm aware. I just need to speak with him about a case."

The neighbor nodded hesitantly. "Okay." She returned to her own home. She paused and looked back at Vivian, frowned, then closed the door.

Vivian hurried to her car. She was checking the YMCA aquatic center next. That niggling in her was gaining a friend called panic.

The drive over was hindered by noontime traffic. Stuck at a light, she made the call she'd been debating.

Larrabee picked up on the second ring. "Counselor Montgomery."

"Sergeant, are you free at this time?"

"Stuck in the office doing paperwork. And reading through those journals Roman told me our guy Porter left behind."

"Finding anything of interest?"

"Not really. 'Course, I've only read through the ones where he's talking about horse rations and rotations and crap like that."

The light turned green, and traffic crawled forward.

"Would you mind meeting me at the Boise YMCA aquatic center?" she asked.

"Thinking of getting in a few midday laps in the pool?" Larrabee's calm and collected voice wasn't doing Vivian's nerves any good.

"Not really." She relayed her suspicions and what the neighbor had told her. "I'm hoping I'm just being paranoid, and he decided to get in a game of golf today."

"But you know full well that's not the case. I'll meet you there. Do not go inside until I'm with you."

"It's a public area," she countered.

"Which don't mean jack shit to someone who intends to do harm. Wait for me."

The man was as bad as T.J. or Dot. If Vivian had learned anything in the last few days, it was to never disregard an order from Sergeant Cassius Larrabee.

SHE ONLY HAD to wait ten minutes for Larrabee to arrive. Ten agonizing minutes.

In that time, she'd circled the parking lot and didn't find Charley's vehicle, a white double cab pickup. She parked and watched people come and go. A lot of elderly folks and working adults on lunch break took advantage of the near empty pool while all the families used the outdoor pools and water parks around the city.

When Larrabee finally arrived in his state-funded vehicle, Vivian had gnawed off two fingernails.

"Do you need to remain in your vehicle while I interrogate the employees?" Larrabee asked as she met him at the front entrance.

"Hell no. I'll remove the rest of my fingernails before you finish. I'm coming in."

"Suit yourself." He held open the door for her and matched her stride to the front desk.

"I asked one of my people to check all the golf courses in case he had gone for a few rounds," he told her.

"Thank you for that. It'll save time searching for him."

"Tell me why you think something bad has happened to him?"

They both stopped walking.

Vivian faced him. "You ever get that special sense something is wrong?" she asked.

"All the time. I'm a cop."

"While I waited for you to get here, I went over everything the neighbor told me. I think Cade was looking for Charley because Hal told him about the second set of files. He needs to take possession of those if he's ever to keep his real identity out of the wrong hands."

Larrabee nodded. "Makes sense. Who do you think the second guy is?"

"Halloway Jones."

"Think you're onto something there, Counselor."

They continued on to the front desk and were greeted by

a bored high schooler.

Larrabee flashed his badge dangling from a stout chain around his neck. "Sergeant Larrabee, state police. I'm here looking for a man."

The teenaged boy frowned. "You'll have to be more specific. We get a lot of men in here."

"This one would have been here early this morning between the times of five thirty and seven," Larrabee replied.

Vivian set her phone down on the countertop with Charley's professional firm photo pulled up. "He looks like this."

The teen squinted at the screen then shook his head. "Never seen him before. But I don't work the desk in the early morning. Hang on." He picked up a desktop phone and punched a single number on the pad. "Yeah, there's a cop up front looking for someone ... I don't know." A moment later he replaced the handset. "My manager is coming."

Two minutes later, a well-tanned, lean man in a pair of white shorts and a lime-green polo emerged from the backside of the reception area. He held out his hand to Larrabee first, then Vivian.

"Jake Starns, I'm the manager. What can I help you with?"

Vivian held up her phone. "Have you seen this guy today? He's a fellow lawyer in my firm, and we haven't seen him in at least two days."

"An eyewitness puts him leaving his home to come here for his daily morning swim," Larrabee followed up.

Jake studied the image, frowning. "I don't think I have. But then, there's a lot of people who come and go here that I don't see. Umm, come with me."

He led them back to his cramped office. Once behind his desk, he sat and brought up his computer. "What's his name? I can look up his membership activity."

Vivian rattled off Charley's full name. After a quick search, Jake was able to find the information.

"It looks like he scanned his member ID at 5:23." Jake squinted at the screen. "But there's no log-out time. That's weird."

"Why's that?" Larrabee asked.

Jake swiveled his seat around to face them. "Certain member plans charge by the hour of usage. Mr. Ash uses that plan. He typically has a two-hour usage window. Today, there's no card swipe to check him out."

"How many people use the pool that early in the morning?" Vivian asked.

Jake returned to his computer and accessed the data. "During the week, we see anywhere from ten to twenty-some patrons during those hours."

"Today?" Larrabee asked.

"Hmmm, it was a slow morning. We had ... five."

"Any camera footage we can see?" Larrabee asked.

Jake clicked away on his computer. "We have cameras set up outside the locker rooms, around the pool for safety measures, and by the exit doors. Nowhere else." After a few more clacks, he rotated his computer screen. "I've brought up the footage from 5:20."

Vivian leaned down beside Larrabee and watched. The camera was angled to get a full scope of the glass walls and the employee-only access door leading directly into the pool, and next to it the men's and women's locker rooms. The seconds ticked past slowly on an empty passageway to the locker rooms. Then Charley sauntered into the screen. He entered the men's room like he hadn't a care in the world. It was a typical morning for him. Ten minutes, then twenty, then thirty minutes went by and no one else entered or exited the locker room.

Jake explained that the locker rooms exited in the pool area so the patrons didn't track water in the main halls. Larrabee had Jake advance the recording to about the time Charley should have exited the locker room. After twenty minutes had crept past, Larrabee asked Jake to advance it farther. A quick two hours later and still no Charley leaving the locker room, only two other men entering and two women in that timeframe.

"Pool cameras?" Vivian asked.

Jake pulled those up. There they spotted Charley leaving the locker room and entering the pool area. He chatted it up with the lifeguard before diving into the pool. He did a full hour of laps. After another quick chat with the lifeguard, Charley headed into the locker room once more. They watched the next few hours in quick time to see if he came out of the locker rooms and left by the pool exits. No Charley. The four other patrons were the only ones to show up at the pool.

"He never came out again." Larrabee straightened. "Are there any exits in the locker rooms?"

"No. In order to make sure our most vulnerable patrons are not attacked or exploited, we have no outside access."

"There are exit doors around the pool," Vivian pointed out.

"Those are locked from the outside so people can't sneak in to use the pool."

"What time does the pool officially open?"

"Five a.m.," Jake replied.

"Did anyone enter the locker room before Charley?"

Jake backed up the recording; no one entered before Charley. The first person to access the pool was the lifeguard, entering through the glass employee-only door next to the locker rooms.

"He didn't just vanish," Vivian said.

"What times do the cameras start recording?" Larrabee asked.

"They're programmed to start at four a.m., right as the employee scheduled to open up comes in. They stop recording at ten p.m., a full hour after the building is closed for the day."

"Back it up to opening time," Larrabee ordered.

Jake did, and they saw the employee reserved to open up appear and unlock the locker rooms and the main pool entrance from the hall. Ten minutes later, the camera blacked out.

"What the—" Jake clicked on a few things and replayed the moment again.

Again, the camera went black. Two minutes passed before it came online.

"Bingo," Larrabee said. "I need access to the locker room."

"I'm coming too," Vivian said.

"Whoa, wait. I can't—"

"Don't you dare tell me you can't let a woman into the

men's locker room."

Jake paled under that perfect tan. "It's not that. There's a lot of people here. I can't just kick them out."

"Tell them it's a police matter. Because it is."

Jake sighed. He picked up the phone and hit a button. "Yeah, it's me. Get everyone out of the locker rooms ... The police are here ... Just do it." He set the handset down. "Give them five minutes."

Vivian, at Larrabee's side, stood outside the locker room entrance and smiled at the half-dressed, confused men who stumbled out into the hallway. Once the last guy had been shooed out and an employee was stationed at the passageway between the locker room and the pool, Larrabee and Vivian entered the men's room.

"What are you looking for?" she asked, scanning the white-tiled room smelling heavily of pool chemicals.

"Check the toilet stalls and the showers for anything that looks remotely off," he said, standing before the lockers.

"You and I both know that if there was something off about the stalls and showers, someone would have reported it."

One side of the lockers were the half-sized kind, just big enough to hang a gym bag inside and other clothing articles. The other side, the ones Larrabee studied, were the full-sized lockers. Three of them had key padlocks on them. He went to work opening all the unlocked doors. Vivian joined in, finding each of the ones she opened either contained some pool-goer's belongings or was empty.

Jake stepped inside and hovered near the doorway.

"You have bolt cutters?" Larrabee asked when they had

opened all the others.

Jake shook his head but walked over with a set of keys in his hand. "The locks belong to us." He checked the back of each lock and found the corresponding key. Once he had each one unlocked, he stepped back.

Larrabee grasped Vivian's hand as she reached for the nearest handle. "I'd rather you not." He shook a finger at her when she went to protest. "Humor me, Counselor."

Grudgingly, Vivian stepped away from the lockers and joined Jake.

Larrabee opened one locker then another. The third one he backed up and hung his head.

"We found Charley."

Chapter Twenty

FOLLMAN WAS PLEASED when Dot and T.J. accepted his offer. Dot couldn't decide if the bemused expression on Follman was from their acceptance or the fact he was setting them up for something. Her suspicions were further heightened when he didn't even bother to haggle over their demand for a higher payout, per Eriksson's insistence.

Follman did have a nonnegotiable in the deal. They had to use the helicopter he kept at the airport for the pickup. He also managed the green light for them to fly out immediately.

Follman's helicopter, a Bell 525 Relentless, while meant for civilian use, couldn't get much closer to a Black Hawk if it tried. A full row of seats was missing from the cabin, and the cockpit was blocked off from the back by a heavy curtain.

Why would they need seating in the back if drugs were being shuttled over the border?

Then there was another issue when flying the 525 Relentless.

Dot glared at the man tasked with prepping the copter for use and maintaining it. "You do realize I need a copilot."

He shrugged. "I do what I'm told and that's about it. If Mr. Follman wanted you to have 'nother, he'd have someone come." He handed Dot a packet. "Here's your flight information."

Dot took the thin envelope and opened it. What the fuck was Follman playing at? These machines were hard enough to handle on a beautiful day with not a cloud in sight. Handicap her with no copilot and if she ran into turbulence or hit a wall with fatigue, they were looking at a downed helicopter.

She read through the single sheet of instructions that gave her the coordinates to the farm where the package was waiting for pickup. And one line of warning—

STAY OUT OF RANGE OF RADAR DETECTION.

Dot was hating this whole operation more and more.

She gave T.J. a hard stare. "Looks like you're my second."

"What do you expect me to do? I don't know how to fly."

"Start learning."

Eriksson had warned them to stay off comms and keep to the flight plan. He was certain Follman had the copter wired and rigged with a tracker. Eriksson also directed that when they did talk to not to discuss anything from their personal lives they couldn't fabricate.

Dot wouldn't worry about that. She'd have her AC/DC soundtrack blaring through the cockpit and be completely focused on keeping this damn bird in the sky.

By midmorning, they were airborne en route to Challis, Idaho. More specifically, a huge farm northwest of the town nestled in the Salmon-Challis National Forest. They kept their chatter strictly to Dot walking T.J. through how to handle the helo if something were to happen.

As they passed the Idaho-Nevada state line, she deviated to the place where Follman had instructed her to refuel the helicopter. It was a long defunct airfield Follman and his people were able to acquire dirt cheap. He'd warned them to stay in the copter during the refuel. So, after she touched down on a resurfaced landing pad, she and T.J. remained in their seats.

While a bedraggled crew of two refueled the helicopter and did a quick once-over, Dot did her own check. Sitting there afforded their phones a chance to connect to a tower, and both chimed with messages.

Dot stared at the text from Vivian warning her that one of her colleagues had been murdered. A follow-up message from her cousin warned that the hunt had intensified for Cade Porter/Caleb Podolsky, whom they suspected of killing the lawyer.

"Shit," T.J. said after reading his, then without a word, handed her his phone with a message from Larrabee.

Not only was Caleb suspected of killing the lawyer, he had also broken into Vivian's apartment. Something her cousin had failed to mention to Dot.

One of the workers pounded on the window next to Dot and gave her the thumbs-up. She returned the gesture and handed T.J. his phone.

"We talk later" was all he said as she put the helicopter back into flight mode.

For the next two hours, she did her damnedest to stay focused on her flight path and not on the fact her cousin had come face-to-face with a trained killer, then couldn't be bothered with informing her about it. She was going to bitch slap Vivian for that move.

T.J., too, kept his own council. Dot couldn't tell by his features what he was thinking. Whatever thoughts were running rampant through his head, some of them better be ways to get them out of this mess.

As she drew closer to their destination, the farm came into sight. It looked … empty. There were a lot of buildings and paddocks and pastures, yet there didn't seem to be any livestock. This time of day and during the summer, horses should be outside. In fact, there was a lack of farm equipment activity as well.

A summons from someone on the ground came through the comms. Dot relayed the required message to grant them unhindered passage onto the property. Cleared by the other end, she directed the copter to the place where the landing pad was located.

Once she cut the engine and the blades were winding down, three men wearing what could only be described as formal tactical clothing—if there were such a thing—exited a building off to her left.

"Incoming," she said to T.J. and unbuckled the seat straps.

The lead man motioned for her to open the cockpit door.

She pushed it out, and he took hold of it.

"You and your partner will exit the helicopter and follow me." His authoritative tone brokered no rebuttal.

After offloading the headgear and shouldering their day packs, she and T.J. hopped out and followed the trio to another building across the way. Before leaving Las Vegas, they had both armed themselves, concealing weapons in areas on their bodies where they wouldn't be noticed but easily accessed if needed. God help them if they got patted down and their bags searched.

Once inside the building, Dot raised her aviators to accommodate for the dimness. It was a small office, and it was empty.

"Come with me." The lead man gestured for the other two to remain at the door.

He led them down a hall to another room, where he opened the door and stepped aside to let them in. A table centered in the room held two silver hard-shell briefcases and a small buffet. Wide, elongated sofas lined two of the unadorned, windowless walls. The place felt like a break room minus the vending machines.

"Mr. Follman asked that we provide you with something to eat," the man said as he closed the door and circled the table.

Dot was picking up on his accent and trying to place his home of origin. He was definitely from the Middle East.

"All fine and dandy," T.J. said. "But why'd we need to leave the chopper?"

"Maintenance purposes." The smile the man gave left Dot feeling like she was facing a timber rattler. "The shipment will be loaded while you take a moment before the return flight. In the meantime, eat and drink. Refresh yourselves. Catch a nap. Do not leave this room." He tapped on a second door—the only other door in the room—opposite the entry. "Here is the restroom."

Dot circled the table, eyeing the briefcases. "What are those for?"

"The first half of your payment." The man returned to the entry door. "The second half will be paid upon your arrival in Las Vegas." The snake smile once more, minus the flickering tongue. "Mr. Follman has requested this. Please, enjoy. I will return for you when it's time to leave." With that, he exited the room.

Dot listened and didn't hear the click of a lock. They were left with some level of trust. Or was it a trap? *Do not heed the warning so that we can kill you.* Except who would be left to fly their shipment back to Las Vegas?

T.J. popped open one of the cases. "Fuck," he said in a hushed voice.

She joined him and stared at the piles of fresh twenties. "I've never seen that much money in my life," she whispered.

He closed the case and moved to the food. "Look." He held up a beer can. "Our country folk ways are being recognized."

With a headshake, Dot wandered the room, studying it. No windows to show them where they were on the property. No indication how many rooms this entire building held. And how many people were on the place. She opened the restroom door to find a single toilet and pedestal sink. Utilitarian and clean. Unused.

It was nice and all, yet the vibe was off. Like they had been herded into a single location to corral them. She was trapped. Confined to a box. Dot was by no means claustrophobic, but she needed her wide-open spaces and the ability to see what was coming.

The silver dish covers clanking brought her back to T.J.'s side.

"Sandwiches and finger foods."

"What do you want to bet they laced it with something?" she said, keeping her voice low in case someone was listening as she eyed a roast beef on a sesame bun.

"And risk us crashing the helo with their precious cargo inside? Doubtful."

"What about the news we received?"

T.J. grimaced and shook his head. Now was not the time to discuss.

"I don't like this," she whispered.

"I don't either." He pressed his hand on his hip, close to the appendix holster and his favored sidearm. "Glad they didn't frisk us."

There was some measure of security knowing they still had their weapons. On the edge of paranoia, Dot refused to eat or drink any of the buffet. Instead, she refilled her own water bottle from the restroom sink and for fuel, downed a slim package of jerky.

T.J. did the same. "We need to make it look like we did eat something," he said.

He took the opportunity to dump two cans of beer down the sink and she several bottles of the provided water. Then they crumbled up some of the food and flushed what they could down the toilet. For special effect, Dot scattered a few crumbs here and there.

Though anticipation crawled along her skin and she craved a joint to calm her, she sprawled out on one of the sofas. She hadn't slept well last night. She was running on pure adrenaline.

Closing her eyes, she listened to T.J. rummage around and mutter to himself. She felt herself drift. She wasn't sure when he did it, but at some point, her upper body shifted, and she felt him settle on the sofa under her head. T.J. would keep up the image of them being married the best way he knew. Dot appreciated his commitment. No matter what the circumstances, they had each other's backs. Even when he acted the fool, like now getting them caught up in this deal with Follman.

She was carrying the brunt of the load in this ordeal by keeping him on task and flying. It had been no different during her days flying for the army or the forest service. She'd been a warrant officer as a pilot and on par or above rank with most of the men she shuttled into the mountains of Afghanistan. Same was true for the forest service. Samo Ybarra had raised his granddaughter to lead. And she did so with a command presence that had always put men of all creeds on notice.

But she was still a woman. And she was woman enough to admit that sometimes she needed some assistance with the load.

Past and present, T.J. had always managed to lighten said load. Never once did he pull the whole macho bullshit on her. Overbearing protector, yes, he was a card-carrying member of the club. She could manage that side of him.

As if sensing her mental wrestling match, he settled his arm along her shoulder and the weight of it helped ease her into a light slumber.

All too soon, she was pulled out of her sleep as T.J.

shook her. She peeled an eye open to see his bearded face looming over her.

"Our escort is back."

Dot sat up, swung herself off the sofa and upright, the moves long practiced and second nature. She was in mission mode. All those days bugging out at a moment's notice were hotwired into her muscles.

The man who'd brought them here watched her with a wary gleam in his eyes. An air of disdain permeated the confines of this temporary, tricked-out holding cell.

He cleared his throat, then grabbed the briefcases off the table. Dot noticed the fresh bruising on his knuckles. T.J. motioned over his own knuckles and Dot nodded.

"We have the shipment loaded and are ready," their escort said. "Apologies for the delay. There were some technical issues."

Technical issues? What could they possibly be hauling back to Las Vegas that warranted this kind of classified level speak?

"Those *technical issues* better not be related to the helicopter," Dot said.

The escort eyed her, then exited the room.

A stillness settled over Dot. T.J. nudged her and they followed the man.

Carrying the cases himself, he led them back through the building and out to the landing pad. Dot noted right off that the Relentless's cabin now had its windows covered. She elbowed T.J.

He nodded his understanding.

Reaching the cockpit, the man handed off the cases to a

shorter male in grease-stained coveralls, who loaded them in a compartment behind the cabin.

Their escort turned to them and held out a sheet of paper. "Please refuel at these coordinates. With the additional weight, you'll need it."

Dot took the sheet. "I need to run through the preflight."

"No need. The crew has everything in order."

Dot glared at him. "Did I clear this *everything in order?*"

The snake grin was back. "As I said, there is no need. The crew has it in hand." His eyes narrowed. "It's the kind of service Mr. Follman expects."

"I don't give two shits what kind of service Follman expects. I'm the pilot, and I don't fly until I've gone over it myself." Dot crossed her arms. "On the ground or in the air? Your choice."

After a bit of a standoff, their escort bent to Dot's will. During her own check, he made certain he shadowed her every move. He was especially twitchy any time she came close to the cabin doors. Other than the blocked windows and the added weight, things looked the same.

She and T.J. strapped in, and once the blades spun up to full speed, she took the helicopter to the sky.

The moment the horse farm was far out of sight, and she had the copter at altitude and speed, Dot scribbled out a quick note in code in case there were extra eyes in the cockpit.

T.J. read it, crumpled it up, and shoved the wad in a pocket. His curt nod was all she needed.

They weren't transporting inanimate objects.

Chapter Twenty-One

A SOUR, MUSTY odor pulled Caleb to consciousness.
Wherever he was, he lay there, eyes still shut, breathing in the noxious fumes until it irritated his lungs into fits of coughing. He rolled over, flopping onto his back, hacking and wheezing. When the fit passed and he was able to breathe, he opened his eyes—at least one of his eyes. The other seemed swollen shut. It was dark, nearly pitch black, and it was raining. A rumble of soft thunder rippled through the air.

Between the throbbing in his head and the foul air, he couldn't get a grasp on what had happened to him. He lifted his hand, and a tinkling sound stopped him. Unable to see what made the sound, he moved his arm, eliciting more tinkling. He tried to move his arm across his body only to be brought to a stop by the bite of metal on skin. The tinkling turned into a rattle.

Caleb bolted upright and yanked his arm, having it jerked back when it met resistance. He was chained to something. With his free hand, he found the links and followed them. As he moved around, he became aware of a strange sensation from his left leg. He stopped with the chain and patted the place where his prosthetic should have been, but it wasn't.

What happened to it?

Abandoning the chain and whatever he was anchored to, he began fumbling around, patting what he deciphered to be musty straw reeking of moldy animal waste, trying to locate the titanium rod that served as his leg. He came to the end of his chain and was yanked backward. He lay there and fumed.

Bit by bit, he remembered what brought him to this situation. Following Manbun to the café. Sneaking in the backside of the café. Stumbling upon the backroom and realizing his stupidity, only to be waylaid by a blackout. And then the horrible beating of his head against a brick wall.

He was the epitome of the cocky ass fuckwad who walked right over a landmine and got blown up.

What an *awesome* undercover operative he made.

Fuck-fuck-fuck-fuck-fuck!

Calming himself, he tried again to locate his missing half of his leg. And again, came up empty-handed. The rain intensified, and the rolling thunder drew closer and louder. A loud plopping sounded behind him. Giving up on the search for his prosthetic, he changed tactics and felt around to get a sense of his surroundings.

He found the chain and located its base, anchored into a cement wall. The cement wall rose above his head. As he maneuvered about on his ass, he was pelted by a stream of water coming from above. He peered up and spotted a tiny bit of light coming from a hole above him. The hole would brighten as lightning flashed.

Caleb scooted away from the water and continued his study. Each time he moved too far, the chain tugged him into submission. The clattering it made each time grew louder along with his frustrations.

Feeling woozy and sick, his head pounding, unable to tell if he couldn't see because his eyes had gone dim or if it was just that dark, he let out a hellish howl.

The noise startled another creature. It bleated a panicked cry.

Caleb stilled.

The sound had been human. Female. Young.

"Hello?" he asked softly, gentling his voice.

There was a shuffling, then a whimper.

"Who's there?" he asked.

A moment of silence passed. It felt like an eternity. His head throbbed, the pain radiating down his neck into his shoulders and chest. The beating against the wall had not done him any favors.

Shit! What if ...

"Who ... are ... you?" The forced words came out lilted and halting, feminine and foreign.

A woman. Possibly a young woman. Fuck, he hoped she wasn't younger than nineteen. If he had to guess her home of origin by her accent, Arabian Peninsula. If he narrowed down even more, Syrian or Afghani.

Damn it. One of the main reasons Eriksson had gotten him to take this undercover assignment was to get as buddy-buddy as he could with Meyer Follman to have an in on Follman's drug operation. As Caleb dug deeper into Follman and his network it was becoming about more than just drugs. Caleb had hoped he was wrong but knew it was more than that.

All the data he had written down in those journals. All the shipments he'd observed coming and going from the farm. It was supposed to be Follman and his cronies bringing in undocumented people for labor purposes. Or even more nefarious reasons like infiltrating nuclear facilities or wreaking havoc biologically on the American agricultural system.

He was fucking wrong. Oh, so fucking wrong.

"My name is Cade Porter," he said. If he dared to use his Jewish given name, he risked losing any trust he could build with her. The false name was safest. "What's your name?"

She delayed, letting the sound of the storm fill the silence. This conversation kept him lucid and holding off the inevitable blackout. When Caleb was about to press the question again, she spoke.

"Mina."

"Just Mina?"

"Yes," she said in Dari.

Fuck! She was Afghani.

"Mina, I'm not here to hurt you." He switched from English to Dari.

She gasped and the rattle of metal alerted him to her own chains. "How do you know my language?"

"The knowing is not important," he said. "Do you know how you came to be here?"

She hiccupped. "My father gave me away to be a bride." Her words were being strangled by her tears. "They killed him. They beat him."

"Why did they beat him?" He had to keep her talking, more for his sake than hers.

"Because I was too old."

Double fuck. How old was too old for these men?

"What about the rest of your family?"

"Gone." Her voice broke on a wail.

The sound of her grief was making the throbbing in his head worse. His stomach clenched in that way that warned of an oncoming bout of vomiting. Talking helped. "Mina, how long have you been here? Where is here?"

"I do not know," she said after a few seconds.

"Do you know how long I've been here?"

"They brought you here when they took my sisters."

Sisters? How many of those *sisters* had been here? "Is it just you?"

She let out a few gut-wrenching sobs, then gasped in her breaths. "Yes."

Why take the other women and leave her behind? Caleb mulled over this, and each path he took brought him to the same conclusion. Mina was being saved for something special. She'd said her father was beaten to death because of her age; she might be for someone who had specific preferences that Mina exhibited.

"Why you?" he asked, wincing as the throbbing transitioned into stabbing and strobing pain.

If she answered, he couldn't hear her through the drumbeat in his ears. He lay on the musty hay and through the agony was able to piece together the logic of his prison. Considering the number of horse farms Follman had bought up in the last three years, Caleb was certain he was at one of them. Which one remained the million-dollar question.

He'd been chained up in a barn with stalls. Mina's voice, while clear and close, was still muffled by objects. She sounded close, maybe right across from him. He couldn't get a sense of how large the building was, but it was cool and clammy, mostly due to the rain.

It seemed to be nighttime. But was it really? He had been knocked unconscious late morning and possibly kept drugged to remain that way until they had him secured. He had no real sense of time. While he was out, they'd chained him up and taken his prosthetic leg. A shackled and crippled man was easier to control. The indignity of it was another blow to his already fucked-up psyche. If he was able to get free, he wouldn't be able to escape without crawling.

Caleb's face burned. If they ever returned for him, they would ensure more humiliation.

"Cade." Mina's broken voice calling him by his false name jolted him from the rage smoldering in his chest.

Bringing his now-quaking body into a semblance of calm, he licked his dry lips. "Yes, Mina?"

"If you are an honorable man, do the honorable thing."

The humiliation and fury leached from him at the despair in her voice. He was fearful of what she would say but needed to hear her say it.

"Mina, my honor to my cause is why they have degraded me. Please, don't make me promise something that goes against my code."

"I beg you," she cried.

"Mina."

"Kill me! Kill me!" Her screams ended in more sobbing.

Caleb sucked in the musty air and listened to the shattered woman's soul die with each passing second.

If he managed to get out of here alive, he would burn Follman's and his partners' worlds to the ground.

Chapter Twenty-Two

THE MOMENT DOT landed the helicopter for the scheduled refueling halfway back to Las Vegas, T.J. did what Eriksson warned them not to do. He jammed all radio frequencies and electronic devices.

Armed, they both exited the cockpit as the two-man refueling crew lumbered toward them. The men were more concerned with saving their hides than putting up any fight. They hightailed it for safety; their vehicles peeled away. Once they were long gone, Dot and T.J. made their move.

The darkening landscape helped to shield their movements as they converged on the cabin. The curtained windows didn't afford them a chance to see what they were up against. But it didn't matter.

"How do we play this?" Dot asked T.J.

"We're going to take the direct approach." He raised his fist then beat it against the door.

With the blades still moving above them, any sounds inside were muffled. It worked both ways, shielding their voices from anyone inside.

There was no response to his first knocking. T.J. did it again, beating harder against the panel.

Dot stayed right on his shoulder, her 1911 pointed at

head level for anyone coming out. None of the curtains moved. Still no response from inside.

T.J. was reaching for the handle when the door cracked open. A rifle barrel poked through. T.J. grabbed the barrel and yanked it. Caught off-balance, the owner of the rifle came flying out of the helicopter and slammed onto the pad. T.J. moved toward him, and Dot slipped inside the cabin.

Another rifle-wielding man was moving to take the place of his missing partner. Dot drilled two bullets into each of the man's thighs, and he dropped, screaming.

His screams were joined by a chorus of female shrieks. Dot ignored them. She needed to take care of the now-wounded rifleman first.

She grabbed the man's ankles and flung him out of the cabin onto the landing pad. His head cracked against the copter floor and then the ground as he was unceremoniously dumped beside his unarmed partner.

T.J. loomed over the other man, his firearm leveled on the man's forehead. "I've got 'em," he said. "Take care of the hostages."

She holstered her 1911 and popped her head inside the cabin. Five shrieking … girls.

A firecracker popped inside of her and molten heat coursed through her veins at the sight of dirt-streaked, terror-filled children chained to the helicopter floor.

Dot abandoned the girls and stalked back to their guards, drawing her 1911 as she went. T.J. had a split second to intervene before she shot them.

"Whoa! Dot, no!" He grabbed her gun arm and shoved it skyward. "We need them alive."

"They're children." Something hot and wet raced down her cheek. "Children!"

Movement in her periphery caught her attention. The uninjured man was making a run for it.

T.J. unarmed Dot. "Have at him," he said and turned away.

Dot broke into a sprint. The fleeing captor barely made it more than a hundred yards by the time she caught up. Unable to outrun her, he slowed and turned to face her. He was raising his fists when she clotheslined him. He slammed to the pavement.

Dot flipped her braid over her shoulder and smoothed away the freed strands as she circled his writhing, gasping body. He flipped onto his back, and she planted her boot on his heaving chest.

His eyes bulged as he managed to catch his breath enough to blubber out something she didn't understand. But she recognized the cadence of his speech.

She took her boot off him, grabbed a handful of shirt, and yanked him up off the ground. "I don't barter with child molesters."

He couldn't understand her, but he understood the righteous anger in her tone. He shut his yammering mouth.

Dot dragged him back to the helicopter and gave him a hard shove to the ground. T.J. cuffed him to his injured partner. There'd be no running again.

"Thank you for not killing him," T.J. said as he returned her 1911.

"He's Arabic. They probably both are."

"That makes it easy to interrogate them." He studied

her, worry straining his features. "Are you okay to take care of the girls?"

She slid the 1911 back into its holster and snapped the strap. "I have to be." She sighed, rubbing a hand over her face. "They remind me of Bethany."

"They're not. You've got to remember that. They need a woman's touch. If I go in there, I'll terrorize them more."

He wasn't wrong. Those girls had been traumatized enough by men.

"Turn off the helicopter," he said. "I'm calling Eriksson in."

Dot climbed into the cockpit and killed the engine. She took a moment to compose herself. The anger that had burned white-hot was a smoldering coal inside. But these girls needed the calm and cool Dot, the one Bethany trusted and loved.

Taking that thought and a cheerful image of her adoptive niece, Dot exited the cockpit and stepped up to the cabin.

All five girls were clutching each other the best they could with the shackles on their hands and ankles.

"You find a key on one of those fuckwads?" she asked T.J.

"Sure did." He passed it off and returned to his little Gitmo Bay.

Dot held up a hand, then the other with the key. The girls didn't make a sound. Their wide dark eyes stared back at her. Their fear heavy in the air, coating her skin with its slime. She caught the distinct odor of urine, and she choked up.

Fuck these fuckwads. Fuck Follman. Damn it, when she

saw that man again, she was going to rearrange his face.

Dot brought her anger back under control and gestured to the key.

One of the girls, who looked older than the rest, but not by much, leaned away from the girl next to her and gave Dot a timid nod.

Slow and methodically, Dot climbed inside the cabin and approached them. She unlocked the chains from the eyebolts anchored into the floor. Then one by one, she freed the girls from their bondage. None of them moved from their seats. Dot wouldn't press the matter. She'd earn trust after the girls realized she was not going to harm them.

Dot was backing out of the cabin when one of the girls farthest from her spoke. Dot hesitated and the girl stopped speaking. Dot and the girl stared at each other.

"T.J.," she called out of the cabin. "You better make sure Eriksson sends someone who can speak all of the Afghan languages."

"Already on it," he said.

Fatigue hit Dot like a ton of bricks. She sank to the floor and sat with her back against the cabin door. She kept silent guard over the girls, thinking of all the ways she was going to use a hot poker on Follman and any of the other men in his circle.

This was how she remained until Eriksson's people arrived with a female translator in the traditional garb of an Afghan mother. T.J. had to help Dot up and away from the helicopter while the girls were taken care of.

"Don't make me go back to Las Vegas," she said. "I'll kill Follman if we do."

"I'm not making you, but we do need to. The helicopter," he said, tucking her tight against him as they walked to the vehicle that would transport them to their next destination. "I'll have Stevo bring our gear to us."

She sagged into T.J. He had redeemed himself in the last twelve hours. They might not be any closer to locating Caleb. But at least they'd done one good deed rescuing these girls.

Yet, the man at the farm had mentioned a technical difficulty. It couldn't have been about the girls? The bruises on his knuckles had been fresh. None of the girls had signs of being beaten. So, what was it?

Dot climbed into the back seat. T.J. held up a finger, shut the door, and turned to speak to one of Eriksson's people. Dot didn't care. She just needed to catch a nap.

She rested her head against the plush seat and closed her eyes. She knew the hunt for Caleb was still ongoing. But a strong pull inside warned there was more to come.

Chapter Twenty-Three

U NABLE TO FACE her apartment alone, Vivian returned to the law firm.

After the news of Charley's murder had been relayed to everyone, the whole building turned into a funeral home. Between the weeping administrative assistances and paralegals to Loren's repetitively stunned *I can't believe he's dead*, she'd had about all she could take.

Everyone had gone home before official closing hours; Vivian remained, locked in her office. The sun had long set and the building was dark except for her lone desk lamp. She had waited all day for a call from Dot, hoping her cousin had received the message.

Vivian's phone remained silent.

She tried to read through the file on Caleb Podolsky, but she kept imagining him murdering Charley and ramming his body inside that gym locker. Any attempt to switch current trial work was thwarted with reminders of Charley's demise. She threw a pen against the folders spread across her desk and slapped her hands down, pushing her body out of the chair at the same time. The wheeled chair careened away from her and banged into the credenza lining the wall behind her desk, knocking over a porcelain kangaroo figurine she'd picked up in Sydney six years ago.

"Damn it," she muttered when the tail broke free of the body.

She picked up the pieces and examined the broken edges, wondering if she'd be able to superglue them back together.

Her cell rang, startling her into nearly dropping the pieces. Blowing out a breath, she set the kangaroo and his tail on the credenza top and went to grab up her phone. An unfamiliar number scrolled across the screen.

Vivian did a quick scan of her office and strode over to the door to peek through the single glass pane into the hall. Except for a lone light down the hall illuminating the janitor's trolley, it was still dark and quiet. The phone continued to ring.

She let it go two more rings then gave in to her unquenchable curiosity and answered the call.

"Vivian?"

She recognized the voice immediately. "Oh my God, Hal?"

"You're being followed. If you value your life, you will get out of the office now."

"Hal, what's going on?"

"Vivian, do what I said." The connection went silent.

"Hal? Hal?" The screen had flipped from the call app to her wallpaper.

Vivian checked the hall again. Same light farther down still on, janitor's trolley still there. Assured that her door was still locked, she returned to her desk. From her briefcase she pulled out the Glock. As a final safety measure, she closed the window blinds, muting the streetlamps' brightness in her office. She was on the firm's second floor but had a wide view of the neighboring buildings. All these beautiful windows were a walking death trap for her if someone was camped out on a nearby rooftop with a gun.

The tone of Hal's voice had toppled Vivian right over the panic ledge. If she was being followed and she left the building, she'd be a sitting duck. No, she couldn't leave. She had to get someone here. So, who did she call for protection? The only people she trusted in that department were in Las Vegas. She paced the length of her office, thumbing through her extensive contact list until it landed on Larrabee's number.

Without a moment to second-guess herself, she tapped the call icon.

He answered on the fourth ring. "Counselor, I was about to call you. Why are you not at your home?"

"You're looking for me?" she asked incredulously.

"Yes. You've gotten yourself twined into a disturbing matter of murder and chaos. Not to mention I've been ordered by your cousin to watch over you. Now where are you?"

He sounded like he was driving, which proved to be a good thing.

"I'm at my law firm, locked in my office." She wandered back to her door to check the hall again. "I was told I am being followed, and I need to get out of the building. Now."

The janitor's trolley was still at the same office. But had it moved a little bit?

"I'm not far from your office. I'll be there in two shakes of a cat's tail."

Vivian spotted a shadow near the far doorway. "Cassius, hurry."

"Vivian, stay on the phone with me."

The shadow moved. Her heart sped up.

"Someone's in the office," she whispered and moved back from the door.

"I'm almost there. I swear it. Are you armed?"

She hurried over to her desk and doused the desk lamp. "Yes. Dot made sure I was able to handle it."

"Good. Find a place to keep an eye out but stay protected. I can see your building."

Vivian chose the open corner between a tall bookshelf and the credenza to wedge herself into. She could still see the door. "This wasn't how I imagined my life as a lawyer."

"We can never imagine our lives to go the way they do," he said. "I'm in front of the building."

She heard the repetitive sound of barking tires outside and through her phone. At the same time, she spotted movement outside her door. She sank down in her corner, using the desk to block her from sight.

"Someone is outside my door," she whispered.

"Hold on, darlin', I'm coming."

Vivian lowered her phone, facedown, to the floor and left it there. With the Glock gripped in her hands as she'd been taught, she raised it, keeping it in line with the doorway and her finger away from the trigger.

The handle rattled softly. Vivian swallowed against the rock forming in her throat and raised the Glock higher. Glass shattered. She ground her molars, resisting the urge to pull the trigger.

Gunfire from the first floor blasted through the building. Vivian had to bite her tongue to stifle the yelp threatening to break free. An all-out gunfight ensued.

It didn't sway her intruder. Over the sound of guns firing, she heard the lock and then the door open. The intruder stepped in, and Vivian did as Dot had taught her hundreds of times.

She aimed for center mass and fired three shots. The intruder slammed into the doorframe and fell back.

Vivian bolted upright. The intruder wearing janitor's coveralls lay on the floor, blocking her escape. How did she get out? She left her cover and inched around the backside of her desk, keeping her weapon trained on the body and the door.

Except the body didn't stay down. With a groan, the intruder rolled onto his side and started to rise. Vivian reacted out of sheer terror and fired the Glock, her aim going wild.

The sound of a bullet smacking into something wet nearly undid her. The intruder's head snapped back, and he slumped to the floor. Even in the muted light from outside, she could tell she had done enough damage to keep this man down for good.

Vivian grabbed the extra clip she kept in a desk drawer and then stepped over the downed man's body into the hall. After a quick check of the hall, she ran toward the light of the other office. Below sporadic gunfire went off, but no sounds of movement or men yelling orders. She assumed Cassius was still alive and trying to pick off the remaining intruders to get to her.

Her trepidation at being hunted fled. She'd turn the tables on the men coming after her. She reached the janitor's trolley and discovered the bloody truth. The poor man had his throat slashed and was left to die on the floor where he'd been dusting a desk.

Swallowing the rising bile, she moved on.

She rounded the corner at the end of the hall, heading for the staircase. More shots fired from the first floor. Vivian let out the pent-up breath she hadn't fully realized she was holding and continued on. A crash from the third floor sent her running for cover. Then she followed the sounds of a scuffle and grunts to the staircase.

She reached the stairs and heard a muffled scream. She jolted back as a body flew down the steps and watched in horror as it rolled to the bottom, slamming into the floor, where it remained unmoving.

A man huffed down the steps. Vivian gaped at a disheveled Loren.

"Move, Montgomery," he barked.

Together they hurried down the remainder of the steps. She had to step over the body to follow Loren to the receptionist's desk. So many of the windows on the first floor were gone, the shattered glass strewn across the carpet. Three bodies were scattered among the wreckage, but no sign of Cassius or any more of the intruders.

Loren led her to the backway into the building.

"I thought you were gone," she said.

"Nights are the best time to get work done." He stopped beside the break room door and pushed her up against the wall. "You were still here. There was no way I was going to leave you alone. Not after what happened to Charley."

Loren checked the break room. "All clear," he said, then grabbed her arm and tugged her along after him.

They were coming on the back exit fast. Until another black-clad intruder stepped into their exit route. Loren slid to a halt, and Vivian slammed into his backside. She spotted the raised weapon and tried to get around Loren.

Shots blasted and she winced, waiting for the pain. Instead, she watched the last man jerk about and then fall to the floor.

Cassius appeared from the hall, his weapon trained on the downed man.

"Who are you?" Loren demanded.

Cassius tilted his head sans typical cowboy hat toward Loren. "Detective Sergeant Cassius Larrabee of the Idaho State Patrol. I'm here for Vivian."

Loren's shoulders slumped. "Oh."

"Is the last of them?" Cassius asked.

"I think so," Vivian said.

Cassius ejected his clip; it clattered to the floor, making a hollow ring against the tile.

He pressed a fresh clip into his sidearm. "We're not going this way. They entered through here."

He grabbed Vivian's elbow and escorted her back the way she and Loren had come. "Who told you they were coming?" he asked as he cleared the first floor.

"Hal Jones." She skidded to a halt, breaking free of Cassius's grip. "My phone."

He reached back and took hold of her once more. "Forget it. We're getting you out of here, now."

"Shouldn't we wait for the police?" Loren asked as he

hurried to follow them.

"And give them time to regroup and send another kill squad? Fuck no." Cassius reached his haphazardly parked and still-running SUV and threw open the passenger door. "Get in."

Vivian did as ordered. Loren climbed into the back passenger seat. Once Cassius was in the driver's seat, he threw the SUV into gear and floored it. As they passed a parked car, Vivian realized in horror the windows were spiderwebbed and blood painted the inside.

"Who was that?"

"Your supposed security detail," Cassius replied coldly.

"My security detail? Why would you put a security detail on me?"

"I didn't."

"Would someone mind telling me what the hell is going on?" Loren demanded from the back seat.

"Mr. McLaughlin, I'd like to know myself."

Vivian sank into her seat. She noticed for the first time that she was massaging a hard grip and looked down at her lap. The Glock lay there, harmlessly. She released the gun and clutched her hands.

She'd killed a man. She had pulled the trigger and ended another person's life.

A warm hand descended on hers. She was trembling. Cassius glanced over and squeezed her hands.

"You did what you had to do. You're alive because of it. Consider that."

Vivian nodded jerkily and let out a shuddering breath as she allowed Cassius to be her anchor. He picked up the

Glock and flicked the safety on, then carefully tucked it into the console as he drove.

With the gun out of sight, Vivian found a way to relax. A little.

"Where are we going?" she asked when they left Boise city limits.

"The safest place for you." Cassius looked at her. "Ybarra ranch."

Chapter Twenty-Four

"HOW'S DOT HOLDING up?" Steve asked.

He and one of his security guys met up with T.J. and Dot at the Las Vegas airport, where they had Eriksson's man drop them off to get the borrowed helicopter.

"She's struggling, man. I had to remind her we needed to come get the helo in order to get back to Boise. She wants Follman's blood."

At least Dot had slept on the ride here. How much good it did her remained to be seen. He'd managed to catch a few zzzs, too, but he couldn't stop the blame playing on repeat. Dot had reminded him this was not about bounty hunting. She was not fully on board with a side gig, even if it was working with federal law enforcement.

The loudest part skipping around in his head? He should have closed up shop in Boise and moved her to Euskadi weeks ago. They would never have been involved with this.

Steve winced. "I feel for her, but she was insulated from what we saw every time we went into the field. Up there, flying those Blackhawks, she wasn't boots on ground and she didn't face the realities we did."

"Don't discredit her, Stevo. She was front and center during Abbey Gate."

"Aww, fuck." Steve's shoulders sagged. "You didn't tell me that."

"Not my story to tell. She don't talk about it anyway."

Steve scratched the side of his bald head. "How you doin'?"

T.J. watched Dot as she finalized her preflight check. They'd already loaded their gear into the copter. "I'm doin' about as good as any man in my position."

He met Steve's knowing gaze. Nothing more needed said.

"By the way, have you told Dot about the other thing?" Steve asked.

T.J. looked away. "There's no reason to get her any more worked up over something that trivial."

"Man, I saw the look on her face when you two showed up at the restaurant the other night. You didn't tell her we were meeting up until you got there, didn't you?"

T.J. gave his molars a good workout.

Steve gripped his shoulder and squeezed. "There's some things you need to stay quiet about because of your job. Then there's hiding things from people who are supposed to trust you because you're scared of the fallout." He leaned closer. "I learned the hard way with Dana. Don't do that with Dot."

"I'll tell her as soon as I can."

"Don't wait." Steve slapped his shoulder.

"You better get back to Dana," T.J. said. "I don't know how good Follman's resources are, but you both should get out of town before he connects us. The payback for his missing merchandise is sure to find a way to you."

"We've got a place off the books. Don't worry about us. Just find this Caleb guy and shut that motherfucker Follman down."

They shared a back-slapping man hug, and T.J. watched his old army friend leave. The admonishment of not keeping Dot in the loop still stung, but Steve was right. God, Stevo giving him relationship advice. The irony was not lost on T.J.

He had to tell Dot. Fuck, the blowback from her, especially in her current state of mind, was sure to be epic. Probably best to lead with his plans to move the business to Euskadi.

As Steve's vehicle faded from sight, T.J.'s phone rang. Larrabee was calling him. Then Eriksson's burner phone went off.

T.J. decided to pass up the Idaho state investigator for now and answered the other phone.

"We've got a problem," Eriksson said.

"And hello to you, too, Agent. How are Dot and I holding up? Why just fucking peachy. I've got a Basque wildcat on my hands who wants nothing more than to commit murder with her bare hands because some *fucktard* decided to steal young girls from the Middle East and bring them here for God knows what purpose. But I'm pretty certain we all know what that purpose is."

"Sarcasm does not become you, Roman," Eriksson rebutted.

"What the fuck do you want?"

"To tell you we've got a problem. One of my other CIs connected with an associate of Follman has reached out to warn me the whole network is on red alert. Your and Dot's little stunt to rescue those girls has reached them and they're coming for you."

"Let 'em."

"Do you forget there is a rogue Mossad agent in their midst?"

"I look forward to meeting him. If he's all about kidnapping and raping children, then let me at him."

Eriksson sighed. "I don't know how involved he is. I don't know how involved any of them are. Cade Porter—"

"We can stop with the fake names with this guy. He's Caleb Podolsky, and that's how he'll be called."

Eriksson's exasperated sigh almost warmed T.J.'s ear. "As I was saying. *Caleb* was getting closer to finding out all that information right before he was attacked and he disappeared."

"Seems to me you don't know much of anything, do you?" T.J.'s phone went off again. "And like an idiot, I allowed myself to be sweet-talked by you into something I should have walked away from." He looked at the screen. Larrabee again.

"I wasn't keen on you or Dot going into this. But I got desperate. You both have the skills necessary for this."

"Eriksson, don't placate me. We did what was right and that was rescuing those girls and turning them over to you. Don't be like every other government agency and fuck it up further. It was not nice working with you, so let's never talk again. Bye." He hung up and answered the call from Larrabee as Dot was walking toward him. "What's up?"

Dot frowned and crossed her arms. She looked like shit.

And now she was planning to put in another two-plus hours in the air to get them home. She probably hadn't done this much flying since her first tour in Afghanistan.

"Where are you?" Larrabee asked.

T.J. put the phone on speaker for Dot to hear. "Getting ready to leave Las Vegas. Why?"

"Someone put a hit out on Vivian."

T.J.'s guts bottomed out. Dot's tanned features turned a darker shade of red.

"I got to her in time, but it wasn't easy," Larrabee said. "Whoever came at her killed a pair of federal agents who had been posted to watch her."

Eriksson. He'd be the only one who'd have Vivian watched. That would be how he knew about the files.

"Where is she?" Dot asked.

"I've got her and one of her colleagues with me. I'm taking her to your ranch," Larrabee said. "I'm pulled over at a rest stop so she could use the restroom. Dot, she had to kill a man."

Dot jerked the phone from T.J.'s hand and walked away with it to have that conversation in private.

T.J. let her go.

The burner phone vibrated in his hand. Eriksson was a persistent pissant.

Should he answer it? T.J. knew what Dot would want him to do. Cut the ties. This was no longer their problem and she'd want to keep it that way.

The phone continued to buzz.

Twenty yards away, Dot was in conversation with Larrabee.

A familiar tingling sensation coursed through T.J. It was the feeling he'd get before every mission. A high as adrenaline pumped into his veins and put him in an elevated state of alertness. He couldn't be that guy anymore. This wasn't a mission into the field where he was seeking out pockets of insurgents.

T.J. dropped the still-buzzing phone to the tarmac and smashed it, grinding it into the pavement.

"Let's go!"

He walked away from the pieces and joined Dot in the helicopter.

Chapter Twenty-Five

D AWN'S GRAY LIGHT melded with the red-orange glow of the sunrise as Vivian emerged from Larrabee's SUV. A chorusing pack of dogs swarmed around her legs; some sniffed and licked her legs, no doubt finding flecks of blood. Vivian stretched her arms above her head and felt the tense, aching muscles in her back give.

Despite the swirl of flashbacks and bouncing nerves, Vivian managed to catch a nap. When she didn't think it would ever happen, she begged Cassius to let her drive some of the route to Euskadi. He flat out refused her offer to reprieve him and gave no reason why. She eventually gave up and somehow succumbed to her exhaustion.

Even with Loren snoring from the back seat.

The clap of a screen door drew Vivian's and the dogs' attention to the house.

Angela Ybarra was a woman cut from the roughened cloth of a bygone era. She carried more of the features of the mountain-region Basque than her daughter. Where Dot was tall, willowy, and a dusky blonde, Angela was shorter in stature, had darker hair, and a larger flat nose. Where mother and daughter were similar was in personality, tenacious and miserly when it came to speaking. Angela had raised a daughter wilder and tougher than herself, and that was saying a lot considering Angela's own upbringing.

They were family to Vivian in more than just genetics and a familial name.

Angela called off her pack and the dogs abandoned their greetings to Vivian, running to their alpha.

Next to her, the back passenger door opened, and a groggy, boneless Loren slid out.

He ran his hand through mussed hair. "Where are we?" he asked around a jaw-cracking yawn.

"My cousin's ranch."

Cassius strode around the SUV and headed straight for the porch. He didn't look one bit like he'd survived a gunfight initiated by men hellbent on murder, then spent the entirety of the night driving all the way to Euskadi.

Damn him.

"Angela," he said as he mounted the steps.

"Sergeant Larrabee. Didn't think I'd have the pleasure of your company again," she said, handing over a steaming mug.

Coffee. Vivian made a beeline for her cousin.

"Neither did I," Cassius said.

Vivian joined them with a lumbering Loren following on her heels.

"Cousin." Angela handed Vivian a mug, then a third to Loren.

The mountains could always be counted on to stay cooler during the summer. The slight nip to the air made the heat of the mug feel blissful.

"Where's Ashley and Bethany?" Vivian asked and took a sip.

"Still sleeping, if the dogs haven't woken them. Ashley will be wanting to come over, especially if Bethany takes off to do chores. Neither of them are still keen on old men." Angela's pointed look at Loren threw the man.

Behind her tipped mug, Vivian smiled at the bewildered attorney.

"Whatever for?" he asked.

"You would remind Ashley of her polygamist cult-lovin' sperm donor and the man she was forced to marry," Vivian replied.

Loren's eyes fluttered, and he jutted out his jaw. "Say what?"

"I'll take him into town and put him up at Cherry's," Cassius said.

"That would be best." Angela reached out and grasped Vivian's shoulder. "Come inside and grab a bite to eat first."

Vivian surrendered to the strength of this woman who was known for her fantastic outfitting business and superb hunting skills. Only Dot surpassed Angela in hunting and tracking.

They entered the house right into the kitchen. If Vivian hadn't been made aware of the incidents from months past when Dot and T.J. had fended off an attack by merciless killers on this very ranch, she wouldn't be able to tell that the house had sustained considerable damage. Not a single bullet hole or bloodstain to be seen.

"Have you heard from *nire alaba*?" Angela asked.

"Not since they left Las Vegas," Cassius said. "They should be in Idaho by now."

"*Berri onak dira.*"

Loren leaned toward Vivian. "What did she say? And how did he understand it?"

Vivian, too, was puzzling out how Cassius understood Basque, and wasn't quick enough to answer.

Angela overheard him and paused by the old-fashioned woodburning stove to look over her shoulder. The perturbed expression on her face was pure Dot. The daughter learned from mother too well.

"She said, 'this is good news,'" Vivian said.

"And the other thing?" Loren pressed.

"My daughter." Vivian patted his arm. "It's Basque."

Loren blinked at Vivian. "You're Basque? You don't look it."

Vivian gave Loren another pat as if he'd grown senile in the last one hundred miles. "I'm not Basque. Angela and I are cousins through her mother's side. Great-Aunt Dorothy was very much British with a touch of Scottish."

Loren did a great impression of a fish out of water. "Wait? How's that possible?"

"Anything is possible in this country," Cassius chimed in as he sat on a stool placed around an island counter.

"My *ama*, mother, met my *aita*, father, during World War II when he was stationed in England before D-Day," Angela explained as she began dishing out food onto three plates. "He vowed to wed her after the war's end. She thought he'd be dead before he got out of the boat and landed on the beach. They were both wrong."

Vivian smiled. She'd heard this story so many times growing up, yet it never got old.

Loren, completely invested in the tale, sat on another

stool at the counter. "Why's that?"

Angela finished dishing out the hearty breakfast of scrambled eggs, sausages, and thick slabs of sourdough bread slathered in sweet goat's cheese. "*Aita* fought all the way to the Battle of the Bulge, where he was severely wounded then sent home to Idaho, the war over for him and no way to get back to England."

She carried the plates over to the counter and set them down. Vivian took the last stool and settled in.

"*Ama* completed her service with the Women's Auxiliary Air Force. She returned home to her family. Her elder brother, Vivian's *aitona*, grandfather, immigrated to America to get away from the reminders of the war. *Ama* came with him. They traveled all the way to Idaho and a chance meeting with a fully recovered sheep rancher of Basque descent whom she'd never forgotten about."

"Two years later, both Montgomery siblings were married," Vivian added between bites of her bread. "That's all she wrote."

"Not quite," Angela said and leaned against the kitchen sink.

"Dot not only shares her grandmother's name but an obvious love of flying?" Cassius asked.

"And many other things she shared with her *aitona*." Angela looked down at her cradled mug of coffee, then looked up, a bit of sadness touching her eyes. "Eat. Ashley will be here soon, with Bethany following. Once the child learns Dot will be here, she will bounce off the walls."

Vivian couldn't deny that Dot, too, had bonded strongly with the girl. It was strange seeing her cousin, whom she'd grown up with at a distance, be motherly. Dot was not the mothering kind.

"I feel like I'm imposing," Loren said. "Frankly, I don't know why I'm even here in hiding in the first place."

"You made yourself involved the moment you decided to not leave the firm last night and watch over Vivian. If anyone was left alive in that attack, they'll be looking for you too," Cassius said.

"Loren, it's safer for you here from those men," Vivian said. "Whoever they are."

Loren looked a little blue around the mouth. Vivian gave him a reassuring rub on the back.

"Do not worry," Angela said. "A few have tried to bring this family down. None have succeeded." She nodded toward his untouched plate. "Eat."

ONCE THE MEN had polished off the majority of their food, Cassius took Loren into town to the quaint bed and breakfast owned by one of Dot's friends. Angela took Vivian back to Dot's old room for a change of clothing and to wash up.

The Coopers had yet to visit.

"Cousin, how is Matlock?" Vivian asked as she stripped out of her blood-flecked and dirty clothing.

A long-time childhood friend of Dot's, Matlock Hargrave was Pyrenees County's acting sheriff and still recovering from serious injuries inflicted on him months ago that would have ended his life had it not been for Dot's intervention. The reasons and the culprits had yet to be discovered. Dot had inadvertently killed the only link to the whole ordeal.

One thing Dot had been certain of—Matlock's attack was connected to his father's unexplainable death. And it wasn't over.

"He does better each day, and then he has a setback. The same is true of Sloane."

Sloane Cross, a friend of both Vivian and Dot, and T.J.'s former bounty-hunting partner. After taking a bullet that nearly ended her life during the raid on the Ybarra ranch, Sloane had been forced to retire out of the business. She now assisted Cherry in running the bed and breakfast. But how much was Sloane actually helping Cherry? Vivian was aware of Sloane's frequent calls from T.J., of which neither knew Vivian knew about.

"Sloane has always been too bullheaded to be waylaid by setbacks," Vivian said.

Angela handed over a towel and took the dirty clothes from Vivian. "She is not the same woman as before. Shower and dress. We will talk more after."

Vivian clutched the towel to her half-naked body and watched Angela close the door to the bedroom. "Cousin ... Angela."

The elder Ybarra woman hesitated, then stepped back into the room. She said nothing.

"You've shot and killed a man," Vivian said.

Angela tilted her head and studied her. "You wonder if these feelings you experience will ever go away?"

"Yes."

After a split second, Angela returned, draped her clothes

over an elbow, then cradled Vivian's face with her calloused hands. "*Nire lehengusu sendo eta ederra.*"

Vivian closed her eyes and dipped her chin. The Basque language always sounded musical to her ear.

"You will experience many emotions; fear and rage will be some of them. Do not let what these vile men tried to do to you steal your soul. You are bred of sterner stuff, enabling you to cope with the evils of this world."

Vivian looked up at her cousin. "I will have to do it again. Won't I?"

"By partnering with Dorothy, you have opened Pandora's box." Angela smoothed back Vivian's hair like a mother would her daughter. "Your parents would be proud of you. Your grandparents more so."

Tears welled in Vivian's eyes. She had been long orphaned in this world and had built a wall to keep her shored up. But she still missed them. Her mother's and grandmother's families had scattered to the four corners. All Vivian had left in her world was Angela and Dot. She could never leave Idaho. Never leave them.

She slipped into Angela's embrace and breathed in the musky odor of horses and goats, and mountains. This was her safe place.

"Shower. It will make you feel much better." Angela released Vivian.

When her cousin had left her alone in the room, Vivian released the pent-up tension in her body in a long exhale.

Angela was right. A shower would do wonders.

Along with the knowledge that Dot was on her way.

VIVIAN WAS CAMPED out on the porch, watching the goats and the handful of sheep graze the yard. Angela had resumed the practice her father had employed when he did not have time to trim the grass and cut back the weeds. Chickens roamed between the herds, scratching at the exposed earth and clearing out the unwanted pests.

There was a soothing effect watching the animals wander about, which freed Vivian from dwelling on the actions from the night before.

Angela, along with Ashley and Bethany, were in the garden harvesting more of the summer bounty to prepare for preservation. Vivian, left to her own devices, just enjoyed being back on the ranch.

The pack of dogs stirred to life when Cassius's SUV rolled into the yard. Vivian stood from the deck chair and, barefooted, moved to the edge of the porch. Cassius slid from the cab, turned back to grab something out, and then headed in her direction.

"How is Loren?" she asked as he mounted the bottom step.

"Plying his verbal skills on Millie and some of the other locals. Don't think anyone is buying it." Cassius held out Vivian's Glock, grip first. "You better hold on to this."

She stared at the black pebbled grip, and kept her hands firmly pressed to her sides.

Cassius drew the gun back to himself. "Vivian?"

"I don't think I could shoot that thing again if I wanted to."

"Even if there was another threat to you?" He nodded his head toward the three in the garden. "To them? Or Dot?"

"You and I both know Dot would never be in a situation where she'd need protection from the likes of me."

"True. Especially with Roman as her partner." Cassius released the clip from the butt and ejected the chambered bullet. "I understand your struggle after last night's attack." He set the empty firearm on the porch rail and placed the clip beside it. "And I know it's going to be some time before you come to grips with it."

"I will never come to grips with it. I went into practicing law, not to enforce it. The hunting, shooting, war stuff, that's all Dot. Angela, too, to an extent. It's not me."

"No one said you had to be Dot. Hell, from my short history with her, I know damn well Dot doesn't want you to be like her. But she's never going to feel any relief if she's always worried about your safety. Face it, you've been caught up in her orbit, which means you're going to be a target."

Vivian sighed and unclenched her fists. She barely knew this man, and he spoke to her as if he'd known her for years.

"Boise PD let me know that they have your phone and personal belongings in custody. When I get back, I'll have them release those to me."

"Did they tell you if they were able to trace Hal's call to me?"

He shook his head. "It was a burner phone." A pensive expression appeared. "I still can't figure out how those men got into the building." Something seemed to cross his mind as his features slipped into a scowl.

"What is it?" she asked.

"Nothing." He checked his watch. "I'm gonna head back to the B and B and catch some shut-eye. If T.J. and Dot get here sooner than I anticipate, give me a call. If trouble pops up ..." He gave her a slow smile. "You know what to do."

Vivian crossed her arms and let herself smile. "I'll let Angela handle it."

"Oh, I know she will."

Chapter Twenty-Six

CALEB PASSED IN and out of consciousness. He knew he'd sustained a significant concussion when his head had been beaten against the wall. He recognized the signs and symptoms. Had suffered through it multiple times before. One of the times when he came to, he threw up, repeatedly. His prison stank of vomit, piss, and shit.

This was worse than a normal concussion. He feared the tumor had burst. With no medical intervention he wouldn't survive this go-around.

Mina had gone silent. The only way he knew she was still alive was by the clinking of her chains. Her caterwauling and pleading ended hours ago. How long, Caleb wasn't sure. A new kind of nausea took hold of him when he thought about the nightmare she would be subjected to when her captors came back for her. He understood all too well why she'd begged him to kill her. Mina knew what was coming too.

The rain had stopped while he was passed out. Time fluxed and twined until he no longer knew what day it was. While in the Corps, he could gauge the passing of time by how long his facial hair had grown. That was no longer the case after he'd grown the scraggly beard to help hide most of the scarring on his face.

Caleb managed to pull himself into a corner and used the walls to support his battered body, away from the makeshift shitter inches from him. He'd gotten only as far as the chain's length.

Above him, a prick of light came through the tiny hole. It had to be daytime if the brightness was an indicator.

Something rattled and echoed through the interior. Too far away to be Mina moving about.

Caleb tilted his head back and listened.

The noise came again and was prolonged. This time Mina stirred.

Her terrified whimper gutted Caleb.

"Mina, be strong," he said in Dari, low enough for her to hear but not be heard elsewhere.

She began sobbing.

The loud squeal of hinges reverberated in his battered brain. He cringed and covered his ears. The squealing stopped with a thud of something heavy hitting wood. Light flooded the building, and blinded Caleb.

"Fuck."

The clap of shoes echoed against hard flooring. Caleb waited until the owners of said shoes stopped close to his prison. His eyes finally adjusted to the bright light, and he made out the metal bars encasing the upper area of the stall, blocking his whole view.

Mina shrieked.

"Leave her alone," Caleb barked, regretting it as the sound of his voice slammed into his bruised brain.

One of the men rotated toward the stall. Through the blurry haze coating his eyesight, Caleb made out the man's features. A slick smile crossed the man's face. If Caleb could still vomit, he would.

"Hassin. Should have known Revach would send his right-hand man to take care of the cleanup." Caleb tried to sit up better. "You like raping innocent children too?"

"Ahh, the consummate hero," he said as he shifted to stand before the metal rails. "Only half a man." He sniffed.

"I'm more of a man than you fuckers who steal, rape, and traffic children."

Hassin tsked. "I don't degrade myself to that level."

"No, you just feed into the system. That makes you worse."

"It makes me rich."

If Caleb had the bodily fluids to do so, he'd spit on the man.

Hassin leaned closer to the bars. "They tell me that some associates of yours have intervened and disrupted the supply chain. You wouldn't happen to know anything about that, now, would you?"

"I have no fucking clue what you're talking about. I have no associates."

"None? Not even say a helicopter pilot woman and her beefy man? No associates of yours?"

Caleb's head hurt from trying to understand what Hassin was talking about. "Fuck off."

Hassin's smirk grew, and he beckoned to the others. Another man stepped into Caleb's sight, hauling Mina into view.

Between the matted black hair was a bloodied and battered face with wide eyes filled with so much terror. She was so painfully young. Not a child, but not a fully grown woman. She was certainly older than they wanted, and it cost her father his life in the process.

Hassin played with a lock of her dirty hair. "Once she's cleaned up and had a change of clothes, she'll make a beautiful bride." He released her hair and grabbed at her childish breasts, earning a shriek from Mina.

"I'll fucking gut you," Caleb yelled.

"That will not be possible if you're dead." Hassin gestured for his people to leave with Mina.

Mina began shrieking in Dari, her words so garbled by her screams Caleb couldn't tell what she was saying but knew by her fear what she was trying to say.

She would rather die than endure what was to come.

"Don't worry. Your time will come."

Caleb glared. "Not before I take the whole lot of you down with me."

Hassin smiled again and left.

Caleb listened to the echo of his fading footsteps. Moments later, the door swung shut on the rusty hinges then locked. Darkness once again claimed him.

Helpless to save Mina. Broken and battered. Left half a man in a stall like a beatdown nag waiting for slaughter. He'd never felt this degraded even after he'd come to in the hospital and realized he was forever altered and his men forever gone from this world.

They'd left him here to succumb to his own demons. A bullet to the brain was too merciful a way for him to die.

His humiliation abated into an exhaustion so strong it

dragged on his shoulders. Unable to stop the inevitable, Caleb gave in to the blackness as his injured and diseased brain pulled him into oblivion.

Chapter Twenty-Seven

D OT WAS BOWLED over by fifty pounds of excited child the second she walked through the front door of the Ybarra ancestorial home. She wrapped Bethany in a tight hug and squeezed her until the girl squealed in laughter.

Damn, it was good to hold the girl and know she was safe. Having Bethany's gangly arms coiled around her neck carrying an ocean's worth of trust in her grounded Dot. She could bury the echoes of those five girls' terror-filled screams and focus on the here and now.

Bethany, and her mother, Ashley, were the reasons Dot had chosen to uproot her life on the ranch and join T.J.

Dot leaned her head back and looked the girl in the face. The wide eyes with a girlish sparkle and the sweet cherub face replaced the memory of those girls' gaunt and dirty visages.

"*Amona* said you were coming. I didn't believe her until I saw you," Bethany said when Dot set her down.

T.J. squeezed past the door into the house behind them. "What am I, chopped liver?"

Bethany giggled and jumped into his arms, wrapping her tiny ones around his thick neck and giving him a raspberry on his bearded cheek. T.J. was the only man Bethany trusted and would allow to touch her. She knew he'd moved heaven and hell to find her not once but twice in her life. It didn't hurt any that he looked nothing like the men who had terrorized or kidnapped her in the past.

For his part, T.J. had never been one to want to be around children except for his own nieces and nephews. He saw them so rarely, he'd come to look at Bethany as one of them. She had filled that hole in his heart. The youngster garnered not one, not two, but three overprotective watchdogs in her short lifetime, the first being her own mother.

Dot spotted *Ama* standing by a sturdy desk Angela used for business purposes. She was on the phone.

Vivian rose from her reclining position on the sofa in front of the fireplace. *Ama* had outfitted her cousin in some of Dot's more comfortable, looser-fitting clothing. Despite the size difference, they were still a snug fit on Vivian's curvier form and made the normally polished and professionally attired Vivian look like an overstressed mother.

Leaving the chatterbox twins in the doorway, Dot strode across the floor and took hold of her cousin's shoulders. "I should have never left you alone."

"No one could have fathomed any of this would happen. You're here now. Everyone is safe. Stop beating yourself up over it."

"You didn't sign up for this life. You have no business being dragged into it."

"Neither did you." Vivian looked past Dot to T.J., who had moved closer to them. "Neither of you did. If we're going to lay blame on anyone, it goes back to Hal and Caleb."

"No." T.J.'s curt reply rumbled through the open space of the living area. "That blame lies solely on the shoulders of the ABCs who decided to recruit people into this fucking dirty business."

"Language!" Bethany chirped.

"Go find me a cookie or whatever your mother has made," he said, placing the girl on the floor.

Bethany held out her hand, palm up, and put on the sassiest expression Dot had ever seen from the child. T.J. scowled.

"What?" he asked.

"You owe a dollar for the swear can," Bethany said.

Dot had to squelch a snort before she earned a spot in the frying pan with T.J.

"Since when?" he demanded.

"Since *Amona* told me you were coming and Mommy started worrying about your potty mouth. Now pay up."

Dot lost it. Oh, how she needed this. Vivian joined her laughter with a snort.

T.J. pointed a damning finger at Dot as he reached into the side pocket of his pants to pull out his cash. "You're being put on notice too."

"Yeah, I don't think so."

T.J. forked over the required dollar, and Bethany skipped over to the kitchen where there was an old coffee can with a white sheet of paper stating SWEAR CAN $1.00 scrawled in childish handwriting taped to it.

God, she missed being here.

Dot felt her mother touch her shoulder and turned. "*Ama*, we will not allow a repeat of before to happen here."

"*Alaba*, there will be no worrying of such things. We are well prepared." Angela caressed Dot's cheek then gave it a loving pat. "Now clean up. You stink of aviation fuel and dirty men."

"I'll take the aviation fuel over the dirty old men smell any day," T.J. said as he headed for the hallway.

"Fuck you," she snapped at his backside.

"Swear can!" Bethany singsonged.

Vivian snickered. "Looks like the favored aunt is doomed to the same fate as big ole bounty hunter."

Dot dug out a dollar and stomped over to the counter, where Bethany beamed up at her. "Traitor," she said.

"Potty mouth," Bethany shot back.

DOT HAD FINISHED showering and dressed in her childhood bedroom. The door opened and T.J., wearing only a towel around his midsection, and his hair and beard glistening with beads of water, slipped inside.

"How did you get in here without being spotted?" she asked.

"They're all outside."

"You could have dressed in the bathroom," she said, reaching back to pull her damp hair into a braid.

"Yeah, about that." He closed the door and moved farther into the room. "I need to talk to you about something in private."

"*Now* you're needing to have a private conversation? We just did a long-ass drive up here from Boise in private."

"You were sleeping. And when we left Las Vegas, you were flying, not the best time to tell you things."

She flung the finished braid over her shoulder. "Then what is it?"

"Eriksson might come searching for us. I cut off his only means of communication back in Vegas."

Dot shrugged. "Good riddance."

The towel slipped, baring more of T.J. He readjusted it. "Hang on here. You're good with this? Even if it means you don't have access to Follman and shutting down his little ... whatever the hell trafficking deal he's doing?"

"Oh, I'm not through with Follman and his lackeys." She closed the gap between them. "In fact, I fully expect Follman to come looking for us."

"Eriksson warned me that was in the works."

"So, we beat him to the punch. Get dressed. We've got work to do." She moved past T.J. to the door.

"What about Caleb? Or Hal Jones?"

Dot paused before leaving the room. "We'll let Larrabee handle Hal. But I think I have a good idea where Caleb is now."

T.J. faced her, the towel hanging lower on his hips. "Care to enlighten me on this revelation?"

"Not when you're mostly naked and dripping water everywhere."

He rotated his hips suggestively. "Why? Do I distract you?"

"Fuck off, Roman."

"Damn, you get bitchy when you don't get sex."

"And you turn into a raging bastard. Save the pent-up

frustration for the oncoming fight."

He grunted. "I paid my celibate dues when I was in the army."

"Ha! Celibate my ass." She pointed at him. "Get dressed." She left the room.

Voices from outside drifted in through the open windows. Despite the summer heat, Angela refused to update her childhood home any more than she had to with no window A/C unit or central air. In fact, the home was still heated by a good old firewood stove. Living near a national forest and at the base of the mountains afforded some perks.

The two blue heelers that favored Dot over Angela bookended the front door, patiently waiting for her. Gidget and Zip hopped to their feet and watched Dot as she stopped by the coffeepot for a mug. When she moved to the door, the dogs quivered. Dot squatted down to their level and gave them permission to greet her. Their trembling, writhing bodies swarmed around her as they licked and nudged her hands and face.

After letting them get out a sufficient amount of affection, Dot rose from her crouch and headed outside, the two heelers at her side.

The entire goat herd roamed the yard. Dot noticed the handful of sheep that had joined the herd since she'd last been home.

"When did you decide to get back into sheep ranching?" she asked her mother as she joined the gaggle of females loitering around the round pen.

Angela glanced over her shoulder at the herd. "Since I decided I needed to have something that would keep the grass trimmed."

A tall Boer doe with a mostly red-brown coat headbutted Dot's hip. She reached down and scratched the herd boss. Dot had hand-raised this particular goat when her dam died after giving birth to the single doeling. Like the blue heelers, this goat belonged to Dot and no one else. And like the dogs, the doe demanded attention from her favored person.

"You've been missed," Angela remarked.

"Apparently." Dot continued to scratch the goat's neck and back while she drank her coffee and observed Bethany riding a leggy gray in the ring.

Standing on the opposite side of Angela, Vivian, too, watched Bethany ride, her chin resting on her crossed hands. Dot saw the strained lines etched into her cousin's face. She wouldn't comment on it. When Vivian was ready, she'd talk about it.

The screen door clapped, echoing through the yard and making the goats jittery.

"Where's Ashley?" Dot asked.

"She ran to town to pick up some supplies," Angela replied.

T.J. joined Dot at the rail and was promptly horned by the territorial goat. "Damn it," he groused, backing away.

"Swear can!" Bethany called from the center of the ring.

"She's never going to let it go," he muttered as he circled behind Dot.

The doe shifted her body to track his movements, throwing her head if he came too close.

"When did you get a guard goat?"

Dot smiled. "I've always had one. She was just locked up

in a pen every time you were around before."

Only after he'd safely planted himself on the opposite side of Vivian did the doe give up her guard duties and resume her need for attention from Dot.

"Now that we're all here, what's next?" Vivian asked.

"We start back at the beginning," T.J. said. "We have more information than we did when this whole thing started. Our primary objective needs to be finding Caleb. We'll leave Larrabee to finding Hal. After that, the rest of this should fall into place."

"How do you propose to do that since we're way out here?" Vivian asked. "On top of that, Caleb and maybe Hal are hiding out in Boise. That's where you should be."

"We have all we need here," T.J. said.

Dot shooed the doe away and hooked her elbow over the top rail to get a better look at her partner. "You're not planning to do what I think you're planning to do."

"She's our best bet," he said.

"She's retired."

He sniggered. "You really think she's left all of that behind? I don't think you know her as well as you think."

Whatever levity and peace she'd regained by coming here fled.

Angela stepped back from the railing, pulling Vivian with her. Dot now had a direct line to T.J. She inched closer to him.

"Tell me you haven't been calling her up and bothering her for the last six months," she said in a low voice. There was no need for Bethany to hear this.

His features were locked in an impassive expression.

"Tell me you have not been keeping Sloane in the loop since I've joined the business." She swatted his shoulder. "Tell me, damn it."

Closing his eyes, he faced away from her and sighed.

Bethany cantered by them on her gray, oblivious to the tension between Dot and T.J.

"Damn you, Roman. Damn you. Sloane nearly died doing this job."

His head whipped back to her, fire smoldering in his eyes. "Yes, damn me for having a hard time telling my former partner to stay the fuck out of this business every time she called me begging for something to do." He pushed away from the rails. "Damn me to hell."

Bethany reined in the gray several yards from their position but kept her wisecracks to herself.

"You've put Vivian at risk by involving us in this whole fucking affair. You're not bringing Sloane into it."

"Too late," he snapped back. "She's already agreed. I'm meeting up with her shortly."

"I can't believe you." Dot pushed on his chest, forcing him to step back. "If something happens to her, I'll never forgive you for it."

"I already have her blood on my hands."

The way his voice cracked when he uttered that statement made Dot want to punch him for his stupidity.

She stalked away from the round pen and made a beeline for the barn. How many more people did T.J. have involved in this that she wasn't made aware of? Fuck! How many more people were going to be put in danger because he couldn't say no. Or worse, killed.

Dot couldn't be everywhere at once. Inside the tack room, she went straight for her secret stash. The marijuana had handled her absence well. By the time she'd dosed out the right amount for a joint and rolled the paper, her mother entered the tack room. Dot held up a finger to stop Angela before she started speaking and lit the end of the joint.

Once she'd got a good burn going and had taken two puffs, she sat on an overturned bucket and continued to smoke. Her fury toward T.J. might take another rolled joint before she felt calm enough.

Angela located another bucket, flipped it over, and sat across from Dot. Each time Dot blew out the smoke, Angela waved it away. Her mother hated the smell of marijuana but never dissuaded her daughter from using it when the need arose.

"How long have the two of you been each other's throats?" Angela asked.

"I don't know. More than forty-eight hours."

"Because of this job?"

Dot bobbed her head, noting with satisfaction the slight lightheadedness creeping in. "More or less."

"Ahh, that explains it." Angela rocked back on her bucket.

"Explains what? That he's a moron."

"Smoke your weed and shut your mouth," Angela barked.

Dot refrained from rolling her eyes at her mother. She wasn't a teenager, and there was no need for such a childish move. She placed the joint between her lips and took a long drag on it.

"T.J.'s right. There would have been no keeping Sloane from doing what she does best. It's good that he still gives her tasks to keep her mind sharp and ready."

"*Ama*, she's unable to defend herself if serious trouble comes for her."

"She's more capable if the time does indeed come, and she has protection. Matlock has ensured it."

Dot finished the last of the joint and smashed the end against the old table holding buckets of medicine and supplements.

"Are you more upset about Sloane or Vivian?"

The weed was doing its thing, but Dot would need another if she was to get through this conversation.

"I will take by your stubborn silence that it is both. You cannot be your cousin's constant protector. You have a job to do. A purpose to fulfill. Worrying about things that cannot be changed is not part of that."

"She is not a fighter, *Ama*."

"She is, but not in the same way you are. That T.J. is. Vivian has taken your teachings well, and she was prepared to protect herself. She did what was necessary and is alive because of what you taught her. Will she be able to face down more than one man at a time? No. But she's been given the tools to ensure she lives to see another day."

Dot gazed at her mother, taking in the lines in her weathered face, the silver overtaking her once dusky blond hair, the hardness of being a mountain woman softening as she aged. When had this all come about? When had the mother she knew all her life changed so rapidly?

Angela reached over and played with the long braid that

had fallen over Dot's shoulder. "*Nire gudari basatia.* You learn what it means to fight, but not how to lead and let go."

"It is only true when you are at war and in combat. This should be neither."

"It is the way of our world now, *alaba*. If I took anything away from the incident with Ashley and Bethany, it is that evil will find a way to us. Your *aitona* had it right when he taught you to the do right thing and fear no man."

That old motto, a philosophy that Dot had lived her life by for decades. A saying Samo Ybarra was fond of repeating when dealing with troublesome people through the years. It had served Dot well during her years in the army when faced with the injustices and hardships she'd seen on a daily basis. She would never outrun it.

"Smoke another roll. Let it relax you. When you have a right head, not one filled with such a pissy attitude, things will be clearer." Angela rose from the bucket.

"And if it doesn't?"

"When has Dorothy Ybarra ever taken a pessimistic outlook on life?"

"Since she witnessed things no human should have seen."

"For all the evil in this world, there is always a balance of good." Angela patted Dot's cheek. "You are that good."

Chapter Twenty-Eight

A BELL OVER the door tinkled as T.J. entered Cherry Valley B and B. A redhead seated behind the antique desk looked up, and a smile crossed her freckled face.

"Took you long enough to get here," she said.

"Hey, Sloane."

She got out of her chair and, with cane in hand, circumvented the desk to meet him halfway across the floor. She lightly punched his arm. "Don't look at me like that."

"Like what?"

"Like you blame yourself for what happened." She started toward a room with a heavy curtain blocking it off. "I've never taken to pity parties, and I won't let you start."

He followed her. "I'm not wallowing in pity over you being shot. And nearly dying. Twice."

Sloane paused to look at him, then pushed aside the curtain. "You're so fucking full of it."

He wasn't. Dot's caustic words thrown at him before he left still echoed in his head. Fuck. Steve had been right. T.J. should have been upfront with Dot from the start. Maybe some time away from her would help her cool off. At least he hadn't told her to calm down. In the history of humankind, when a man told a woman to calm down, it never went over well.

T.J. entered the room at Sloane's beckoning and found himself greeted by an array of computers.

"So, when did you decide to upgrade to full-blown hacker?"

She gimped past him and slid into what looked like a high-end, highly expensive chair that conformed to her disabled body. "My body might need a lot of TLC, but my brain is still firing on all pistons. When you're recovering from a bullet that nearly kills you, you have time to educate and research."

"And Cherry lets you run a side gig from inside her business?" T.J. asked, taking up a position at Sloane's side.

"She's the one who insisted on it." Sloane keyed in several passwords and the computers came to life. "What do you need?"

"With Vivian's avenues of getting information shut down, we need to start doing a deep dive on some people. Chief among them Agent Kurt Eriksson."

Sloane cracked her knuckles. "Of what federal agency?"

T.J. crossed his arms and spread his stance out wide. "He never said."

Sloane swiveled her chair around to look up at him. "And you just took his word he was a federal agent?"

"No, we really didn't. But after the fact, he seems legit enough."

Sloane snorted as she swung back to her screens. "They always do in the end."

While she hacked her way into files normal civilians weren't allowed to see, T.J. scoped out her digs. The three computer towers and the single large server in the room called for a secondary cooling unit, which came in the form of a window A/C in the only window in the room.

The floorboards creaking above distracted him from the scrolling code on three of the five screens.

"You have guests?"

"Only Larrabee and that lawyer he brought. Cherry says this is usually the slow time for her until hunting season kicks into gear."

"I need to talk to Larrabee," T.J. said, turning to the doorway.

"Wait." Sloane swiveled back his way. "Give me a list of names of the people you want me to search for. I can run more than one scan at a time."

He took a pad and pen from her and scribbled out all the characters in this whole messy business. "Do a really deep dark dive on Follman and his connections to Israel and a group associated with the Revach family."

"Israel? Really?"

"Did you know they have crime families too?"

Sloane beamed. "Oh, I'm so going to enjoy this. Larrabee's in room five."

She went back to her search, and T.J. headed upstairs.

He lucked out when he reached the top landing and Larrabee was exiting his room.

"Roman, good of you to make it. Where's Ybarra?"

T.J. stiffened. "Doing her thing. Who's the lawyer that came with you?"

"Loren McLaughlin. He's one of the main partners of Vivian's firm."

There it was again. T.J. had caught on to the fact that Vivian kept referring to Larrabee by his first name, and now Larrabee was doing the same. T.J. wasn't sure what the deal was between those two.

"The old lawyer is wiped out from last night's ordeal. We'll let him sleep," Larrabee said, moving past T.J. to head downstairs. "Hungry?"

"Starving."

"Let's hit up Millie's diner."

They left the bed and breakfast and walked the block and a half to the diner owned and operated by Cherry and Matlock's mother, Millie Hargrave. It was late afternoon, too late for lunch and too early for the dinner crew. The whole diner was quiet.

Millie wasn't at the counter. The employee managing the front said the owner was in the back doing inventory. Both men sat at the fifties-style counter with stools and ordered up Millie's famous open-face hot beef sandwiches with bottomless sweet tea and two slices of pie each with ice cream. The young gal taking their orders eyed them both, then with a shake of her head, headed back to the kitchen to get the cook on it.

"Comfortable with telling me what happened last night here in the diner?" T.J. asked.

Larrabee checked the swinging doors dividing the kitchen from the rest of the diner. "As long as we keep our voices low."

"Do your commanders know where you are?" T.J. pressed after the other man turned on his stool to face him.

"They do, and they are aware to keep things radio silent

until I reach out again. One of the crime scene people found something during evidence collection they weren't sure about, and it turns out we might have located Hal Jones, or his family at least."

T.J. gestured for Larrabee to go on.

"While going through the Jones house, a tech picked up a wireless gaming device from one of the sons' rooms and bagged it. Not sure why, but the tech has a gaming background and figured it might be worth it.

"Turns out they were right. IT charged it up, and they found out it was still logged on to a gaming site. After a bit of trial and error, they were able to get a lock on the son and his location."

"Where?" T.J. asked.

The waitress returned with their sweating glasses of tea. Once she'd returned to the kitchen, Larrabee resumed their conversation.

"Texas. Dallas to be exact. Don't get the connection since Jones and his wife are from Idaho and Oregon respectively, but I get the appeal of being somewhere least expected. We're in touch with the Texas Rangers and Dallas PD to check on them but staying out of it otherwise to make sure no harm comes their way." Larrabee took a big gulp of his tea. "But Halloway is not with them."

"How do you know that?"

The dark-skinned man eyed T.J. "Because he was the one who gave Vivian the heads-up she was in trouble."

T.J. digested this news. If Halloway was still here in Idaho, in Boise to be exact, then there was a chance they could find him, and thus find Caleb Podolsky.

"I'm headed back to Boise as soon as we're done here," Larrabee said. "Loren wants to stay to be near Vivian, he claims. I'm not going to fight with the old coot."

"Why'd Vivian call you?" T.J. asked.

"Because your partner told her to if things got hairy. Don't ask me why, but I'm glad she did. I was able to get a more recent description of Caleb Podolsky, something we never had before."

"What did he want from her?"

"Files Jones left behind that her colleague Charley gave her." Larrabee pinned a hard stare on T.J. "Files, she says, you and Ybarra have."

"And you're not getting. There's classified shit in those you have no business seeing."

"Which you and Ybarra are qualified as having special access to them?"

T.J. smiled as the waitress brought out their slew of food. With the plates arranged in the order they would be eaten from, the waitress topped off their teas and disappeared.

"I like her. She's whip-smart to know when to stay away," Larrabee said as he dug into his gravy-ladened mound of roast beef, mashed potatoes, on a thick slice of homemade bread. "You were telling me how you and Ybarra got clearance."

"I don't recall saying I was." T.J. shoveled a forkful into his mouth.

They ate in silence a moment. After the meals on the go and the junk food of the last few days, Millie's diner food hit the spot.

Larrabee wiped a wrinkled napkin across his mouth.

"What did you learn in Las Vegas?"

"That we're dealing with a helluva big international mess that involves trafficking of very young girls."

"Ahh, fuck, don't tell me that."

"Too late. There's some federal ABC entities involved, and I expect the guy in charge to show up anytime. It's a good thing you're planning to get back to Boise. You might find yourself on the wrong side of things and forced to choose sides."

"I know which side I belong on, Roman. It's the side of justice."

"Not the vibe I'm getting from this guy. It's the usual bureaucratic bullshit of getting what he wants at any cost and using anyone by any means with no regard to the fallout. Unfortunately, I get the sense Caleb Podolsky is just a means to an end and his involvement in all of this is over. If he's dead, they don't care."

Larrabee tapped his fork against his pie plate. "The whole 'you're on your own if captured, because to us, you don't exist.'"

"Precisely."

"Dot was right." Larrabee set his fork down and shifted to face T.J. "You're too personally invested in Caleb."

"So what if I am?"

Larrabee considered T.J. a moment then nodded as he turned back to his dessert. "She'll know how to straighten you out."

"What's that supposed to mean?"

Larrabee paused before eating a piece of lemon meringue. "Exactly what it's supposed to mean."

They finished in silence, which was a good thing because T.J. wasn't in the mood to hear any more of Larrabee's witticisms. Millie came in as they were paying their checks. She spoke briefly with them and then returned to her tasks before the dinner crowd showed up.

T.J. walked Larrabee to his vehicle parked beside the bed and breakfast.

"If I learn anything new after I get back to Boise, I'll call," Larrabee said as he climbed into the driver's seat. "I should have the autopsy results back on our dead lawyer. It was evident how he died, but we might get lucky on finding something left behind."

"Be careful. These are the kinds of people not to be un-derestimated."

Larrabee studied T.J. "What aren't you telling me, man?"

He thought hard on whether to tell the law officer the truth or not. Not preparing others had cost them before. T.J. would be a fool if he didn't pay Larrabee the respect he deserved.

"I'm not kidding about the international stuff and the classified files. The people coming after Caleb, Hal, now Vivian, who got to Charley, they're deadly. You got lucky last night. I think they keep underestimating us."

"That's going to stop now," Larrabee added.

"It is. I fully expect the experts to come this time."

Larrabee slapped T.J.'s shoulder. "Thanks for the heads-up. I'll be extra cautious."

T.J. watched the lawman leave Euskadi, then headed back inside the bed and breakfast.

He returned to the room where Sloane reigned supreme.

"What did you find out?"

She swung her chair around, and the expression on her face made T.J. regret all that food he ate.

"What the hell have you gotten yourself caught up in?"

Chapter Twenty-Nine

T HE TREE FROGS joined the chorus of crickets making for a beautiful serenade as the sun dipped past the mountains of the Payette National Forest.

Rested and less pissy than earlier, Dot sat in an Adirondack chair, smoking one of the cigars she'd left at the ranch. There was a charge in the air, and the National Weather Service was calling for an unusual summer thunderstorm to pass through the area. This was the dry season for Euskadi— for the whole of Idaho—and weather that threatened lightning put residents on notice.

Dot's time in the forest service taught her to pay attention to weather patterns, especially in the summer. Forest fires were becoming too prevalent these days. One bad lightning strike could burn thousands of acres and put hundreds of lives at risk, including those sent to fight the fires.

Angela had mentioned the odd rain shower that passed over their region a day before. With another one coming so soon, it was cause to worry. Dot would take a blizzard any day over a lightning storm.

Gidget and Zip collectively gnawed on an elk leg bone. Where they had scavenged it up was anyone's guess. They hadn't left Dot's presence since she'd emerged from the barn.

The rest of the dogs were behind the house, helping the livestock guardian dogs keep watch over the animals. Bears and coyotes were known to wander down from the mountains and get a whiff of the goats during this time of the year. Then there were the smaller, more annoying mammals, raccoons and possum, that liked to kill chickens or steal their eggs.

Gidget and Zip came to their feet and hustled to the edge of the porch. Dot heard the approaching vehicle the moment they took up barking.

"*Nahikoa da! Eseri!*"

The heelers ceased their barking and plopped their hind ends on the porch but did not take their eyes off the Suburban as it pulled in beside Angela's old baby-blue Ford. T.J. killed the engine but didn't leave the vehicle right away.

Dot called the dogs back to her and continued smoking while she waited for him to make up his mind. Having paused their night song when T.J. had pulled in, the frogs and crickets took up their chorus once more.

By the time Dot passed the halfway point of her cigar, T.J. rolled out of the vehicle. In the dimly lit landscape, she could see he was exhausted. His steps dragged and his shoulders slumped. He carried a folder.

The dogs did not rise when he mounted the steps. They knew him, knew he wasn't a threat. But he wasn't their human, thus he didn't deserve a welcome greeting.

"Where's your guard goat?" he asked, leaning into a support post.

"Bedded down with the rest of the herd."

The frogs and crickets filled the silence between them while Dot smoked, and T.J. propped up the porch roof.

"Dot—"

"A wise woman once said—" She cut him off. "That men with an agenda will do some of the stupidest, most irresponsible things in order to achieve their objective. It's why God made women to counteract those meathead responses and make sure they live to an old age." Dot set her cigar in the ashtray. "That wise woman was *nire amona*, and she would speak from experience."

"I will not make excuses for what I did or didn't do."

"I would think less of you if you did." She pushed out of the deck chair and moved to stand in front of him. "I accepted the fact you couldn't let this go. Learning what I have, I can't let this go. What I won't accept is you not keeping me in the loop. We're not in the army anymore. There are no layers of denial to keep us out of the know in the event one of us is captured. We're bounty hunters, not federal agents."

He bowed his head for a few seconds, then looked up. "Sloane chewed my ass too. Did you call her?"

"Fuck yeah, I did."

"Potty mouth."

Dot clenched her jaw, trying not to smile. "You still walk a fine line with me, Danger Ranger."

"Wouldn't have it any other way, Fly Girl." He flicked her braid. "Larrabee went back to Boise. He's supposed to give me an update on things back there. They found the Jones family but not him."

"They're safe?"

"As long as the Texas Rangers can convince them to go into their protective custody. Larrabee is certain Jones is still in Boise."

"How would he know that?"

"Because Hal Jones was the one who warned Vivian of the incoming attack. He had to be in the vicinity in order to alert her."

Dot mulled on that. "We'll let Larrabee see if he can work his magic and find him. We need to focus on Caleb."

"About that." T.J. extracted the folder and held it out to her. "Eriksson is legit. Way in over his head, but legit. If he shows up, he better come with receipts."

Dot took the folder. "Why?"

"He didn't warn either of us who was running this whole operation. Follman is the middleman, that's true, and he definitely knows more than he let on. From what Sloane was able to find, he was the idiot who sent the first and second inept kill squads. Sorely underestimated Caleb and wasn't expecting us at the Jones's place."

Dot moved closer to the door to catch the light from inside the house and opened the folder. More than twenty pages of printouts were fastened in the center with prongs. The first handful of pages were on Follman and his history. The next pages were on the men associated with Follman, including photocopies of their passport photos.

First dossier was Armand Revach, a prominent businessman in media and communications from Israel up until five years ago, when it was rumored he was making his millions illegally. To avoid prosecution, he defected to Morocco, where he managed to secure citizenship by aligning himself with a Moroccan family with strong ties to the monarch. Two years later, Revach disappeared from Moroccan society and was later spotted in the United States at an embassy event.

Revach was of Moroccan-Berber-Jewish descent, his grandparents having immigrated to Israel from Morocco after the founding of Israel's own state. It was the same for the rest on the men in the files. Nearly identical timing of family migration and rise in socioeconomics or politics. Shlomo Drahi and Yitzhak Ben-Asher had not left Israel as of the last reporting—they and their families were living in comfort far from any disputed zones.

Then there was Yonatan Hassin, a former Israeli Forces soldier with questionable ties to intelligence. His dossier was so thin, it filled only a third of the page. Everything about it screamed this was the Mossad man.

The icing on the cake came in one sentence at the end of Shlomo Drahi's dossier. He had familial ties to former political party members of the Islamic Republic of Afghanistan, who had recently disavowed their party affiliation and joined the Taliban.

Dot lowered the folder and turned to T.J. "What the fuck?"

"Exactly." He pushed off the support post and took back the folder. "I had Sloane compare Caleb's background to Follman's."

"They were connected?"

"Podolsky's father was employed by Follman's father. Follman Senior ran a slew of casinos in Las Vegas during the eighties and nineties at the tail end of the Jewish and Italian mafia control of the city. Podolsky worked the gaming tables until Follman caught him skimming money. Learned about Podolsky's little secret trick to always make the house lose and sent him out to rival casinos to work their tables and rake in money.

"Caleb was a kid back then, no mother, no relatives, just him and his father. The gig worked right up until one of Follman's competitors found out what he was up to and had Podolsky killed. Caleb witnessed the whole thing."

"For fuck's sake," Dot groaned.

"Kid was thrown into the foster system and did what most of them do at that age: defy and survive."

"Let me guess, typical shithole homes with abusive foster parents."

"Winner, winner, chicken dinner." T.J. massaged the back of his neck. "Somehow, he got out of the system and joined the Marine Corps. Made something of himself only to get blown up by an RPG and lose his friends and fellow Marines."

Dot compared what T.J. recently learned with what she remembered from Caleb's file they'd left back in Boise. Not once had there been any mention of a connection to Follman or Caleb. "Do you think Caleb took on this whole under-cover operation for personal reasons?"

T.J. stopped his personal massage parlor administrations, his face scrunched in thought. "It would be a legit reason. But Follman Junior was a teen and in his early twenties when Caleb's dad would have been messed up with Follman Senior. Would he have even been aware of it? And Caleb was just a kid."

"He had a shitty upbringing and a lot of time to stew on what he'd do to the people responsible for his dad's murder. Was Sloane able to find out more information on his dad's case?"

T.J. rapped his knuckles against the post. "Yeah. With Caleb's testimony, they put away two of the men who had actually killed him. What they weren't able to do was pin down the man who gave the kill order."

"How did Follman Senior die? How'd Follman Junior get the keys to the kingdom?" Dot asked.

T.J. chuckled. "You sure you don't want a PI license?"

"Just answer the question."

"First, both Follman Senior and the man suspected of ordering the murder of Caleb's dad were found dead six years after the trial. Their deaths were believed to be power moves by family members to take over their businesses. But no one could verify it." T.J. frowned. "Wait. You think … Caleb did it? By that point, he would have been fifteen or sixteen."

"About the time he started to rack up a criminal record for breaking and entering and petty larceny." Dot poked his chest. "What do you bet those were just practice runs until he found who he was looking for? If my memory serves me right, some of those homes were suspected mob residents."

"Oh, shit."

"Why would Follman send out an inept kill squad to take out Caleb?" Dot circled a finger. "Because he figured out who Caleb really was? And possibly learned that Caleb was informing on him? Two solid reasons to eliminate the guy."

"I get Follman having Caleb taken out if he figured out

the connection to Eriksson's task force. But how would he know Caleb killed his own father? For all anyone knew, Follman whacked his old man to take over the family business."

"Everyone else would suspect that. But say Follman really didn't kill his father, and somehow Caleb slipped up and Follman figured it out. Eye for an eye, Old Testament style." Dot crossed her arms.

T.J. stared at her then began shaking his head. "Fuck." He sighed. "Do you think he killed Vivian's coworker, Charley?"

Dot studied on his question. What she came to realize about Caleb and with what she knew about his tenuous connection to Halloway Jones, it didn't jive. "No. I think there's another party involved in this."

"Hal?"

She waved him off. "Let Larrabee work on that whole mess. We've got a bigger problem to deal with."

"So, oh great one, where do we begin to find Caleb Podolsky?"

"We need to get back to that farm where we picked up the girls. I'd bet anything there's information to glean there. Drive time is about four hours—we could make it easily."

He thought it over then nodded. "I need some sleep though."

"I got some in. I'll drive; you sleep."

"Not exactly fair there."

"You want to wait until you've fully rested up?"

T.J. winced. "Not really."

"Then let's go."

Chapter Thirty

V IVIAN HATED THAT she was without her own mode of transportation. Loren had summoned her to Euskadi for a meeting, and that meant leaving Angela without a vehicle. Ashley offered up hers, but Vivian couldn't take the mother's car and leave the three females without a means for all of them to get off the ranch if needs be.

Dot and T.J. had left in the wee hours of the morning going God knew where. They hadn't left a note or any message to tell anyone where they had gone. Vivian wasn't sure if it was out of a need to protect the rest of them or give them deniability if things went wrong.

Vivan hadn't bothered to stick around for breakfast at the ranch; she drove straight to the bed and breakfast. Cherry greeted her with a kiss to both cheeks. The five-foot woman wore a flowing floor-length tank top dress the color of pink lemonade and a matching bow in her wild hair piled at the top of her head.

"Your lawyer friend is eating breakfast in the dining room," Cherry said.

"Where's Sloane?"

"Hasn't even rolled out of bed." Cherry pointed Vivian toward a side room. "She had a late, late night, and I'm shocked she even went to sleep."

"Doing what?"

"What she does best. Shoo. He's waiting for you."

Vivian entered the dining room to the heavenly aroma of Denver omelets, French toast, bacon, and coffee. Loren was seated at a small circular table meant for two plowing into one of two heaping plates.

"Grab some food," he told her, waving at the self-serving sideboard.

Vivian did as he ordered and loaded up. Cherry was as good a cook as her mother, Millie, and when she was in a real slow season, she sold homemade pies and jams at a booth every Saturday at the farmer's market.

After setting her plate down on the table across from Loren, Vivian grabbed a mug of coffee and a glass of orange juice. Once she settled in her chair, she gulped down some of the juice.

"Your state patrol officer has gone back to Boise, so I'm told."

Vivian cut into the Denver omelet. "He's in the middle of an investigation. I would expect him to do so."

"And leave us behind?"

"We'll figure out a way to get back. Just hang tight."

Loren wiped his mouth with a napkin. "Where's your cousin and her partner? I thought they were supposed to be here."

Vivian gave him a long, hard look while she chewed her food. He returned the same look while he waited.

She swallowed. "To be frank, I have no clue. They arrived and then left again."

He made a *hmm* noise and resumed eating.

"Why did you call me here?" Vivian asked.

"I think I know where Hal's been hiding out."

Vivian took a moment to digest what he'd said and the few bites of food she'd consumed. If they could find Hal, maybe she could get some solid answers on who had sent the kill squad after her. He obviously knew something.

"How long have you suspected you knew?" she asked.

"It hit me last night. When I went to tell Sergeant Larrabee, I found out he was gone. I wasn't going to disturb your sleep, and I have no way to contact your cousin."

"You could have told Sloane. She's a retired private investigator and friends with us."

Loren's craggy face scrunched. "Who?"

"The redhead who works here."

Loren shook his head. "I don't recall seeing a redhead."

"Cherry could have done it too." Vivian held up her hands. "That's beside the point. I'm here now. So, where do you think Hal is hiding?"

The old lawyer continued eating and downing his coffee, speaking between bites and chewing. "North of Boise, there's a golf course he and Charley would play hooky and visit. I overheard a conversation between them one time about an abandoned church that sits across the road from the golf course property."

"You think he's hiding there?"

"I do."

"What golf course is this? I'll call Cassius and have him check it out."

Loren reached across the table and grasped her hand. "No."

She scowled.

He released her and held up the offending hand in surrender. "If I'm wrong, the last thing I want is a lawman giving me grief. I'm already seen as losing my edge and should just hang up my hat and retire."

Vivian softened toward him. "You were wanting Dot and T.J. to check it out, weren't you?"

"They are bounty hunters, aren't they?"

"But Hal isn't a bounty. This Cade Porter that Hal associated with is. That's their first priority."

Loren sighed and tapped a meaty finger against the tabletop. "Then I'm left with the only other option."

Vivian didn't like the tone of his voice. "Loren, the only option is to have law enforcement check it out."

He shook his head. She grabbed his still-tapping hand and squeezed.

"You better not be thinking what I think you're thinking."

He leaned closer to her and lowered his voice. "You can't tell me the other night didn't light a fire in your belly."

"It most certainly did not. Loren, I killed a man. And so did you," she said, her voice pitching a bit higher than she liked.

"My dear, I'm an old man on my last leg. I haven't felt this fired up in a long time. But I don't like to be the butt of anyone's joke, and we both know how law enforcement gets when they're sent on a goose chase."

"See, even you think this is bad idea and Hal's not there. There's no need to run off halfcocked over it. Besides we're hours away. Even if we did go, and *if* Hal is there, he could pack up and move locations before we ever arrived."

Loren sat back against his chair and gnawed on his lips.

"Loren, I know you mean well, and I understand your motives, but this is a bad idea all around. Those men will still be looking for me and probably you too. Take my advice and sit this one out. I'll talk with Cassius. He's not like the rest."

The old lawyer threw his hands up in surrender. "You're right. You're right. You call that statie and let him know."

"I will. I'll ask him to keep this between us. If Hal is there and Cassius finds him, then all the better, right?"

Loren smiled. "Right."

Suspicion slithered through Vivian at the way he spoke, but she left it alone. "Let's finish breakfast."

BEFORE SHE RETURNED to the ranch, Vivian met up with Sloane, who loaned her a phone to call Cassius. He didn't answer, so she left a message and asked him to call Sloane to let her know he received the message and would check in on Loren's suspicions.

After reassuring herself that Loren was set for at least another day or two at the bed and breakfast, Vivian headed back to the Ybarra ranch.

She arrived to chaos. The ranch yard was covered in chicken feathers and some of the yard furniture was broken and scattered. Was that a rooster's head? Vivian bailed out of the Ford.

"Angela! Ashley!" Good God, if something had happened

to them while she was gone …

"Behind the house!" came Angela's shout.

Vivian ran to the back and came to a sudden halt.

Angela knelt beside one of the guardian dogs. His body was ravaged and bloodied. Two dead goats, their bodies ripped open, were dangling from the fence. Chicken carcasses littered the ground mingled with an array of feathers.

And lying dead, half its skull blown away, was a huge brown bear.

"Oh my God. Angela?"

"I'm fine. The girls are fine; they're inside. I have the vet and the wildlife people coming. Get me some towels. Do *not* let Bethany out here to see this."

"Yes, ma'am."

Vivian ran inside and slammed into Ashley. The young woman's face was white as a sheet.

"Is she okay? Angela?" Ashley stammered.

"She's fine. Keep Bethany in here and away from windows."

Ashley nodded.

"Towels?" Vivian asked.

Ashley perked up at this. Give her something to do and she was all business. She ran into the laundry room and came back with a stack and a bottle of iodine balanced on top.

"I know Petey got in a fight with the bear. She'll need this to help."

Vivian took the stack. "Watch Bethany."

Outside, she hurried back to Angela's side as the older woman worked to save the life of her guardian dog.

But Angela's pack and the two other guardian dogs were

missing. "Where are the rest of them?" Vivian asked.

"I've got them all locked in the barn with the goats and the chickens that fucking bear didn't kill."

The dog whimpered and heaved. Angela pressed an iodine-soaked towel to his injuries.

"Damn it. I'm going to lose him."

"Why is a bear this far out of the forest?" Vivian added another towel to a gruesome wound on the dog's hind end.

"I think it was sick. There was so much wrong when it attacked."

Over the sound of the dog's agony, multiple vehicles arrived. Seconds later, the vet, followed closely by the wildlife wardens, joined them.

"Oh, Angela," the vet said as he dropped beside her. "I don't know if I can do anything to save him," he said as he peeled away the towels to examine the wounds.

Angela sat back on her heels and looked the vet dead in the eye. "Make him comfortable. It's all I ask."

Vivian climbed to her feet and backed away to let the vet do his thing. She watched the wildlife warden examine the bear.

"Shit," he spat.

"What?" Angela barked.

"Ms. Ybarra, this bear has a tracker on it. And it doesn't look like anything of ours."

Angela glared at the man from her kneeling position, refusing to leave her dying dog's side. "I don't give two shits if that bear belonged to the fucking president. It killed my livestock and nearly killed me and has killed my guardian dog. I want all of this documented, and I want to know why it came on my property."

The wildlife guy nodded. "Yes, ma'am. I just thought you should know."

The vet returned and Angela turned her focus on him and the dog. Vivian wandered closer to the wildlife agent, careful to stay back from the bear as far as she could.

"Is there some kind of significance to tracking devices?" she asked.

He glanced at her, then gave a grim nod. "There is. We usually have them on animals we're monitoring. Sometimes we put one on an animal that has been reported to be a nuisance in case it becomes a repeat offender."

"And the collar on this one?"

"Is nothing like any collar we or the State of Idaho Game and Wildlife Department uses." Using the end of a pen, he lifted the collar from the deceased bear's neck. "I've never seen anything like it. It almost looks like one of those devices people use to administer drugs to their system."

Vivian was about to ask more about that when Ashley called for her.

She hurried to the other side of the house. "What is it?"

"Sloane just called. She said your lawyer friend is gone."

"What?"

Ashley shrugged. "Apparently, he bought a vehicle and left Euskadi. He's going back to Boise."

Chapter Thirty-One

DOT AND T.J. had been hunkered down on a hilltop, looking down at the farm for the last two hours but saw no activity. Nestled as it was in the foothills, it afforded lots of rocky outcroppings and gaps to hide in, but it lacked tall vegetation to shield them from the sun. Neither of them had any blinds the color of this landscape.

The midmorning sun beat down on them. Sweat left streaks in the dirt that coated both her and T.J.'s skin.

"What do you think?" he asked, lowering the binoculars.

"I think they were only here when we arrived, and this place is completely abandoned."

"I don't. I think they're lazy asses and sleeping in. There are no animals, that's for certain. But they are people here."

Dot shifted around, careful not to raise any dust, and faced the opposite direction toward the place downhill where they'd parked the Suburban. "I say we get out of this sun and reassess in the car." She titled her head back to look at T.J.

"Fine," he groused. "I'll set up a camera."

She waited for him as he rigged a digital recording camera to stay focused on the farm. Once he was satisfied with its positioning and made sure it worked correctly, they headed back to the Suburban.

Camped out in the cooling interior, they rehydrated and snacked on jerky and energy bars.

"What I wouldn't give for a good ole MRE," T.J. muttered around a stick of jerky.

"I'd take this over those any day. They were complete garbage."

"Says the pilot who got to fly back to the base and eat a hot meal instead of being stuck out in the field."

"Not my fault you chose the wrong MOS." She popped the last bite of her energy bar.

"Cook was not an option when I enlisted."

His phone dinged and the camera app activated. "We've got movement."

He tilted the phone so she could see the screen along with him. The recording went for five minutes, and still no footage of human beings appeared.

"Might have been wildlife," Dot said as she repositioned herself in her seat.

"Maybe." T.J. continued to watch the screen. "I think that far building is where they brought the package out from." He turned the phone and pointed to the building he was referring to. "Looks like an old stable."

"It does. They made sure we couldn't check things out, that was for sure."

The makeshift pad where she'd landed the helicopter was hard to see from their stakeout vantage point. The building where they had been holed up in while they waited to leave was smack in the middle of the whole facility. Less than fifty yards from it was a house. This was where they'd centered their focus.

"Bet they have all the vehicles and any other equipment hidden in the outbuildings," T.J. said.

"I still don't think anyone is there," Dot countered.

Her phone vibrated against her leg, and she dug it out. They were in a region they could pick up signals from local towers yet remain hidden electronically from anyone seeking their location. It was Vivian via text.

You're not going to believe this, so here it goes.

She looked at T.J. "Get a load of this. A bear attacked my family ranch. Killed some of the animals before *Ama* put it down."

"What the fuck?"

What the fuck indeed. Dot was hundreds of miles away from the ranch and this shit happened. Yes, Angela was there, and her mother was more than capable of handling situations like this. But she was getting older. What if Bethany had been outside when the bear attacked? Or Angela had been too slow? Or severely injured?

Dot felt the weight of T.J.'s stare, he probably wanted to know the rest. "No human was hurt, but we lost a few goats and most of the chickens." She drew in a steadying breath and let it out through her mouth. "One of the guard dogs had to be put down."

He gripped her hand. "Dot?"

She shook him off. "Vivian says the wildlife people are doing a necropsy on the bear, but they suspect it was drugged." Dot lowered her phone and looked at him directly. "Also, the head of Vivian's law firm left Euskadi and is going back to Boise. She thinks he knows where Hal Jones is and is going after him. Vivian is going after her colleague."

"What the fuck?" T.J. repeated.

"Swear can," Dot said. She needed some humor to pull her out of this dark place.

T.J. got the memo and grinned. "Bethany is not here; it doesn't count." His grin faded and he tapped the side of her head. "Don't go there, Dot. We can't be everywhere at once."

"It's still not right, T.J."

His mouth turned into a thin line under his beard.

Not ready to hear whatever he might say, Dot reread the text. "A drugged bear?"

"Have you had problems with bears before?" T.J. asked.

"Never. I mean, they roam the perimeter of the ranch and test the dogs but never actually came onto the property. I think we had a mountain lion take a nap in a tree when I was a kid, but it stayed away from the sheep. Wolves and coyotes are our biggest threats."

"Movement again," he interrupted her.

This time, the camera had picked up actual activity on the farm. A door on the side of the house facing the camera's direction opened. She and T.J. watched as a man carrying a rifle in a crossbody sling exited the house.

"I was right," T.J. said in a singsong voice.

"I don't want to hear it from you."

The gunman walked to the old stables, paused by a set of doors, and did something. It was hard to tell from this distance and with his body blocking his actions.

"I think he was checking a lock," T.J. said.

"You'd only check a lock if you were keeping something inside from escaping. Or keeping people out."

"This might be a rescue mission if they have more girls imprisoned in there."

"We've done it before." Dot twisted around in her seat and then rolled down the window to listen. "I think someone is coming."

T.J. drove the Suburban down a smaller path off to their right that was the perfect size for ATVs. It was just wide enough to fit the Suburban in without getting stuck between the rock and raised ground creating a tunnel of sorts. Once he had the tail end out of sight of the road, he killed the engine, and they waited.

Unable to see who was coming, Dot climbed over the seat—surprising T.J. in the process—and crawled into the back.

"Lift the hatch," she ordered.

The latch disengaged, and the hatch began its ascent. Dot grabbed the internal handle to stop it from going farther and slid out through the gap. She pushed the hatch closed and, staying low to the ground, hurried to the mouth of the earthly tunnel in time to see two vehicles pass in a cloud of dust.

Dot gave it a few minutes to make sure there were no stragglers, then hurried back to the Suburban. She smacked the hatch.

"Back up, we're clear," she said as she hopped in and sat with her feet dangling over the end.

"It's Follman and his bodyguard," he told her as he maneuvered the beast of a vehicle back to their original spot.

"Who's in the second?" Dot asked as she twisted around to assess their weapons options.

"Can't tell for sure, but it might be Yonatan Hassin and a man with a fashionable manbun."

"Why would Follman be up here with Hassin?" Dot pondered.

"I can think of only two reasons," T.J. said, his voice heralding doom. "They have more girls that need inspecting." He twisted around and met her gaze. "Or they have Caleb."

Dot looked down at the Mossberg tactical shotgun she was doing a finger dance on. "Or it's both."

"It's just the two of us against we don't know how many," he told her.

She smiled, a sad smile. "It was just me against an entire squad of killers."

"You had backup. We were just a bit behind. That won't be the case here."

The idea hit her. "What do you want to bet Eriksson has eyes on Follman and they're back on the main road?"

"It would make sense." T.J. gave her a sly grin. "One way to find out."

"I'll go. You sit tight and keep an eye on what's going on down there." Dot holstered her 1911, slid in an earbud connected to his wireless comms, and scooted out of the Suburban's backend with the Mossberg in hand.

"Be careful and watch your six," T.J. warned.

She saluted him and hurried up the hillside. She took the narrow footpath that forked with one path going up to where they'd planted the camera and the other continuing on along the most level point of the hill. For the most part it kept her hidden if she stayed bent over.

Dot went about five hundred yards, reaching a dip in the path that exposed it to the roadside below. Making herself blend into the bland beige landscape best she could, she belly-crawled forward and checked the road.

Sure enough, just over seventy yards directly below her position, there was a tan-colored POS four-door sedan parked on the opposite side of the road, facing west. Using a small pair of binos, she zeroed in on the interior of the car through the windshield. Two men, both in the front seat, both looking behind them and possibly talking to each other.

Dot surveyed her surroundings, using the binos to check both ways on the road. No one else was out here.

"See them?" T.J. asked over their link.

She touched the mic button on the stem of her earbud. "I do. Two of them."

"Can you get down to them without being spotted?"

"Negative. I'll need a diversion and hope it doesn't go south and alert those at the farm that someone else is here. Update on your end?"

"All targets are standing in the middle of the yard talking. No movement from the stable, and none from the house."

Dot didn't like this news. What was Follman up to?

She looked up over her shoulder. The hillside blocked her from the other side. If she got the two men to get out of the car, she could easily step into the open with the shotgun trained on them. The Mossberg was loaded with slugs and in her hands could easily put down a threat. But she didn't intend to shoot them.

She wiggled back behind the cover of a rock outcropping. She dug up some decent-sized rocks and chucked one then a second down the hill, watching them bounce along the loose dirt, and then checked to see if the men had noticed. They hadn't.

By the time the second rock had finished its descent, hitting the road with a clack, she'd thrown another one. The men in the car noticed.

First the driver, then the passenger opened their doors and slowly emerged as the third rock hurtled over the roadway and smacked the front end of their POS.

"About to engage," she warned T.J.

With a silent plea that the men at the farm were distracted and far enough away they didn't hear this, she pumped a round into the shotgun and stepped out from behind her cover.

Both men aimed their service weapons at her. They both looked like they were plopped out of the same mold, lean and muscled, high and tight haircuts, same aviator sunglasses, desert tan T-shirts and pants paired with desert tan boots. Only difference was, one was pale blond and the other a dark brunette.

She wedged the shotgun's stock into her shoulder and lifted her left hand to her lips to make a shush motion.

The blond lowered his weapon and said something to his partner. After the other man had holstered his pistol, Dot moved downhill. She didn't give them the same courtesy and kept them at gunpoint. Despite the loose dirt and rock falling with her, she managed to descend the hill without incident and hit the road.

"Dot Ybarra," the blond said in a civil tone.

"Take it you're Eriksson," she said.

He looked over at his partner. "Told you she was a quick one."

"What? You decided enough of your people fucked this whole thing up that you'd make yourself more involved?"

He crossed his arms. The man's voice did not match his physique. "I've been involved from the onset of this task force. Just not in the same circles as you would imagine."

Dot lowered the Mossberg. "Why's Follman here?"

"One of my UCs in another part of this whole operation got word to me that Follman was out for blood, and he wanted the both of you on a platter. You gave him enough information to come seek you out here in Idaho. Which I warned Roman about and he chose to ignore."

"You didn't exactly give him much of a choice."

"If he'd given me more time, I also would have told him what else we learned."

Dot checked her watch. "You're wearing my patience thin."

"There was another shipment of girls brought in through Mexico. My other UC was there on arrival. These girls didn't fare as well as the ones you and Roman rescued. Three of them were dead." Eriksson's features morphed into a spot-on replica of an enraged Norseman. "The UC had to dispose of the bodies, which he turned over to my task force."

Dot let the Mossberg dangle in her arm, the barrel point-ed at the ground. How many more girls were out there unaccounted for? How many brought here before Dot and T.J. became entangled in this mess? Was that what Caleb figured out and Follman tried to have him taken out before he blew the whistle? This was a damn good reason to give Follman and his lackeys some Vlad the Impaler treatment.

Dot let the thought of Follman's head on a pike settle her. "Why were these girls brought here? And where the hell are they getting them from?"

Eriksson and his partner exchanged looks.

"I'm not a hundred percent on that," Eriksson said. "But my guess is as brides for some of Follman's business associates. Cade ... Caleb was tracking this information in a coded journal, which I can't seem to find."

"A leather-bound journal?" Dot asked.

"Yes." Eriksson's once-furious face turned contemplative. "You saw it."

"I did. But I didn't read them. T.J. did. And last we knew, those journals were in the custody of the Idaho State Police investigator's office."

"Shit."

Her earbud came to life. "Dot," T.J. said.

She touched the mic. "It's Eriksson and one of his men."

"Better bring them in. Now. More have come from the house. And they've got a young woman with them."

"Fuck."

Eriksson frowned. "Mind updating me on what just happened?"

"Are you prepared for infiltration and an extraction?" she asked.

"We came with equipment, yes, but not to—"

"You are now," Dot broke in and moved to the passenger seat of the car. "Get in."

Eriksson opened his mouth to protest Dot taking his original seat but shut it when she shot him an ugly glare.

"Now, *Agent*."

Chapter Thirty-Two

B Y THE TIME Vivian was given a phone and a vehicle to borrow, Loren had at least a half-hour head start. She still wasn't able to reach Cassius personally. She was, however, able to reach one of his commanders and let him know what was going on.

"Do you know which golf course he was talking about?" the commander asked.

"He never gave me a name, just a general location north of Boise."

"Counselor, there are more than thirty golf courses in the city, and at least ten of them in what could be considered north Boise."

"I'm sorry I can't be more specific. Is there any way to narrow it down by type of golf course someone would go to? Or even the surrounding community geography?"

The commander faded away from the phone connection as he spoke to someone. He had to have muffled the microphone, as his voice and the respondent's were garbled.

Vivian choked the steering wheel. If she could only drive faster! But ID-55 was not the road to play Russian roulette on. She took satisfaction in knowing Loren would be hindered by the same speed limits and reductions. If he'd chosen this route.

"Counselor Montgomery." The commander's strident voice dragged her back to the task at hand.

"I'm still here."

"I have a few of my people working on this. They're going to need a bit more time to narrow down our options and get some people out to look. What can you give me that might help?"

She relayed what she'd learned about Hal Jones and his habits and what Charley's paralegal had told her days before about his own habits. She also added in what little Loren had said to her.

"If you would, also check our law firm. I have a sinking suspicion Loren will return there for something."

"Boise PD hasn't released it. The building is still an active crime scene."

"I understand, but he's the head partner, and I doubt a lowly patrol officer is going to be able to sway him from going in."

"Why would he go there?"

Vivian had been mulling over this exact question, trying to come up with a reason, any reason for Loren to return. The only logical reason was he had a weapon hidden in his office. A weapon he conveniently did not have on hand when the gunmen stormed the office for Vivian.

"Knowing him, it could be any of five different reasons, and I couldn't begin to guess which one he'd use."

"We'll work on narrowing them down," the commander said. "If you come up with anything, call me back."

With the call ended, Vivian focused on her drive, and in

the silence let her mind run wild. Topics ranging from Loren wanting to be some kind of superhero to the most absurd, that Loren himself was the main instigator behind this whole sordid affair. She was really playing in a fantasy world with that idea.

Right?

Vivian needed to come at this logically. Like a lawyer. Piece by piece, she analyzed the evidence she had and cross-examined it against what she suspected.

First, there was Loren's odd behavior during her first visit with him. He'd seemed a bit too eager to get her out of his hair, but a bit more intrigued by what she knew. Then came Charley's warning about someone in the firm being a mole. Or maybe it was someone who was not who they seemed.

Damn it, she couldn't remember what he told her exactly. What she did recall was how adamant he'd been about her not letting anyone in the office see her leave with that box holding Caleb Podolsky's actual file. Charley had been antsy, maybe even scared.

But if he was so scared, why did he allow two men to visit him at his home the day before he was murdered? One of them was certainly Caleb, by the description the next-door neighbor gave Vivian. But Charley and Caleb hadn't talked because Charley hadn't been home at the time Caleb showed up.

What about the other man? He'd come the night before. This man Vivian assumed was Hal. He was a tall, good-looking man who like to dress in expensive clothing.

So was Loren.

She should have pressed the neighbor harder on her actual descriptions. Vivian had told Larrabee about the neighbor after they discovered Charley. Hopefully, he or one of his team was able to interview the woman. Vivian really needed to see those notes.

She brought her wandering thoughts back to Loren. On the day they found Charley, Loren had showed up in her office with Caleb Podolsky's juvenile file and acted very out of character. Vivian was certain Loren had read through the file. The bigger questions begged, why had he read the file?

She had. And something … a sentence in the file had stood out to her when she read it, but she hadn't dwelled on it too hard.

The name of the attorney who'd represented the men accused of murdering Caleb's father.

Lawrence Maltsberger. L.M. Did it equal Loren McLaughlin?

No! She was grasping at straws. No way Loren and Lawrence were one and the same.

Vivian disregarded that bit of information and focused on why Loren was there the night the kill squad came for her. He shouldn't have been there. His excuse of keeping an eye on her felt off. Why was he keeping an eye on her? Did he suspect she knew something about him? Was he aware Charley had given her the actual file on Caleb?

Cassius questioned how the killers got inside the firm. Had Loren let them into the building?

If he did, then why did he throw that one down the stairs? It could have been for show and went wrong when the man's neck was broken.

Vivian groaned. What was she doing? She had to stop

this and focus on driving. She couldn't recall the last sixty miles.

Her phone rang, echoing through the vehicle cab. A welcomed reprieve from her mental gymnastics. She touched the Bluetooth.

"Vivian, I got all of your messages," Cassius said. "Where are you?"

"I'm about a half an hour away from Boise. Loren should be there already."

"I think we figured out which golf course he was referring to. The Sapphire Greens golf course—it's east of Star and a bit north of town—has a historical church sitting across the road."

"How sure are you that's the place Loren was referring to?" Vivian asked.

"I'm about 100 percent certain."

"Only *about* 100 percent?" she pressed.

"I'm giving myself some wiggle room here. But it feels right, because I was able to connect with the family in Texas. One of the boys is into golfing as much as his father, and he told us about the church across from the golf course."

Vivan sighed in relief. Now if they could just beat Loren there. Or better yet, Hal was somewhere else and safe from any danger.

"What about the firm? Did Loren go there?"

"If he did, he found a way in no one knows about. PD added a few more guys to keep an eye out, and crime techs are still working the scene. No one has seen or heard him there." Cassius paused. "Vivian, I don't think you should come to the golf course in case this turns sideways. Especially after what you've already been through."

"Cassius, I've come this far. I'm not backing down now. I really think something is not right with Loren. And if Hal is there ... I need to know. He can't end up like Charley."

"He won't end up like Charley. I promise. You said yourself, you're a lawyer. Not law enforcement."

"Oh, screw what I said. You also told me I'd get past what I did. This is me getting past it."

"I don't think Dot would like this."

"Dot needs to let it go. I'm a grown-ass woman."

His chuckle warmed her unexpectedly. "Call me when your ETA is minutes out."

Vivian focused on the rest of her journey, plotting her best route to get to the golf course as fast as she could. Cassius was right—she shouldn't be there. But something deep inside her warned her she had to be. Who else would Loren listen to otherwise?

Chapter Thirty-Three

T HE STABLE DOORS opened, letting in bright light. Caleb blinked against the harshness.

It took a bit for him to realize he'd tipped over and was lying on his side. In the next second, he felt the tingling sensations in his right arm and shoulder where it had fallen asleep. His arm would be useless until it regained feeling.

A moment later, footfalls echoed through the building. He did his best to prop himself up just as the first face came into view.

"Well, good morning, Caleb Podolsky."

More men flanked Follman. Caleb recognized Manbun from the café where he'd been ambushed and Follman's ever-present bodyguard. Next to the bodyguard was Yonatan Hassin, decked out in full tactical regalia. The man couldn't pull off a posh businessman if his life depended on it.

One other man Caleb recognized—and couldn't believe was here—was Armand Revach.

Caleb ignored the rest and focused on Follman. "Finally figured it out, did ya, Meyer? How does it feel knowing that the son of your father's biggest fuckup got to you?"

"Your father's death is on his own head."

"Funny you say that. Your old man kept blaming mine

for his own death right before I ended him. I so enjoyed listening to him plead for his life."

Follman's face turned a deep shade of red, and he lurched toward the bars. He was stopped by Revach's outstretched hand.

"This is the man you are afraid of?" he asked, his heavily accented English doing nothing to hide his true origins.

"I'll be fucked. Armand Revach in the flesh."

The Israeli mafioso glared at Caleb. "How does a man missing half a leg worry you?" His heated look swung back to Follman.

"He took out an entire hit team. Alone."

Hassin sniffed. "You sent amateurs. What did you expect?"

"I had expected a man missing half a leg and obvious mental disabilities to die," Follman countered.

Hassin guffawed and threw his hands up, then walked away. Manbun followed, leaving Revach, Follman, and his bodyguard behind.

Revach faced Follman. "We've lost enough merchandise and time in the past week. Finish him and be done with it. We have work to do."

"It's not that simple," Follman said.

"It *is* that simple. If you value your position, you will do it." Revach left the stable.

That left just Follman, his bodyguard, and Caleb.

"So, you brought them in here to show off your incompetence?" Caleb asked as he shifted himself upright now that his arm no longer burned.

Follman jabbed a finger through the bars. "Shut your

fucking mouth, you bastard Jew."

"That's rich, coming from you."

Follman composed himself by adjusting his jacket and stepping back from the stall door. "Who sent you to infiltrate my business?"

"Why would anyone send a crippled and scarred man into your domain?"

"Enough with the sarcasm. You are in no position to fuck around."

"Really, and you think I haven't already found out? What did you do with Mina?"

"Who?"

"The child who was caged in here with me like an animal. Mina."

Follman stared at him as he fiddled with a gold ring on his finger. He inched closer to the stall. "The woman?"

"She's a child."

"For her soon-to-be husband, she's a woman."

Caleb wished he could be sick, but that reaction had long dried up.

"The men asking for our services like their wives to be young and fresh. And we found the perfect place to obtain them."

"From desperate villagers under Taliban control who think they're giving their daughters a better chance. And here I thought you couldn't get any lower."

Follman's gaze burned. "They have a rich husband, clothing, good food, and no lack of care. All that is asked of them in return is to produce an heir. Much better than living in the squalor and poverty they came from."

"Exchanging them from one prison to another doesn't make you any better. God will smite you for such evil. They're little girls, Meyer! They don't even fucking know what sex is. And you sell them off to men to be violated."

"They were created to be vessels for man. Nothing more."

"I should have killed you the night I ended your father."

Follman canted his head. "You know, I should be thanking you for that. Saved me the trouble of figuring out a way to off him myself and get away with it."

"Burn in hell."

Follman's gaze brightened. "You'll have the luxury of enjoying it first." He looked Caleb from head to toe and then back. "By the looks of you, you're not much longer for this world."

"I have enough in me to take some of you with me."

Follman made a dissatisfied noise deep in his throat and turned as if to leave, only to stop and turn back with audible flourish. "One more thing. The couple. Dorothy and Titus. Who are they to you?"

Caleb scowled as best he could considering his faltering brain. "How the fuck should I know who two old birds are?"

"Oh, they're not old. Nowhere near it. But they do owe me."

"What? A blowjob."

There was a hesitation on Follman's part. Caleb wondered if he was trying to decide to be offended and react or let the comment slide.

A slick smile creased the man's face. "You know, that wouldn't be a bad idea."

From outside the stable came an explosion of metal on metal and things shattering. Follman and his bodyguard jolted and turned to the doors.

Caleb smiled. "You better run."

Chapter Thirty-Four

THE CHAOS THAT erupted when T.J. plowed the Suburban into one of the vehicles was glorious.

Dot, Eriksson, and Peters, his partner, bailed out of the Suburban and opened fire on the men loitering in the yard. T.J. slammed the gas to the floorboard and pushed the SUV across the gravel drive, creating a dust cloud for cover.

He ducked down as bullets peppered the bulletproof windshield, but he continued to inch forward.

The heavy slap on the hatch made him let off the gas and throw the car into park. He killed the engine just as the hatch opened. Dot grabbed out the rest of her weapons and darted away.

T.J. threw the driver's-side door open and slid to the ground, keeping the door as a barrier. Over the sound of the gunfire, he heard the terrified screams of a girl. Everything in him demanded he move toward the screams, but Dot had ordered him to the stable. She would handle getting the girl.

Logic dictated she be the one; it was evident that another man, despite rescuing her, was going to cause more problems for the girl than if Dot were to do it herself. His objective was the stable. Eriksson was Dot's backup and Peters would be T.J.'s.

"They've scattered." Dot's alert came over the comms.

"Move out," T.J. ordered. "Peters, with me."

He peeled away from the door and hurried to the back of the Suburban, where he grabbed a second loaded shotgun and slung a shotshell bandolier crosswise over his body. T.J. drew his pistol as Peters materialized beside him, and they took off for the stable.

"Revach and another man with the girl are headed to the house," Eriksson said. "Did anyone see Follman or Hassin?"

"Negative," T.J. answered.

They hadn't seen Follman leave the stable with the rest of the men. T.J. only assumed Follman had stayed for some reason.

Behind him, T.J. heard Dot make contact with the enemy. It took everything within him to not do a one-eighty and run back to help her. She was more than capable of taking care of herself. He had to disregard what she was doing and focus on his mission parameters.

He and Peters came to a stop behind the second unscathed SUV and waited. When no gunfire came their way, they broke from cover and ran for the building. Bullets chased their heels as they made the last few yards. They returned fire, then slammed up against the stable walls.

"Hassin is nowhere to be seen," Dot relayed over the comms.

"Shit." T.J. looked back at Peters, then looked around him. "I see a back door."

Peters nodded. They left their position, firing in their wake, and rushed along the wall. T.J. exchanged his emptied pistol for the shotgun, readying it to use as a doorbuster. T.J.

pumped a shell into the chamber, and fired two rounds into one hinge, and then fired two more rounds into the second hinge. He swung to the left of the door, readying to reload as Peters stepped back to kick it in.

Peters was waylaid before he could kick the door as a gun blast came from his right. Peters jerked and fell. Dead.

T.J. lifted the shotgun and pumped it as a figure started to come around the corner. He fired the final round just as the figure yanked back from the edge. T.J. tossed away the shotgun and grabbed the man's hands as he whipped around the corner again. T.J. twisted the man's hands upward, causing the gun to go off.

As they struggled for control over the weapon, T.J. met the man's steely gaze and recognized him as the asshole who had been his and Dot's escort slash handler the day the girls were loaded onto the helicopter.

Yonatan Hassin gave him a cruel smile. "You're out of your league, American."

"You just keep on believing that," T.J. said through clenched teeth as he fought to keep Hassin's hands and the gun pointed away from his body.

"I should have killed you that day," Hassin snarled in his face. "Took that woman of yours and put her in her rightful place."

"You talk too much."

"And you are weak."

"Fuck you," T.J. roared and threw his substantial weight into Hassin, forcing the somewhat lighter man backward.

T.J. leaned harder into Hassin, propelling them behind the stable and into the open space between it and another building. Hassin swung his body around, veering them off course, and T.J. was thrown off-balance, jerking Hassin's hands down with him. The momentum between them toppled them both to the ground.

Dust billowed into the air as T.J. skidded across the dirt. When he came to a stop, he swept his bulky frame around and froze. Hassin was already on his feet and raising the pistol he managed to hold on to.

T.J. scooped up handfuls of dirt and flung them at Hassin's face. The dirt exploded. T.J. charged into the dust cloud and tackled Hassin midbody. T.J. felt something fly past his head. His tackle slammed Hassin into a wall, where he tried to pin him.

Hassin managed to free an arm and drove his elbow into T.J.'s neck. The right side of his body went numb. T.J. staggered back, and the other man drove his fist into the side of T.J.'s head, sending him reeling away.

Hassin grabbed T.J.'s arm and swung him into the wall. He rotated at the last second and let his shoulder absorb the impact. Hassin cupped the side of his head and tried to push it into the wall. T.J. resisted, instead headbutting Hassin. Hot liquid hit his face, and Hassin released him.

T.J. pushed Hassin, who'd managed to entangle his arms with T.J.'s and fell backward, dragging T.J. with him. The momentum of the fall threw him over Hassin's body, and somehow the other man kicked up and propelled him farther. The impact with the ground rattled T.J.'s teeth and must have winded Hassin, as he'd released his hold.

T.J. lay there a moment, trying to catch his breath. With a groan, he rolled onto his side and spat out a stream of blood. He pushed upward and glanced over.

Hassin was coming at him, this time brandishing a knife. T.J. got to his feet and avoided the first two swipes by backing away, only to ram himself into the wall again. Hassin threw himself at T.J. He grabbed the knife-wielding hand and shoved it aside as Hassin leaned into his body, punching T.J. in the side.

Twisting to avoid more blows, T.J. freed Hassin's knife arm and had to throw his body out of the way as Hassin took another swipe at him. The knife glanced off the wood wall, and Hassin bent forward.

T.J. punched him in the head once, then twice, forcing the man back and giving T.J. the space to get away from the wall. Having no weapon of his own, T.J. was fucked.

With a frustrated yell, Hassin rushed T.J., swiping the blade at his torso. T.J. smacked the knife arm away on the first swipe but missed the return and felt the blade slice through his forearm. They did this dance for five more steps, T.J. receiving two more slashes before he was able to capture Hassin's knife arm and bend it backward.

The other man grunted as T.J. applied more pressure and propelled his body into the stable wall. He bashed Hassin's knife hand into the wall repeatedly until the knife fell. Then T.J. stepped back and kicked Hassin into the wall.

Heaving, T.J. glared at the bloodied man.

"You're supposed to be one of the good guys. You fucking prick."

Hassin laughed and coughed up a wad of blood. "Americans. Always fucking things up."

T.J. punched him. Hassin slid down the wall and sat on his ass.

"I'd rather fuck things up than be known as a kiddie rapist." He spotted Hassin's discarded pistol inches from his boot.

Hassin saw it too.

T.J. dove for it at the same time as Hassin. T.J. managed to grab the pistol and was wheeling around to aim when Hassin's knife sliced across his calf. With a yell, T.J. reeled back and fired repeatedly into Hassin's chest until the slide jammed.

Stepping back from the lifeless body, T.J. dropped the useless pistol. He wiped away sweat and staggered back to the stable, drawing his own pistol and ejecting the empty clip to replace it with a fresh one. He holstered the pistol, picked up his shotgun from next to Peters's body, and ejected the last shell casing.

From the bandolero, he reloaded the shotgun. Once the last round was in, he placed the stock against the door and forced it open. The wood door fell off its blasted hinges and landed on the stable floor. T.J. stepped inside, giving the shotgun a pump.

"Follman, I know you're cowering in here!"

A sound came from his right; he swung the shotgun that way, saw the armed man, and pulled the trigger. Follman's bodyguard was thrown off his feet, and he slammed into a stall wall. His body made a slow slide to the floor, a path of blood streaking down the wall.

"Sounds like you just lost," said a voice from halfway down the aisle.

T.J. set his shotgun aside and brought out his pistol. He stepped over the bodyguard's corpse, wincing as his calf burned, and hobbled down the aisle toward the lone man standing in front of a barred stall.

"You?" Follman spat as he backed away.

T.J. grinned. "Yup, me."

"Go ahead … kill him …" the voice said.

T.J. glanced inside the stall. The quick look was enough to make him see red.

"You must … be Titus."

"You must be Caleb Podolsky," T.J. responded, keeping all of his attention on Follman. "You don't look good, man."

"I've … been worse," Caleb said.

"I doubt that."

"What the fuck is this?" Follman demanded.

"This is two old war vets conversing," T.J. said.

"You've messed in my affairs for the last time," Follman snarled.

"Yeah, about that." T.J. hacked up a wad of bloody snot. "It was never about you. Until you pissed off my woman." He chuckled. "Shouldn't have gotten into kidnapping little girls."

"Just who the fuck do you think you are?"

T.J. licked his lips. "I'm the exorcist here to wipe out the devil."

Follman jerked, a gun coming up from his side. T.J. fired before the man could level the pistol. Follman's head rocked back with a neatly placed hole in his forehead and then fell backward.

"Any more in here?" T.J. asked Caleb.

"Only those two … and me. They have a young … Afghan girl … somewhere." Caleb was beginning to slur his words. Something was more seriously wrong than being chained up in here and beaten, if the bruising on his face and upper body was any indication.

"We know. My partner's getting her," T.J. said as he holstered his pistol and threw open the stall door.

He avoided the pile of mess left in the hay and followed the chain to the anchor in the wall. It was bolted into the wood and looked manageable to remove with the aid of something sharp.

"There's a key around here on someone," Caleb said weakly. "Hassin probably has it."

Maybe the dead man still had it on his body. T.J. would have to go look for it.

"Man, I can't leave you in here."

"Don't waste any bullets on trying to get that out. Where's Hassin?"

"Dead." He was going to have get the key, but T.J. wasn't about to leave the man unarmed, not with more men with guns still prowling around. He removed his pistol from the holster and held it out to Caleb. "I'll be back."

Caleb gave him a weak smile and nodded. "I know you will. You rangers never leave a man behind."

T.J. gaped at him. "How did you ..."

"I can smell one from miles away. You all have a certain swagger."

"Hang tight. I'll get you out of here," T.J. said.

"I'm countin' on it."

Chapter Thirty-Five

DOT AND ERIKSSON reached the house only to duck down when the windows began shattering.

"Split up," he said and headed left.

Dot went right, for the door where she and T.J. had seen a man exit earlier. She'd lost comms with TJ and had to trust that he was fine and taking care of business in his typical hell-bent fashion.

More gunfire ripped from the house, along with the girl's screams. Dot lay flat on the ground and waited for the shooting to stop. When it ceased, she was up and moving in a low crawl toward the door.

"This doesn't end well for you," Eriksson yelled from the other side of the house.

He was rewarded with more gunfire directed his way.

Dot knew what he was doing—the man was smarter than he let on. The only thing bothering her about this whole scenario was the missing Hassin and Manbun. When she'd bailed out of the Suburban and the dust cloud blew up, she'd lost sight of them both.

She just hoped T.J. was handling one of them.

By the door, she quietly rose into a squat and rotated the Mossberg from behind her back over her shoulder into her hands.

"Might as well come out!" Eriksson's voice echoed across the now-silent property.

Dot scanned her surroundings and found not a fidget of movement. The dust had long settled and revealed a few bodies of men scattered in the yard who hadn't been lucky enough to escape a bullet.

By Dot's count, there should potentially be five men left, and two of them, Follman and his bodyguard, were still in the stable. That left three unaccounted for, and Dot knew Revach and one of his men were in the house with the girl.

"You ready?" Eriksson's voice in her ear put on her on point.

"In position," she responded.

"I'll draw fire. You go in," he said. "Go."

Dot bolted upright, plastering her body against the wall beside the door. Within seconds, gunfire rattled through the house. No bullets passed her.

She threw her body away from the wall and, with practiced precision, stepped back and kicked at the door jamb. The door blew inward. Dot followed it with her Mossberg raised.

There was a flicker of movement to her left. A tattered curtain fluttered. She heard the scrape of a boot against debris to her right and was on the move.

Through two darkened rooms into a short hall, she burst into what had been the kitchen. A man spun, weapon coming around. In the space between fully registering his face and Dot pulling the trigger, he flinched.

It was the one they had dubbed Manbun. He took the

slug to the chest and flew back into the sink and cabinets. As he sank to the floor, his once-white shirt blackened with blood, his hair coming loose from the bun and falling across his face.

Dot turned away from him and went back to clearing the rest of the house. One down. One to go.

She touched her mic. "First floor is clear," she told Eriksson.

"I'm coming in."

A creak of the floorboards above sent her to the base of the staircase. From her position, she could see to the top where the floor teed. Two, possibly three rooms above.

Eriksson joined her and stared upward. "How do you want to play this?"

"I go first, you cover me. I think it's Revach up there with the girl."

"Lead the way."

Taking the stairs with slow and light steps, she ascended, Eriksson one step behind her. The moment Dot's head came in line with the floorboards she paused to get the lay of the land. Two bedrooms on each side and what looked to be the bathroom straight ahead. The doors were closed or mostly closed.

Eeny, meeny, miny, moe.

Light came from under the bedroom doors but none under the suspected bathroom. Dot gestured for Eriksson to hold. If their target was in the bedrooms, he'd get antsy when neither of them made it up the stairs. If he moved toward the door, she'd see his shadow.

She pointed for Eriksson to hunker down, and she took a

position to see back and forth between the doors. If the target was hiding in the bathroom, he might come bursting out.

Outside, the echo of gun blasts reverberated through her head. She recognized the gun. T.J. was alive and well.

Her attention never wavered from watching the bottom of the doors.

Another blast, a shotgun blast, followed the other rounds of gunfire. Someone had passed from this life.

Something flickered in the corner of the left side bedroom. Dot waited. There it was again. Her brain flashed back to the moment she'd entered the house—the flicker of a tattered curtain. The movements from under the door were similar.

Then came the creak.

Eriksson was on his feet. Dot rushed the stairs, and before the target could react, she kicked in the bathroom door. It slammed into a body, and there was a shriek from the girl.

Dot hit the deck, Eriksson following suit as the man fired through the door. Dot took stock of where the bullet holes were coming through, leveled her shotgun dead center, and pulled the trigger. The center of the door splintered, flecks of blood shot through the hole. There was a thud and the door swung shut.

When no other sound except for the girl's screams came out of the room, Dot hopped to her feet and approached. Using the barrel of her gun, she pushed the door inward. It stopped mere inches away from the frame. The girl's volume increased.

Dot reached inside and managed to find the light switch.

Light flooded the room, shutting the girl up. Dot shoved against the door and felt the body slide. She poked her head inside and found the wisp of a girl tucked inside the bathtub. When the girl saw Dot's dirty face, her eyes grew wide.

"Do you speak Dari?" Eriksson asked quietly behind her.

"No." She pulled her head out and turned to him. "Do you?"

A pistol shot cracked through the air. Dot felt a momentary stab of panic at the sound.

Eriksson held up a finger. "Stay with her. I'll be right back." He rushed down the stairs.

Dot pushed the door open farther and checked on the dead man. Revach. That left only Hassin unaccounted for, if T.J. hadn't already taken care of him.

She slipped inside the bathroom and took up a crouched position next to the doorway and gave the girl enough space to not feel threatened. The girl's gaze bounced back and forth between Dot and the body for a bit until she finally settled on staring at Dot.

Not knowing what else to do, Dot fell back on the one thing that had always worked for her when dealing with a skittish animal or Bethany when she'd had a horrible nightmare and Ashley wouldn't do.

Dot began speaking to the girl in Basque. She wouldn't understand a word, but the lyrical words of the story of a fisherman who encountered the first pods of cod fish and brought the secret back to his people began to wipe the fear from the girl's eyes. By the time Dot had come to the end of the story, she heard voices downstairs.

She held up a finger to the girl and left the bathroom.

She spotted the three men at the bottom of the steps. T.J. looked like he'd taken a beating from Mohammad Ali but with Eriksson's help was holding up a sickly looking Caleb Podolsky. He was missing the prosthetic, and he was struggling to keep his head from flopping around. Dot wasn't too sure he was going to make it out of here alive.

"He speaks Dari," Eriksson said.

"We're not getting him up these stairs," T.J. said.

"Just set me down," Caleb said weakly.

The two men gently sat him on the bottom step. Caleb leaned against the wall and let it cradle his head. He looked upward, his face so bruised and bloodied, Dot didn't know what he could actually see.

"Mina," he called up in a strained voice.

Then he began speaking to her in her native tongue.

Dot heard the creak of the flooring in the bathroom, and she stepped aside. The girl appeared, hesitating when she saw Dot.

Caleb continued to speak to her, his voice and words losing steam. Mina moved to the top step. Her hands flew to her mouth, and when the sleeve of her dirty dress fell away, Dot saw the bruises on her wrists.

Mina answered Caleb and began crying at his response.

Caleb rolled his head to T.J. and Eriksson. "She begged me to kill her when she learned I could understand her."

"Why in the hell would she ever ask that?" Eriksson asked incredulously.

"Because in her culture, if there is any sign of impurity on her, she will be killed," Caleb said. "Her family sold her to the men. They got rid of her to keep her from Taliban rule, and they'll never take her back. If there's anyone even left. She said her father was killed because of her. If she goes back, the Taliban leaders will have her executed."

"Fuck," Eriksson said.

Dot inched closer to the sobbing girl. She had no one. She was alone in a foreign country and left with no options. She would rather be dead than live out her life in fear of being captured and slaughtered in the name of some unholy rite.

"T.J.," Dot said softly.

Mina looked up at her, startled by her closeness, but didn't shy away.

"I know that tone of voice. What do you have up your sleeve?" he asked.

"I think we know a couple who would love to have her around and treat her like one of their own."

He didn't speak, and neither did the other men. Dot let T.J. digest her idea.

"You know, Fly Girl, I think you're right. Steve was the one who worked with the translators, and he picked up on Dari."

A low moan came from Caleb. He slumped over and slid into T.J.'s hold.

"We've got to get him out of here. He's going to die if we don't."

While he and Eriksson got Caleb up in their arms and hauled out of the house, Dot coaxed Mina down the stairs and into the last remaining unharmed SUV.

As they were driving out to the car, Dot realized they were minus a man. "Where's Peters?"

Eriksson shook his head. "He didn't make it."

"Hassin?" Dot asked.

"Dead. Along with Follman and his bodyguard," T.J. answered as he drove away from the farm.

She twisted around and looked out the back window at the property through the billowing gravel dust. All of this carnage just so a couple of men could make themselves rich. She looked at Mina.

Lives ruined. For a fucking dollar.

Chapter Thirty-Six

SOMEHOW VIVIAN BEAT Cassius to the golf course, and she found the church easily enough. She drove the loaned SUV along the street at a crawl looking for the vehicle Loren had taken. The previous owner had given Sloane a good description and the license plate number. There was no sign of the truck.

The street was more like a county road with the golf course on one side and farm or commercial property on the other. Sporadic croppings of old trees lined the seal-coated gravel road. Vivian slowed the SUV to a stop and parked across the street from the small church. A bungalow-style home sat behind the building: the parsonage Sloane had told her about. The property was registered as a historic landmark and held special services certain times of the year but otherwise was left shut up and monitored by the historical society.

Vivian rolled down all the windows and studied the surroundings. *Cassius, where are you?*

She turned to the golf course. A yellow flag flapped in the breeze. She was too far away to see which hole she was near. Judging by the location, she'd guess she was at one of the later greens. Except for the hum of wildlife and breeze rustling through the trees, it was quiet and peaceful. Not a human in sight. Had Cassius gotten management to corral their patrons and steer them away from this side of the course? Was that why he wasn't here?

Why would this place be the first thing to pop into Loren's head as Hal's bolt-hole?

Vivian felt like a sitting duck. There was no place to hide her car, and with no traffic coming along here, it was harder still to blend in.

Loren had to have it wrong.

She shifted out of park and was about to pull away, then movement behind the church caught her attention. She let the car creep forward until she was under one of the trees and had a better view of the church.

A man loitered near the parsonage.

Vivian's breath caught in her throat. Hal!

He was crossing the yard to the church. Vivian didn't see a vehicle and wasn't sure what he was doing.

With Loren's whereabouts unknown, and what his current state of mind was like, Hal had made himself a moving target. Vivian was preparing to turn the SUV around, but Hal jerked and stumbled forward.

The tell-tale crack of a rifle shot reached her as Hal fell to the ground.

"No-no-no-no!" She whipped the beast of a vehicle around and stomped on the gas.

The car plowed through the miniature yard, Vivian driving straight for Hal. Something pinged against the SUV's body, and she shrieked, ducking down.

She stomped on the brakes, using the car to block Hal from the shooter. He was on his knees, pressing a hand to his right shoulder. Blood seeped through his fingers.

"Hal! Get in!"

Another shot hit the back window, splintering the glass. Where the bullet went, Vivian didn't have time to care. Hal managed to stagger to the car and crawl into the back seat as another shot shattered the back window.

Gritting her teeth, Vivian hit the gas the minute the door behind her shut. She peeled out of the yard and circled around the back of the church. She could stay there, wait for Cassius and crew to show up. She should stay there, but a gut-twisting groan came from Hal. He didn't have time to wait.

And the last thing she wanted was to wait for the shooter to get into a better position and shoot them.

"Fuck it!" Vivian gunned the engine and tore out of the churchyard.

The tires hit the sealcoat and the SUV fishtailed. Vivian drove through the slide and was flying down the street. As she navigated the street at seventy miles an hour she called Cassius.

"Where are you?" he answered.

"Where the hell are you?" she yelled at the same time.

"At the golf course," he said.

Vivian heard the squeal of tires and looked in the rear-view mirror. The truck Loren had taken was in hot pursuit.

"Shit!"

"Vivian, what the hell?"

"Cassius, shut up. Loren shot Hal, and now he's chasing me down."

"What the fuck?"

"I'm on River Birch Lane going south." She blew right past the golf course's main entrance and caught a brief flash of Cassius's vehicle in the parking lot. "And I just went past you."

She glanced at the mirror. Loren was catching up.

"Vivian, get out of the residential area. We don't need a car accident."

"I don't have a choice."

"In two more blocks, there's a construction area." Vivian heard the slam of a door through the connection. "Drive into there. I'm coming."

"This is getting real tedious having you run to my rescue, Sergeant."

She shouldn't have taken her eyes off the pursuing vehicle. The SUV jerked, and she struggled to maintain control.

"Hurry!"

"I'm coming."

Vivian saw the site he'd told her about. She glanced in the mirror and found Loren preparing to ram her again. Taking in a fortifying breath, she threw the car into neutral, hit the brakes, and yanked the steering wheel to make the turn. Thank God no one was on the road.

Loren flew past her, barely missing the bumper that would have sent her into a spin. Vivian shifted the engine back into drive and manhandled the SUV into the dirt lot, bouncing over ruts and tiny piles of gravel. Construction employees and heavy equipment operators were scattered about the lot. A man in a neon orange vest and yellow hard hat ran toward her waving his arms.

Vivian blew past him. "Sorry!"

She glanced in the mirror and didn't see Loren's truck. She slowed the SUV and swung it behind a parked dump truck.

Seconds later, the wail of sirens flew past the construction site.

"Vivian, where are you?" Cassius asked over the speakers.

"Behind a dump truck." She twisted around and looked back at Hal.

He was staring at her and still breathing. His shirt was completely soaked in blood.

"Cassius, hurry. I don't know if Hal will make it."

The shouts of men and the sound of an approaching vehicle made her jerk. Cassius's car pulled into view.

"Follow me, Counselor."

"What about Loren?"

"My guys are on him. Let's get Hal to the hospital." Cassius turned on his sirens.

Chapter Thirty-Seven

D OT ALLOWED THE gelding's easy gait to lull her. A bite to the air warned of the incoming snow. Next to her, T.J. rode a sturdy roan. Ahead, keeping a brisker pace than the two behind her, Bethany led the way along the trail around the Ybarra ranch.

Dot and T.J. had taken the last few months off from bounty hunting to recoup. In the days and weeks following the shootout at the abandoned horse farm, they had been forced to reassess their business setup. The discussions hadn't gone well at times, eventually leading Dot to declare neutral ground.

They'd moved quarters to Euskadi and the ranch. To get her mind off the changes, Dot had taken two trips up the mountain with Angela and hunting parties. T.J. had relented on the second trip and came along. The excursion had helped him move further through his own decompression process.

Caleb Podolsky had died as they were rushing him to the hospital that day. T.J. had taken the death hard, despite not knowing the man personally. He was still a fellow veteran. Eriksson later admitted at Podolsky's funeral—the last time they'd spoken to or seen the man—he'd found out that

Caleb had had stage four brain cancer with no chance of survival. He'd kept it from everyone involved on the task force. It hadn't made T.J. feel any better about the ordeal.

Dot had seen him perk up for a few days when they—with a few strings pulled on Eriksson's part—were able to see Mina settled in with Steve and Dana. The Afghan girl had taken to their newborn daughter. T.J.'s moment of respite was short-lived. It wasn't long after they returned to Boise that Dot moved them to Euskadi.

Vivian had come out a few times to do her own decompression trips, her brush with death having left a few mental scars. Yet, there was a gleam of strength Dot had not seen before in her cousin's eyes. She'd faced down killers and a former colleague hell-bent on seeing her dead to keep up his façade of a respectable lawyer and she'd survived.

Between Vivian's and Larrabee's accounts of what she'd done to save Hal Jones and slam the jail cell door shut on Loren, Dot still marveled how Vivian managed it all without Dot there to save her. Vivian did reiterate that this was the last time she'd ever do anything this reckless and dangerous again. She preferred her nice, quiet job as a lawyer, *thank you very much*.

Dot and T.J.'s prolonged visit was stirring up Bethany's desire to see them stay. On this windy, chilly autumn Saturday, she'd coaxed them out on a ride, trying to eke out every last drop of attention from them she could get. And lob pointed comments about how nice it was out here.

T.J. reached out and grabbed Dot's free-swinging hand. She looked over.

"I've been thinking long and hard about this. For the last

six months or more," he said.

"About what?"

He released her hand and reined in his mount, and she did the same. Bethany, oblivious to their halt, kept right on riding.

"I had every intention of moving Shadow Force Solutions out of Boise to here," he said.

She frowned. "There's not enough work to keep us afloat up here."

"You'd be surprised what work will fall our way, especially with the PI business side of things." The roan shifted under him and danced around to face Dot's gelding. "I know I've apologized probably a hundred times now for getting us caught up in that mess ..."

"It turned out to be a good thing. So shut up already."

He sighed. "It could have gone a lot worse. You're right, we're not on missions anymore."

"Meh, I think we still are."

T.J. chuckled. "Okay, in a way, we still are. But we're too fucking old to keep that shit up. Sloane's got everything set up for us to run both the bounty hunting and our private investigation services here."

"So, what kept you from saying something sooner?" she asked.

"I wanted to make sure you were ready and able to handle the bounty hunting side."

"That can't be all."

He crossed his arms over the saddle horn and leaned into them. "Yeah, Dot, that can be all."

Bethany, who'd finally realized they weren't following

her any longer, was making her way back to them. Gidget and Zip, and one bossy Boer goat, danced around the gray's legs.

"You thinking of expanding our services to a bigger region?"

"I'm working on it, yeah."

"And when we're slow on work?"

He sat up and swept his hands the width of the land around him. "We help your *ama* out with the ranch and the outfitting business."

Dot smiled and shook her head. "You're crazy—you know that, right?"

"I want Bethany to have her favorite aunt around more. And I want you to continue being who you are, Dorothy Ybarra."

"Bethany needs you too. Needs to know what a good man is." Dot reined her gelding around to come alongside the roan and T.J. "And you need her to remind you that there are good things worth fighting for."

"Is that a yes, we're moving up here?"

Dot gave him a playful shove. "Fuck yes."

"Swear can!" Bethany shouted, then she spurred her gray. "Race you back!"

The gray and the two dogs shot past them. Dot gestured for T.J. to pursue.

"Hurry up."

"You're not coming?"

She pointed at the goat bleating after the fleeing horse and dogs. "She's not going to keep up."

"She needs to be locked in a stall. She's a bitch."

Dot laughed. "Only to you."

With a "Ha!" T.J. spurred his roan, and the gelding took off like a rocket. Far ahead, Bethany's gleeful laughter drifted back.

Dot looked down at the doe, who stared up at her. "Come on, Pineapple, let's go." Dot shook her head at the name Bethany had bestowed on the goat, one that had stuck and the only one the goat responded to. "Pineapple for a goat."

She'd have to get used to it.

Dot looked over the rippling blades of grass and the towering trees surrounding her home.

T.J. was right, this place was in her blood. Deep in her bones. They could make a real go of it with the business here.

Dot had no doubt about it.

The End

Acknowledgments

I'm a faith-based woman, and with that comes the assurance that everything I write will touch readers in whatever way, shape, or form it needs to. I always give thanks to the Almighty Who cultivated this gift and drive to write.

My family has long since flown the coop, and in their place have flooded in nephews and nieces who keep my husband and myself hopping. I marvel at the gift of being the aunt able and willing to always be there when they need her. I loved researching the Basque way of life and really tried to thread in their strong ties of family into Dot and Angela. In all ways, I think we should all take a page from the Basque and treasure our families deeply.

The one person alive who is allowed to remind me that I'm procrastinating and goofing off is my husband. As much as it pains me that he reminds me of this, I love him still. Now if he'd only stop sending all those videos and memes in my Facebook Messenger so I can focus on writing.

Writing a book is a taxing endeavor, and it's not possible without some kind of cheer squad or, in my case, prodders to keep me going. My editor, Julie, never wavered in her belief that I'd come through with this book. She might have received the worst draft I've ever given her, except maybe the very first book we ever worked on together, but receive this book she did. To her credit, she gave me too much credit on how little work there was to be done on it during the editing process. But the book you hold before you is one we spit-shined and polished.

Along with Julie were my beta readers, Jenn and Rachel, whose long-distance loathing toward me for not having a new chapter sent to them drove me on.

I couldn't have asked for a better dream team than the one at Tule. From the promotion team to the cover art team, this group is a fantastic one to work with.

I belong to a wonderful organization that aids authors in so many ways. Sisters in Crime and my local chapter SinC-Iowa have been a great motivator in the last few years for me. It's always a good thing when I can make a meeting in person, but belonging to this organization always fuels me and keeps me dialed into the mystery/crime fiction world.

I have made great connections with Iowa-based bookstores and look to expand into surrounding states. I will always support our independent bookstores and local libraries, even the little share libraries that have popped up in your hometowns.

Finally, I'd like to acknowledge all the readers who have supported me in reading and reviewing all of my books so far and continue to come back for more. Welcome to all the new readers I gain each year; come find my backlist and catch up. Most of you are strangers to me, some are actual family members, but you are all great in my eyes for being readers. Continue to support us authors by reading, reviewing, or just plain spreading the word. It means a lot.

If you enjoyed *Bait the Devil*,
you'll love the next book in...

A Bounty of Shadows Series

Book 1: *Ride a Dark Trail*

Book 2: *Bait the Devil*

Available now at your favorite online retailer!

More Books by Winter Austin

Benoit and Dayne Mysteries

Book 1: *The Killer in Me*

Book 2: *Hush, My Darling*

Book 3: *Straight for the Kill*

Book 4: *A Requiem For The Dead*

Available now at your favorite online retailer!

About the Author

Winter Austin perpetually answers the question: "were you born in the winter?" with a flat "nope," but believe her, there is a story behind her name.

A lifelong Mid-West gal with strong ties to the agriculture world, Winter grew up listening to the captivating stories told by relatives around a table or a campfire. As a published author, she learned her glass half-empty personality makes for a perfect suspense/thriller writer. Taking her ability to verbally spin a vivid and detailed story, Winter translated that into writing deadly romantic suspense, mysteries, and thrillers.

When she's not slaving away at the computer, you can find

Winter supporting her daughter in cattle shows, seeing her three sons off into the wide-wide world, loving on her fur babies, prodding her teacher husband, and nagging at her flock of hens to stay in the coop or the dogs will get them.

She is the author of multiple novels.

Thank you for reading

Bait the Devil

If you enjoyed this book, you can find more from all our
great authors at TulePublishing.com, or from your favorite
online retailer.

TULE
PUBLISHING